CONTENT WARNINGS

A WARNING to the reader:
This BOOK contains subject material
that may be disturbing or upsetting,
including grief and bereavement,
bullying and homophobia, abusive
relationships, alcohol and substance
abuse, sexual assault, and suicide.

"If you're looking for a raw, unfiltered journey into the heart of a difficult and complex queer experience, *An Ugly World for Beautiful Boys* is a must-read. Rob Costello has crafted an unflinching coming-of-age story that dives headfirst into the chaos of self-discovery, loss, and redemption through Toby Ryerson: an imperfect, impulsive young man trying to survive when everything falls apart. An unforgettable debut novel."

CHRISTOPHER BARZAK

AUTHOR OF STONEWALL HONOR WINNING NOVEL
WONDERS OF THE INVISIBLE WORLD

"Gritty, lyrical, and refreshingly honest, Costello's debut novel pulses with realness, as raw and resilient as its oh-so-human protagonist. A triumph."

NORA SHALAWAY CARPENTER

award-winning author of *Fault Lines* and *The Edge of Anything*

"Rob Costello has crafted an exquisitely haunting, gorgeously-written portrait of survival and resilience with *An Ugly World for Beautiful Boys*. This story is necessary, especially for anyone who has ever felt alone or misunderstood. All too real, it is at once painful and gritty yet brimming with hope and the profound power of love and understanding. Toby's story will stay with you long after you've turned the last page."

AMBER SMITH

New York Times and *USA Today* best-selling author of
The Way I Used to Be and *The Way I Am Now*

"This novel shines in its exploration of the various ways masculinity manifests in the lives of young men, highlighting the damaging effects of toxic masculinity in every scenario. Costello has created multi-dimensional characters who are raw, imperfect, and utterly human. Readers will find themselves swept up in Toby's joy, only to feel frustration when he makes mistakes… *An Ugly World for Beautiful Boys* is a deeply moving novel about finding self-acceptance and communal joy amidst life's messiness."

SAMANTHA HUI

Independent Book Review

AN UGLY WORLD FOR BEAUTIFUL BOYS

ROB COSTELLO

LETHE
PRESS

When this city's got you down,
Let my love lift you up.
Higher and higher,
Into that wide blue yonder,
Where we'll touch the dawn.
And those that used you and blamed you,
Those that shunned you and shamed you,
They'll be gone, baby.
They'll be gone.

—Ravisha Mann, "Manntasia"

NOTHING EVER HAPPENS IN SHELTER VALLEY

CHAPTER ONE
F*CK THIS SHIT!

I GAZED DOWN UPON THE Diva with the ardent longing of a beautiful boy who dreams in stardust but lives in the dirt. *A Weekend in the Andes With Ravisha Mann.* Below the magazine headline, a breathtaking, full-page shot of the world's greatest genderqueer superstar wearing a pink satin ball gown and eight-inch stiletto knee-high boots, climbing the steps of Machu Picchu. Ravisha glowed: towering, strong, and regal—Mom, I imagined the ancient Incas falling to their knees at the mere sight of her magnificence.

I quivered with envy—or maybe that was just the Mini Mart air-conditioning blasting through your silky coral camisole tucked into my cutoffs. I knew Ravisha's was a look I could never pull off—though I will admit to my pixyish charm thanks to your super-fly genes, Mom. God bless our high Scandinavian cheekbones, our eyes the algae blue of

Shelter Lake, and our sun-blonde hair that's 100% natural (although the proof of that has been Naired away since the first pubes appeared on my little patch of heaven). But despite these gifts, I'm seventeen now and still shorter than a fire plug and skinnier than a piss stream. I stand about as likely to pull off "regal" as a Chihuahua in a parade of Great Danes.

Undaunted by the Diva's clear superiority, I scanned the article, nibbling a fleck of Limerick Green off my fingernail. The bio, written to be inspirational, was dull: Impoverished queer boy, DeShawn Morris, grows up in a shack deep in the Mississippi Delta, catches the eye of DJ Uri Cohen at a New Orleans nightclub, and quickly ascends the global EDM ladder. There were also a few tasty nuggets about the Manntasia World Tour I'd already read online, including that the upcoming grand closing show would be at the infamous Terminal City in Hell's Kitchen.

My heart ached. Mom, I would have sold my left kidney to go to that show, but it wasn't going to happen: Jimmy would've sooner sworn off beer than entrusted me with a night on my own in Manhattan. He didn't understand that I belonged there, that the city already beat in my blood, the pulse and heat of it, the energy and noise. The city was all the future I'd ever desired. It held beautiful boys that looked like me, thought like me, and wanted the same things out of life I wanted: concerts and clubs, fabulous clothes and killer looks, all-nighters rolling on the latest chemical enhancers, followed by loud, raunchy sex with a different beautiful man every night of the week.

Manntasia was just a taste, a distant glimpse of sky from the bottom of the deep, black well that was my life in Shelter Valley. Our shithole town was too small to contain me forever, and so was my brother. I'd find a way to climb out and reach the sunlight someday. I refused to fall back into darkness here.

I owed you better than that.

I just needed to do it without breaking Jimmy's heart.

When I finally closed the cover on my Manntasia daydreams, I cringed at my tawdry surroundings. Abe's A-Plus is the same mildewy den of buzzing fluorescence and dangling fly strips you'd remember. It's the only "grocery store" left in town since Rozella closed the One Stop, and Abe keeps the usual collection of dusty sundries in stock— chips, road maps, breath mints—for the occasional passers-by who take the wrong turn on their way to the touristy parts of the Adirondacks. For us locals, he supplies the usual fare: a ready assortment of chewing tobaccos, scratch offs, prophylactics, live bait, six-packs of Utica Club, and the only source of culture in town: a well-stocked magazine rack.

Admittedly, the rack's an anachronism, although that's typical in a town that didn't get cell service until the tower went up on Connecticut Mountain a couple of years ago. The rack runs almost the entire length of the back wall and features a wide array of supermarket tabloids, hunting and fishing journals, untouched stacks of the *Kayoga Gazette* and *Adirondack Life*, and a stash of outdated hetero-porno magazines from back before we had reliable Internet. Not much has changed about it since your time, except that in the far corner, gathering dust beside the national news magazines screaming the latest election headlines, sat Abe's shrine to Donald Trump, with bright red MAGA hats (don't ask), buttons and bumper stickers, as well as a human-shaped rifle target taped to the wall with Hillary Clinton's face pasted over the head, her chest riddled with bullet holes. (She's running against him, and she's going to kick his ass, although nobody around here wants to believe it.)

That's progress in Shelter Valley.

I was about to buy my magazine and leave when the entrance bells jangled. A spasm of teenage boy laughter followed which for me is the equivalent of gunfire to a doe.

The Schlee Posse strutted into the store, and my whole body went rigid.

Shad and "Scarface" (née Eddie) Schlee led the way, dressed as if auditioning for the roles of Thugs No. 3 and 4 in some random PSA on the dangers of teenage drug abuse. They were wiry blond twins living with their beleaguered grandmother on Townline Road. The main distinguishing feature between them was the jagged scar that ran along the side of Eddie's face from where their since-incarcerated old man had pushed his head through a plate-glass window. The twins made the leap during junior year from shaking down freshmen for their pocket money, to selling them the dirt weed they grew under the heat lamps in their basement. Though Shad could be decent when you got him alone, Scarface was a foul-mouthed hothead who'd earned a reputation for calling anyone he didn't like a faggot, me especially, ever since I'd accused him of checking out my ass in eighth grade gym class.

Behind them, Owen Betts shuffled in, his basketball shorts slung so low on his beefy hips you could read the brand name of his boxers. Lumbering, doughy, and as dim as a nightlight at high noon, he wasn't much of a threat on his own, although the Schlees had figured out ways to put his sheer bulk to use as their personal enforcer.

But to be honest, Mom, all I cared about was, God help me, Dylan Falcone. Yes, Donna's boy. Doing his best to mimic the testosterone swagger of his buds but wearing it like a suit he hadn't grown into yet.

Trouble.

You wouldn't have recognized Dylan. The goofy nerd-spawn who used to bring over his G.I. Joes to play dress up with my Barbies had transformed into a delectable specimen of boyhood. His chocolatey-brown eyes glistened when he laughed. Ribbons of licorice hair bounced when he walked. Small, plump lips that swelled into a mouthwatering smile that could melt hearts at a Klu Klux Klan rally. His was the kind of classical boy beauty the Old Masters immortalized on canvas, the kind that in the real world seemed too untouched to be believed as if anything so pure and effortless must be divine by its very perfection.

No wonder it still hurt so much to look at him.

As soon as I saw him, my heart skidded into a brick wall. This was the first time we'd run into each other since our rendezvous the previous week at the Marsh Trail. I was hardly prepared for another encounter.

The foursome made a beeline for the porn at the far end of the magazine rack. I knew I should leave before they saw me, run, never look back. But I was only human and couldn't help myself. While the boys fingered through copies of Wet Snatch and Horny Lesbians, I gazed dreamily at Dylan from the corners of my eyes, picturing again how beautiful he'd looked half-naked and trembling above me in the Marsh Woods.

"What're you staring at, fag?"

Of course, it was Scarface who noticed me first.

"Nothing," I said and flashed him my patented shit-eating grin. "I'm looking at absolutely nothing, I assure you."

Though his eyes narrowed as he worked out my insult, he seemed to drop it, returning his attention to the glossy porno he'd plucked from the rack.

I, however, stood my ground, waiting for the other Jimmy Choo to drop. From personal experience, I've learned, Mom, that backing down only invites more aggression. Rolling with blatant homophobia has become as much a part of my daily routine as lamenting the sorry state of dental hygiene in Kayoga County. Despite how many surveys show that today's youth are cool with all things gay and glorious, this attitude has yet to pay a visit to Shelter Valley—along with Grindr, hybrid cars, and the merciful death of the mullet.

Scarface was hardly the first person in town to call me a fag to my face, and I'd decided a long time ago that it no longer bothered me. I am a faggot. A queer. A cocksucker. Pick your pejorative, and I'll own it. I'll own them all.

Unlike certain closet cases I could mention.

Of course, Dylan still hadn't looked at me. But this was clearly on purpose. For nearly a year, he hadn't looked at me or talked to me, answered my texts or any of the pathetic notes I'd periodically stuffed into his locker. He barely acknowledged my existence except to laugh half-heartedly if Scarface cracked some joke at my expense or tripped me in the hall.

But after the Marsh Trail, I'd allowed myself to hope again, just a little. And now here I was, peering at him as if I could will him to look at me, to see me, to give me some sign that what we'd done alone in the woods together meant there was still a chance for us.

But again, it was Scarface who saw me gawping. "Hey, D," he said with an elbow to Dylan's ribs. "Take a look at this one here, all spread-eagle. Don't she remind you of Ryerson's Mom?"

"Um…" For the first time Dylan flashed me an uncomfortable glance.

"I wanna see," Owen said, trying to peer over Dylan's shoulder at the magazine.

"That's cold, man," Shad said in vague disapproval, though he, too, leaned over to get a better look.

"Come on, D," Scarface insisted, smirking right at me as he shoved the magazine in Dylan's face. "You knew her better than us. Tell me there ain't a resemblance in the, uh—eyes."

"I dunno." Dylan gave a half-hearted shrug and shifted his weight from one foot to the other. "Sure, I guess I can see it." He flashed me a sheepish look as the others leered closer. "Though Ryerson's mom was, um, too skanky for porno."

I felt the knife jab straight to my heart.

Not that I haven't heard countless variations on this theme my entire life, Mom. After thirteen years, people still say the same cruel and ignorant shit about the notorious Bonnie Ryerson. Living fast and dying young in a place like Shelter Valley has guaranteed you a kind of messed-up local celebrity that makes the unwashed rabble feel perfectly entitled to say whatever they damn well please about you.

Even to the son you left behind two months shy of his fifth birthday.

But this was different. Dylan knew you. The *real* you, not the she-got-what-she-had-coming cautionary tale version that most people espouse. I could still picture him in the little black turtleneck Donna dressed him in to come to your funeral, bawling his eyes out alongside the rest of us. Although I'd put up with a lot of shit from him over the past year—shunning, indifference, standing idly by while his buddies hurled their insults in my face—he'd never uttered a single word against you. Not once. It was our last, unspoken bond. The one bridge left unburned.

Yet now he'd gone and torched it, the only shred of decency still lingering between us. As I stood there paralyzed in disbelief, it dawned on me that this single betrayal hurt more than all the others combined.

Still transfixed by the model in the magazine, Scarface added, "Well, I'd fuck her."

"You could've, too," Dylan replied, followed by a needy laugh that only twisted the knife in deeper. "She was everybody's good time."

Scarface grabbed his crotch. "One more reason to buy this then," he said, smirking at me. "Just think, Ryerson, we could've all taken turns being your daddy."

Shad glanced at me with something like pity and smacked the back of his brother's head.

"Leave it," he said. "We've got better shit to do."

"I wanna see, too," Owen pleaded, reaching out a meaty paw that Shad slapped away.

"Let's go," Shad insisted.

"Yeah, dude, don't waste your money." Dylan wrapped his arm around Scarface's shoulder, doubling down on this chance to elevate his status with the pack alpha. "You can score way better pussy than that. Skanks like this are always junkies anyway. This one's probably already OD'd, just like his mom.... Ain't that right, Ryerson?"

My breath caught like nails in my throat.

Scarface shrugged off Dylan's arm, but sneered at me anyway, crinkling up his fleshy disfigurement like a shiny pink ribbon to adorn my broken heart. He jammed the porno back in the rack and swaggered toward the counter with the casual savagery bullies the world over have perfected to demonstrate their mastery over the weak. While he paid Abe for a few bucks worth of gas, Shad and Owen slipped outside without further comment.

Only Dylan hung back, daring me with his eyes to say something more. God help me, but he still smelled of that same dreadful body spray that I sometimes spritzed on my pillow at night to cry myself to sleep. I felt dizzy, almost faint with my desire for him. Yet, I stiffened my back and forced myself to hold his gaze. I wanted him to see me again, like I knew he'd seen me before, as someone worthy of love. I wanted him to burn for me the way I still burned for him, my skin prickling hot to the touch. I wanted him to whisper his old pet name for me—T-bone—in my ear, to ache as much as I ached for our lost kisses, how they tasted of strawberries and mouthwash, how we melted into each other's bodies so perfectly and completely there were moments when we'd forget where one of us left off and the other began. I wanted him to crumble under the sheer weight of regret and finally admit to me just how much he still missed me—how much he still missed *us*.

But somehow, I couldn't speak, and if he felt anything like remorse for all the awful things he'd done and said, he kept it to himself. So, we just stood there like that, poised on the brink of all that ugliness, until he finally threw up his hands and shrugged as if to say, *What else could I do?* and followed his crew outside.

And that was that, Mom. His answer to the Marsh Trail and all that'd come before it. To you and your memory. To the secret history we shared that he'd spent the past year doing everything possible to deny. He gave me a shrug—a goddamned shrug!

Well, fuck that shit.

Hungry for my long overdue payback, I took a deep, cleansing breath, carefully replaced Ravisha's magazine in the rack, and marched outside to follow the Schlee Posse.

CHAPTER TWO
BLATTO! A GUARDIAN ANGEL KICKS ASS

I MARCHED FROM THE AIR-CONDITIONED Mini Mart into the armpit of the sultry afternoon. The brothers Schlee had already forgotten about me and were busy hitting on a trio of college girls gassing up their fancy red convertible. Owen slumped against the fender of Scarface's pickup anxiously watching. Dylan stood apart from the rest and smirked.

The girls were strangers to these parts. They exuded the whiff of a glossy perfume ad, with pristine manicures, Hermès sunglasses, and gold bangles jangling on their wrists. I knew the type. Girls like these often found their way down to the Kayoga Cinema from the great camps on Diamond Lake, seeking summer blockbusters to alleviate bouts of rainy-day boredom. They were typically loud and ungracious, chatting throughout the movie and displaying the withering disdain of lesser nobility toward the locals. I often pictured such girls flitting moth-like around posh young heirs with perfect teeth and names like Bradley and Bennett, soaking up the sun in string bikinis or squealing with delight on the backs of speeding jet skis, their arms wrapped around the sort of well-oiled abs I could only ever dream about someday caressing myself.

Or maybe I'd just watched too many mean girl movies.

The driver, a statuesque brunette wearing a pained expression, stood filling the tank. The two others absorbed themselves in their phones. All three were working overtime to ignore the advances of Scarface and Shad.

"Trust me, gorgeous," Scarface said, leaning so close to the driver his breath disrupted her hair. "10B takes you to this great lookout on the far side of Little Tip Mountain. You can see for miles up there. If you want the best scenery, that's the way to go."

"Naw, bro," Shad protested. "They outta take Townline up to Little Tip." He reached his arms above his head to stretch and flexed his scrawny biceps for the benefit of nobody. "It's quicker that way, plus they'll get all the scenery along Black Dove Pond and Kenner Lake."

"Asshole," Scarface said and puffed out his skinny chest for all he was worth. "Townline is dirt and potholes. Trust me, ladies. Stay on 10B. Smooth rides are my specialty." He made the international "smooth ride" hand gesture, and somewhere, a seismometer registered the tremor of three pairs of female eyeballs rolling in unison.

I took this as my cue. "Hey, Dylan," I called out, sweet as honey on a sugar cube. "Why'd you leave me hanging at the Marsh Trail last week? It's not cool to cum and go like that." I strode toward the pumps, delighted that the smirk had vanished from his face.

"What's your problem now, Ryerson?" Scarface said. "You got your period or something?"

He threw the girls a laugh as if to assure them that dissing faggots and making menstrual jokes were only two among his myriad charms.

The driver replaced the pump in the cradle and slipped back behind the wheel.

"Maybe I'm not your type anymore," I said, focusing all my attention on Dylan as I sashayed toward him like a cartoon prostitute. "But all you have to do next time is bend over, close your eyes, and call me Eddie." At the mention of Scarface's name, Dylan turned ashen, and I realized my shot in the dark had hit a bullseye.

"The Marsh Trail was just a taste, baby," I continued, grabbing my crotch. "Don't you remember how well I took care of you last summer? I miss your sugar buns."

For a moment, it seemed as if all the air in the world had been sucked into outer space.

Then Scarface whirled on Dylan.

"Fuck he say?" he barked.

"Marsh Trail?" Shad asked.

"Sugar buns?" Owen added.

"You dirty lying faggot!" Dylan lurched toward me. "Say that to my face." Though he flexed his outrage for the benefit of our little audience, his eyes were shot through with terror.

I stood my ground. "I can let everything else slide, asshole, but not what you said about Mom." I turned to Scarface and Shad, both gawping at Dylan in gay-panicked horror, and announced, "Yeah, that's right. I sucked your boy off at the Marsh Trail last week. It sure as hell wasn't the first time. I've been his good time for a while now. Or didn't he tell you he's a 'mo, same as me? Hope you never showered together."

Then I blew Dylan a kiss, and with rich satisfaction coursing through my veins, I turned on my heels and marched in the direction of home.

"You gonna let that faggot talk shit about you?" Scarface barked.

"Is it true?" Shad asked

"Sugar buns?" Owen added.

"Get out of the way so I can back up," the driver yelled, and then something between a cannonball and an anvil struck the base of my skull.

The world exploded in a shower of stars.

I staggered forward, toppling face-first into the parking lot, my forehead shredding like a juicy plum against the jagged gravel.

Dylan shouted, "Say it again!"

I tried to push myself onto my hands and knees. Tears swam down my cheeks as I hocked out a loogie of blood-coated asphalt and glanced over my shoulder to see Dylan looming above me. He looked more horrified than menacing, like he couldn't believe what he'd just done to me, like it was second grade again, and he'd accidentally knocked me off the monkey bars at school with another head-cracking thud. I knew he'd never hit anyone like that before in his life, and I realized I'd just taken a second, more terrible kind of virginity from him.

Shad, Scarface, and Owen all rushed over to watch. They stood several paces behind him, trading looks of disgust and confusion.

"What are you waiting for?" Scarface said. "Beat the shit out of that lying fag."

"Why did he say he sucked you off?" Shad said. "Is it true?"

Though Dylan flexed his fists priming for another blow, his eyes pleaded with me to lie to them, to deny everything and stop him from doing what we both knew he'd have to do.

But I was done letting Dylan Falcone off the hook.

"Of course, it's true," I blurted. "Just look at his face. He's gonna bawl."

"Motherfucker!" Dylan shouted, tears streaming down his cheeks as the heel of his Adidas plowed into my ear.

I collapsed, my temple slamming hard into the parking lot. Sparks shot across my vision as he ground my face into the pavement, my brain quivering like Jell-O. A fistful of bile punched up my esophagus, and I gagged, but at least this made him jump back.

"Don't hurl on my kicks, you dirty liar!"

He shouted for me to get up and fight like a man so he could beat the lying shit out of me. But there was no point. It's not as if I've ever been able to fight back, Mom. My mouth has always been my only weapon. But what good is stinging wit in a fistfight?

Dylan seemed to be circling me, or maybe the whole planet had begun to spin madly. Someone said, "Why the hell are you crying, D?" I caught a glimpse of the blazing sun above me, then of sneakers, then blackness. I began to shiver as a female voice said, "Leave him alone," while another said, "Let's go." A car horn blared as tires kicked up gravel, and I flinched, certain I was about to be run over. But when I tried to push myself up to get out of the way, Dylan's foot torpedoed into my gut.

"Get up," he shouted. "Get the fuck up!"

It was then that I caught sight of a blurry shape approaching from the gas pumps behind him. The shape moved fast, massive and fearsome, wielding something that looked like a sword or a sledgehammer.... Shit, no, it was a pickax!

"Don't," I slurred, just as the figure whaled the business end of Abe's windshield squeegee into the side of Dylan's head.

Blammo! A shower of windshield fluid rained down as Dylan careened sideways into Shad.

The sight of the impact shocked me back into awareness. I managed to scramble out of the way just as Dylan whirled around and received a sharp uppercut to the chin. His neck snapped back, he lost his balance and tripped over his own foot, landing squarely in the pool of my spit and blood.

Scarface lunged for the squeegee, but the stranger bitch-slapped him across the cheek.

Owen bolted for the pickup like a gun-shy mutt at a shooting party.

Shad, always the wisest of the crew, simply put up his hands and backed away.

That's when my mysterious savior turned to me. He was about Jimmy's age, blonde, tanned, and built like a brick shithouse on steroids. Dressed in felon chic, he wore mirrored shades that glinted in the sunlight, black leather biker boots, a threadbare wife-beater, and crotch-tight Levis that left little to the imagination.

"You okay?" he said, offering me a hand up, but I only managed a feeble nod.

Clutching his stricken cheek, Scarface shouted, "What the fuck, asshole? The little faggot had it coming. We oughta call the cops on you for assault with a deadly weapon."

"Deadly weapon?" The stranger laughed. He offered Scarface the handle of the squeegee and said evenly, "Let's skip the cops and settle this for real. I'll even give you the first shot."

Scarface's eyes fell, and he backed away.

"Yeah, that's what I thought," the stranger said. "You're only a badass when it's somebody you can take down easy." He tossed the squeegee away and turned to Dylan, who was rolling around on the ground, cradling his formerly beautiful face. "Next time, pick on somebody your own size." He gestured to Scarface's pickup and added, "All of you, get the hell out of here before you piss me off anymore."

"You can't tell us what to do," Scarface muttered, but Shad grabbed him by the arm. With shoulders slumped, they shuffled back to their truck, where Owen cowered in abashed silence.

Dylan was left to drag himself to his feet, which he did with agonizing slowness. His shirt was soaked in bloody spittle, though whether it was mine or his own, I couldn't tell. His Adidas were scuffed, his eyes bloodshot and teary. The whole left side of his face shone as ripe as a well-slapped ass. Yet, while the stranger had done plenty of damage, I could see that I'd landed the killer blow, though it gave me precious little satisfaction to know it.

"This isn't over," Dylan said to me with much-reduced menace.

But the stranger was having none of it. "If you ever touch this kid again," he growled, "I'll come for you, you hear me? And next time, you won't walk away."

Dylan had no choice but to nod. He wiped the blood from his mouth with what remaining dignity he could muster and staggered to the pickup, where Owen gamely tried to heave him into the bed.

"Is it over yet?" Abe called from the Mini Mart doorway, all 350 pounds of heavy-breathing disgruntlement, baseball bat in hand.

"No thanks to you," the stranger said.

"I would've broken it up," Abe said defensively. "Only, Princess there had a lesson coming first."

The stranger didn't reply. Instead, he hoisted me to my feet and said, "Can you stand on your own?"

"I'll manage," I said, locking my quivering knees beneath me. "Who—who are you?"

"Fournier. Gabe Fournier."

"Gabe," I repeated, testing the weight of the name in my mouth as I offered him my wet-noodle handshake. It was a good name. Gabe.

"You like it? It was my Granddad's. Short for Gabriel."

"Like the angel?"

"Yeah, just like that." He laughed and wrapped a beefy arm slathered in tattoos around my shoulders. I inhaled his scent, sweat and pot and manhood. "Let's get you cleaned up," he said, maneuvering me back to the Mini Mart.

Before he could usher me inside, I stole a parting glance at Dylan, whom Owen had finally managed to heave into the back of the truck. He was staring off into space like he'd just witnessed the whole world come crashing to an end.

Mom, he looked afraid. Stone-cold afraid.

CHAPTER THREE
TOUGHER THAN YOU LOOK

GABE FOURNIER HOVERED OVER ME in the Mini Mart bathroom, using a dampened wad of toilet paper to scrub away the streaks of dirt and blood from my face. He'd hooked his sunglasses on the collar of his wife-beater, and in the unforgiving fluorescent glare, I could see that his stormy blue eyes were puffy, tired, and rimmed in red. He looked as if he'd just come off a weekend bender, and despite the half-grin nudging the corner of his mouth, he gave off the impression of a dude who lugged sadness around on his shoulders like a mountain that would someday bury him. He reminded me an awful lot of Jimmy.

As he hunted through the dregs of Abe's first-aid kit to find an alcohol swab that hadn't dried out, I took the opportunity to reassemble what little armor I had left.

"So, you've rescued your damsel in distress for today," I said. "Achievement unlocked. I can take care of the rest from here."

I tried to pull away as Gabe started to attack the last smear of filth on my cheek.

"Hold still," he commanded, pincering my chin between his thumb and forefinger. "You're shaking like a leaf."

"I'll be fine." I jerked my chin loose and flashed him my patented I-have-already-risen-high-above-this-bullshit grin. Then, I turned to the mirror to inspect the damage. It wasn't pretty. The skin on my forehead looked shaved raw by a cheese grater. A nasty, weeping gash ran the length of my eyebrow, while the thin trails of black eyeliner I'd applied that morning had run into dark smears. My stomach and ribs still throbbed, and the cut in my lower lip had swelled into an Atomic Fireball.

Mom, your lovely coral camisole was bloodied and torn, but it would take more than a few love taps from Dylan Falcone to permanently mar my America's-Next-Top-Model fabulosity. "As God is my witness, I shall be lovely again," I said, shaking my fist in my best Scarlett O'Hara.

This drew a genuine smile to Gabe's lips. "You're tougher than you look." He pasted the only good Band-Aid left in the first aid kit across the gash above my eyebrow.

"Don't let my gorgeous face and killer fashion sense fool you. Nobody takes a hit around here better than me."

"Why is that?" he said and tossed the bloody wad of toilet paper into the toilet behind us.

"Practice makes perfect." I yanked up the spaghetti strap of your camisole back over my shoulder. "You like my look? I call it Guantanamo Queer."

"I'd like it a hell of a lot better without the cuts and bruises. Does it hurt anyplace else?"

"Just my pride."

"How about your ribs? That little prick got in a couple of good kicks."

"They're fine," I lied and forced myself to straighten my posture without wincing.

He scowled. "You should have a doctor check you out."

"I said I'm fine."

"Okay, okay." Gabe threw up his hands. "So, what the hell was that all about anyway?"

"I'd rather not bore you with tawdry details."

"Why not? The only thing I've got planned today is to sit by the lake and drink beer. Besides, I'd like to get my story straight for when the cops haul my ass away for assault with a deadly squeegee." He laughed, and it was like the clouds parting after a thunderstorm. He thumb-scratched the adorable dimple on his chin, and I felt a stirring in my belly that wasn't the result of Dylan's kicks. "Seriously," he continued, "I know it ain't my business, but I'm standing right here if you want to talk about it."

"That's sweet, but you've done plenty. I don't even know you."

"Sure you do. I'm Gabe, and you're?"

"Toby—Toby Ryerson."

"Jim Pettinger's kid brother?" He arched an eyebrow as the clouds swept back in. "No wonder you're so tough."

"You know Jimmy?"

"Knew." His lip curled slightly. "Graduated a year ahead of me at Kayoga Unified."

It was obvious they hadn't been the best of buds, Mom, but then your elder son rubs most mere mortals the wrong way. I decided to let it drop. "And you're a Fournier, huh?" I asked instead. "Any relation to Harold?"

"My old man."

"Ah, so you're the prodigal son."

His eyes narrowed. "Why? What have you heard about me?"

"Just that you exist." I shrugged. "I know more about your sister... Connie, right? She's got a couple of kids. Lives in Georgia or something?"

"North Carolina."

"Yeah, that's it. I overheard Harold telling Abe about her once."

"Sounds about right," he said. "My old man don't brag about me." He flicked on the hot water to rinse his hands, his whole body tightening up like a fist.

"I heard he was in the hospital," I said cautiously. "Is that why you're back in town?"

"Something like that," he replied.

But when he offered no further explanation, I mumbled my sympathies and let it drop.

Harold Fournier was still the same miserable bastard you'd remember, Mom. He had the nerve to corner Jimmy at your funeral, demanding the $300 he claimed he lent you before you died. Though Jimmy eventually paid him back with interest—along with the dozen others around town you'd stiffed on your way out—he was the only one who held a grudge against us afterward. We didn't shed tears for Harold when the county shut down the Sunset Grill for back taxes a couple of years ago, and I certainly wasn't crying about his heart attack now. Still, I knew better than to speak ill of a dying old man to his son.

I was angling for a way to change the subject when my phone rang—Jimmy's ringtone blaring "Ball and Chain" from Ravisha's Mann Bites Dog E.P.

"You need to get that?"

"Naw, it's just my brother. He lives to check up on me." I powered the phone off and stuffed it back in my pocket.

"Sounds like Jim," Gabe muttered, drying his hands on his jeans. "Anyway, last chance: you going to tell me what that was all about, or do I have to go overpay Abe for a lousy six-pack of Saranac and get shit-faced all by myself?"

"Enjoy your beer," I said airily, and returned to my reflection. "Jesus, I look like something Ru Paul's cat puked up." I licked my fingertip and tried to rub away my melted eyeliner but only succeeded in smudging it more raccoonishly than before.

"Damn," he said, watching me. "You really are a hard-ass."

"I just have a genetic aversion to heart-to-hearts." I caught his eye in the mirror and smiled. "There's nothing to talk about anyway. I get under people's skin. Sometimes, they get under mine. Fireworks ensue. I'm not trying to be a jerk here, but I'm totally fine, thanks to you. I don't know why you saved my ass like that, but I appreciate it."

"Maybe I've got my own genetic aversion to bullies."

"Lucky for me," I said, and added sincerely, "Thank you, Gabe."

"It's alright," he mumbled, almost embarrassed. He picked up the first aid kit and moved for the door. "Look, I'll be staying at my old man's place a few more days. You have any more trouble or decide you feel like spilling your guts, come find me, and we'll hash it out over some beers, okay?"

"You do realize I'm only seventeen, right?"

Gabe cocked an eyebrow. "Do I look like I'm gonna call the cops on you for having a beer?"

"You'd better not, or I might have to report an assault with a deadly squeegee."

He smirked. "It's been a trip, Toby Ryerson. Here's hoping I see you again." Then he pushed out the door.

As soon as he was gone, I deflated against the countertop. My ribs throbbed beneath my skin, hot and angry. I lifted the hem of your camisole to discover a mass of swollen red flesh puffing up into the shape of Florida.

Exhaustion overcame me. I collapsed onto the toilet and hung my head between my knees. Dylan's fear-stricken stare had seared itself onto my retinas like the afterimage of the sun, although my anger with him had already burned away.

Dylan was weak—I knew that. Dylan was terrified of what he was. I was not.

My skin had grown thicker than boxing glove leather from all the hits I'd taken over the years just being myself. I knew my wounds would heal, but Dylan—he wasn't built for this.

Not that I regretted what I'd done. Not exactly. He'd had it coming for a long, long time. Maybe I had it coming, too. After everything I'd gone through with him last year, desire had short-circuited my self-respect the moment I saw him leaning against that tree on the Marsh Trail. He'd licked his perfect lips, his cheeks flushed and ripe, his dark eyes darting and hungry. I didn't demand an apology or ask him to explain why he ghosted me at the end of last summer. Hell, I didn't even make him say my name before I dropped to my knees in the mud. And when he'd finished, and I stood up and tried to kiss him, I just let him push me away like garbage.

No wonder he treated me like shit… *I let him.*

Yet now, I'd fucked up his life in a way I couldn't take back. In the sobering clarity of my solitude, it felt like a much heavier burden than I was prepared to bear. People would find out the truth about him now—Donna would find out. That irrevocability made me anxious—not for me, but for him. God help me, but I was afraid for Dylan Falcone, only there wasn't a damn thing I could do about it now. I'd done this to him. I'd outed him, and for the rest of his life, he would have to live with the consequences of my actions.

Abe pounded on the bathroom door. "You gonna die in there, Princess, or what?"

"Shit." I jerked upright, a fresh stab of pain knifing my side. "I'm coming."

"Good. Rozella just called and wants you to bring her cigarettes and beer. Turn your damn phone on. I ain't your messenger boy."

It took me a few minutes to gird my loins and hobble out of the bathroom. Abe was at the counter bagging up Rozella's Utica Club and Newports, so I shuffled back to the magazine rack and then up to the register.

"I didn't bring money for all this," I said, gesturing to Rozella's bag. "Put it on her tab... this too." I handed him the music magazine.

"She gonna be alright with this?" he said, pointing at the magazine.

"I'm not a delivery service. She owes me."

"Fine, whatever," he said. "It's your funeral."

As Abe added the cost of the magazine to Rozella's tab, I said, "What do you know about that dude. Gabe Fournier?"

He smirked at me. "What is it, Princess? Puppy love?"

"Just tell me."

He scowled and said, "He's trouble, that's all."

"What else?"

"I ain't your social secretary. Go ask your brother. Old Saint Jim'll give you an earful."

"Or you could just tell me now," I said. "Unless you want to explain to Saint Jim how you just stood there and watched as Dylan kicked the shit out of his defenseless little brother."

I've never been above a bit of blackmail, Mom.

Abe's eyes narrowed and he shifted uncomfortably. Despite Jimmy's reputation as the town Goody Two-Shoes, nobody wanted to piss him off.

"Don't you worry about Jim," he said, sounding like he was trying to convince himself. "He knows about your big mouth. He'll see you had it coming."

"That's your story then?"

He flashed me a smirk. "The bigger question is what's your story going to be when he hears about what you've been getting up to at the Marsh Trail."

The air seized in my lungs.

"Ha! You didn't think about that, did you?"

No, actually, I hadn't.

But though panic began to melt my knees, I refused to give Abe the satisfaction of knowing it. Instead, I beamed my widest shit-eating grin, grabbed Rozella's bag off the counter, and was lurching toward the exit when he threw me a parting shot.

"Already turning tricks down to the Marsh Trail. A chip off your 'ole ma's block. Your poor brother. Ain't he suffered enough."

CHAPTER FOUR
BLACK SHEEP

THE PROBLEM WITH LIVING WITH secrets, Mom, is that they never stay secret forever.

Despite the afternoon's blistering heat, what Abe said had turned my blood to ice water. He was right: Jimmy would hear about the fight from somebody—news still spreads like head lice in a preschool around here—and then he would find out about Dylan and the Marsh Trail, and my life as I'd known it for the past seventeen years would be over.

Not that your elder son was clueless about my sexuality. Hardly. After you died, he really stepped up to the plate on that score. He happily dressed up as Beast so I could be Belle for our first Halloween. He grudgingly sat through countless episodes of Real Housewives and Drag Race, and let me wear whatever I wanted with only an occasional complaint. Hell, he even left me a vintage Playgirl on my pillow once, after he caught me jerking off to a feature in his Sports Illustrated on the Men's Olympic Diving Team.

In theory, he was fully supportive of his little queer bro. But the reality—*my reality*—was not something Jimmy was prepared to take. I'd been lying to his face for over year. He knew nothing about what'd happened between me and Dylan, let alone that I'd been sneaking off to the Marsh Trail practically every day since school let out in June. This behavior was most definitely not on the Jimmy-approved program. Being queer was one thing. Cruising for random dick was something else entirely. Something that would hit way too close to home.

Meaning way too close to you.

Not that Jimmy could even bring himself to spit out your name. After you died, he turned his back on you and your memory so thoroughly it was as if you'd never even existed.

But I refused to play along.

You remained the dark core of all the friction between us. Like a black hole we orbited on opposing sides, you exerted a crushing pull that neither of us could escape, though that never stopped Jimmy from trying. He wouldn't talk about how tough his life had been growing up alone with you before I came along, but I'd heard enough gossip over the years to guess what it must have been like. The parties and booze. The revolving cavalcade of strange men. No money, no rules, at times not even a slice of bread in the house to make a sandwich.

After you died, he did all he could to ensure a stable life for me that was in opposition to everything he hated about his own childhood.

He quit his classes at K.C.C.C. to work full time. He broke off an engagement to a fiancé I didn't remember. He surrendered all his own hopes and dreams to give me a better life than the one he'd been given as the son of, well, you.

But none of this was a sacrifice I'd asked him to make, and the price he'd set for me to repay him was too damn high. I'd never turn my back on you, Mom. Not even for Jimmy.

I owed you better than that.

Besides, his master plan for my future was like a master class in everything I wasn't and would never aspire to be. It began with college and career, followed by husband, kids, and a house in the suburbs with a white picket fence. All of it so sweet and upstanding and Disney-gay dull it made my teeth ache just thinking about it. It was an oppressive vision, starched and suffocating, yet it was so all-consuming, whenever he looked at me, all he could see was *that* Toby, *that* future, *that* dream.

He saw everything except for who I really was: *your* son.

But when he heard about Dylan and the Marsh Trail, his eyes would finally be opened about me. The thought of it made me ill. I lived in constant dread of letting him down. I'd played along with his college daydreams, kept my grades up, aced my SATs. I'd concealed the most dangerous parts of me and what I desired, all because the last thing in the world I ever wanted to do was hurt Jimmy. Yet, how could I keep on avoiding that and still be myself? He'd have to find out the truth eventually. Maybe now was as good a time as any. Maybe Rozella would let me crash on her couch until I turned eighteen. Maybe then I could get my GED and hit the road for the city. At least that way I wouldn't have to look Jimmy in the face every single day and see in his eyes what a colossal disappointment I'd turned out to be.

These thoughts hardly made the walk home a pleasant one. Not that the slack-roofed houses and boarded-up buildings constituting the barely beating heart of Shelter Valley ever made for a delightful stroll. The town reminded me of a drunk after closing time who's passed out in a pool of his own sick. Jimmy says the party ended here years before I was born, when the logging company went bust and took with it the last outpost of industry in this corner of the Adirondacks. Then the state swept in and bought up all the land the company owned around the lake and mountain, designating it "forever wild," a veritable death sentence for the town.

No rich summer downstaters building fancy lakefront camps.

No tourists.

No jobs.

Shelter Valley curled up into a ball and began the long, slow roll to oblivion.

Consequently, nothing ever changed around here. The few landmarks were the same as before you died, just more rundown. There was the First Methodist Church plastered in For Sale signs, Jobie's ramshackle snowmobile and chainsaw repair shop, the shuttered ghosts of the Sunset Grill and Rozella's One Stop, and the white clapboard municipal building that used to be the schoolhouse. A couple of rotted picnic tables and an elbow of gritty sand were all that remained of the public beach. The old mill still sat crumbling and derelict in a jungle of barbed wire about a mile south from where they dammed up Fallen Creek. The same trailers and hunting camps were still scattered throughout the woods, and nestled in the hollow halfway up the mountainside sat the Shelter Mountain Mobile Manor, where Jimmy and I still lived in the same drafty doublewide you got in your divorce settlement from Earl.

That's pretty much it, Mom, except for J.J.'s Tavern, which remained at the center of town in all its faux-log cabin and deer-antlered glory. It endured as the hub of Shelter Valley social life, just like it was when you tended bar there, still the best and only place in town to get drunk, trade gossip, or meet that special someone with whom to share your STIs.

Or make a baby.

In fact, the only thing you would've found unfamiliar as I walked home that blistering afternoon were all the MAGA and Confederate flags that flapped in my face in practically every yard—although you would have totally recognized the small-minded bigotry behind them. Every time there was a new election, Jimmy and I argued about putting up a Democrat sign, but he kept insisting he didn't want us to stick out any more than we already did. Which is why his refusal to even think about pulling up stakes and moving away from our dead-end existence here made no sense to me at all.

Jimmy didn't belong in Shelter Valley any more than I did. He was too good for this town. Even if he couldn't see it, I sure as hell could. He didn't think like everybody else, socialize like everybody else, hate like everybody else. He was decent and kind and fair. He worked hard and never bitched about it. He treated everyone who earned it with respect. He even loathed to gossip and kept his drinking to himself, which meant there was nothing for him to do around here and nobody to do it with except me. Besides, it was damned inconvenient for him to live out at the ass-end of nowhere. There were times in the winter, before the plows cleared 10B, that it took forever to get to his shift at the paper mill. What he shelled out in gas money each month commuting to Kayoga could've covered the mortgage on a new trailer somewhere closer to civilization. Yet, whenever I asked him why we didn't just get an apartment in Kayoga, or better still, move down to Gloversville or Albany, he would get all tight-lipped about it or change the subject and never mind what I wanted.

That's another thing you would've recognized, Mom: Jimmy's obstinacy...

Anyway, by the time I reached the driveway to the public beach, my ribs were screaming. I decided to take a break and slumped against the buckshot-riddled sign that welcomed visitors to the Shelter Valley Municipal Park: No Swimming After Dark. My body felt like a wet sock somebody had wrung out to dry. I dreaded the agony ahead of me: home was still half a mile away, straight up the mountainside. Cicadas droned like oven buzzers in the languid air. Globs of gritty sweat percolated on my forehead. I peered out at the lake where the sunlight rippled across the surface like ribbons of shimmering gold, and I flashed on my memories of when Donna used to bring Dylan and me swimming here when we were still little kids.

This was after you died, Mom, during those few summers when Donna stepped up to take care of the babysitting and other stuff that

Jimmy was too proud to ask for help with. Sometimes, she'd bundle Dylan and me into her old Explorer and drive us to Enchanted Forest to ride the waterslides or over to the Fun Zone in Schenectady, where we'd get sick on pepperoni pizza and the bounce house.

But the best times I remembered were when she brought us here. She'd pack us a little lunch of peanut butter sandwiches and Pepsi, and we'd spend the whole day spread out on the sand, Donna in her swimsuit working on her tan, while Dylan and I chased each other in the shallows. Sometimes he'd bring along his granddad's old fishing pole and attempt to teach me to tie a lure or bait a hook. He was always so serious about it, as if he were trying to prove to the universe that he'd earned the right to be called his mommy's "little man" by teaching someone else what he'd been forced to learn all by himself.

Yet, despite how important it was to him, he never got angry when I failed to replicate whatever he was trying to show me. He never yelled when I grew bored or refused to spear the nightcrawlers with a hook—because it was gross, I'd said, though the truth was I simply couldn't bear to hurt the squirmy things. He never poked fun at me, never called me a sissy, never made me feel like he was sorry I was there. He just persisted in that quiet, determined way of his, and though we never caught a single fish, on those afternoons, this ugly patch of sand seemed like the most beautiful place in the whole world. Maybe because back then I didn't know any better than to be blissfully happy when I was with Dylan.

Too bad I knew better now.

"There could at least be a breeze today," I grumbled to the

universe. I set Rozella's bag on the ground and lifted my arms to air out the swampiness in my pits. That's when I noticed the white Silverado backed up to the water's edge on the far side of the park. Gabe Fournier was sitting on the tailgate, sipping a beer and gazing out at the water. He hadn't spotted me, so I toed at the ground, dislodging a half-buried blue bottle cap in the dirt. With the edge of my sneaker, I gave it a sharp kick that sent it careening in his direction.

But he was too far away. The cap landed well short of the mark, and if he'd heard it strike the asphalt, he didn't bother to turn around to look.

I was just about to call out his name when his phone rang. The conversation that followed was brief and unpleasant, though from so far away I only managed to catch snippets of what he said: "I'm sorry... possibility of another stroke... longterm complications.... He keeps asking for you, Con.... You're the only one he gives a shit about anyway.... I'm garbage to him."

Poor Gabe. I hadn't wanted to say anything earlier, but that day I overheard Harold telling Abe about Connie—I also heard him say something about his only boy: "He's as good as dead to me."

It must suck being unwanted by your own father... although I could kind of relate. No wonder Gabe was getting drunk by the lake instead of playing the dutiful son at his old man's sickbed. Did it even matter to Harold that Gabe was the only one who'd bothered to show up in his hour of need? Probably not. That's what being the black sheep meant: nothing you could do would ever make things right.

I wondered what Jimmy would have to say about me once I was gone.

When Gabe finally hung up the phone, he downed the rest of his beer and hurled the empty bottle into the lake. I decided to leave him in peace, though I hoped I'd have the chance to take him up on his offer of a beer sometime before he left town.

If Jimmy didn't kill me first.

CHAPTER FIVE
AH, ROZELLA

YOU'D THINK AFTER THIRTEEN YEARS, the Shelter Mountain Mobile Manor might have freshened up a bit. But no, like everything else in town, it's exactly as you left it, Mom, a sad hodgepodge of a dozen or so weather-beaten house trailers nestled among the spruce and pines. Rozella keeps the rent cheap, so our neighbors have all stayed put: the same crew of retired busybodies, layabouts, and Shelter Valley-lifers you once knew and loathed. Nobody's hauled in a new trailer since Earl bought our doublewide when Jimmy was a newborn, and I've seen pictures of the place from twenty years ago that, save for a fresh coat of paint or a potted begonia, look no different than today.

Rozella still lives in the dumpy, seventies-era single-wide you'd remember, with the pink aluminum siding and the original tin roof that Jobie has to tar for her every summer. As I skirted around the patch of dirt that passes for her front yard, I was surprised to find her outside waiting for me, rocking beneath the patio awning in flip flops and a blue gingham house dress, a cigarette in one hand and her cordless phone in the other.

She looked at me and barked, "Jesus Christ, puppy, get inside before you melt to nothing!" She flicked the cigarette into the dirt and groaned to her feet, but when she spied the plastic bag dangling from my wrist, she added, "That six-pack better be cold, or you're running your scrawny ass back down the hill for another."

Ah, Rozella....

Jimmy says that along with the cockroach and Ebola virus, Rozella Ames is the only creature on earth obstinate enough to survive a nuclear holocaust. She still wears the same bouffant wig you'd remember, with the stiff blonde curls that resemble yellow baling wire. Her skin has grown even more worn and crumpled over the years, like a paper bag that's been reused too many times. She's sailed undaunted through breast cancer scares, crippling arthritis, and the worst case of bunions known to mankind. Even getting ditched by her skirt-chasing ex-husband and disowned by her only daughter couldn't take the piss and vinegar out of her, and at seventy-two, she's the same loud, salty, opinionated old broad she was on the day you died.

I wouldn't have her any other way.

At least the trailer was cool inside, courtesy of the box air conditioner wheezing like a dying relation in the front window. A miasma of cigarette smoke and cheap perfume hung in the air. Rozella slammed the screen door behind me and grabbed my chin to inspect my face.

"You look like hell. Wanna tell me about it?"

"No, not really."

She hesitated, and I got the feeling she wanted to say something more, but instead she clucked her tongue and yanked the plastic bag from my hand. "You need aspirin or an ice bag?"

"Naw, I'm holding out for a couple of Jimmy's Percocets when I get home. I could use a beer, though."

She flashed me a wry grin. "You're lucky I'm a soft touch."

She retreated into the kitchen while I hung back by the door, waiting for an invitation to sit down. I needed a shower badly, but I didn't feel like going home to wait alone for Jimmy. Rozella was easier company. Whenever I felt like escaping from my life for a few hours, she was here, ready to hand me a beer, shoot the shit, and watch TV. Nothing too deep or too complicated. She liked to bust my chops, but she didn't judge or intrude. She never snitched to Jimmy or demanded to know my private business. I appreciated the space. It made it safe and comfortable, and though there were definitely subjects better for us to avoid, that was mostly fine by me.

I didn't need Rozella to be my confidant. I just needed her to be my friend.

The refrigerator door slammed shut, and she strode out of the kitchen carrying two cans of beer and the magazine I'd forgotten in the bag.

"Did I pay for this, too?" she asked, handing it over with a beer.

"Call it a delivery fee."

"Like I'm made of money," she grumbled and swept past me into the living room, where she slumped into her recliner with a weary sigh. She gestured to the couch, and I took a seat. The TV was on mute, featuring some bleach-blonde Fox News fembot who glowered her Angry Barbie face through a report on the trade deficit with China. Rozella cracked open her beer and said, "Why is your phone off? I had to listen to Abe bitch about being your messenger boy."

"I didn't feel like talking to Jimmy."

She snorted. "Can't blame you there." She threw back a swig of beer and grimaced. "Warm as piss." Then she fished into the pocket of her housecoat for her cigarettes and lighter. "How's Jim doing these days? The doctors finally yank that stick out of his ass?"

"No, not yet."

I cracked open my own beer and took a sip. It wasn't *that* warm, but then Rozella was only happy if she had something to complain about. Poor Nicki. I glanced up at the dozen or so framed photographs of Rozella's only child scowling down at me from the wall above the recliner. Even in her First Communion picture, Nicki looked pissed off, as if her mother had spent the minutes before the shutter clicked belting out orders for how she was supposed to pose.

I've always felt sorry for Nicki, Mom. Though I never met her, and Rozella rarely mentions her, considering the rough ride they had after Duke ran off, a special place in my heart bleeds for her. Who can blame Nicki for going a little bit wild? Certainly not me, that's for sure.

I noticed Rozella peering at me, nursing her cigarette. I worried she could tell I was thinking about Nicki, so I focused on the TV, until she finally turned up the volume on the remote, shattering our awkward silence with some right-wing Senator's prissy nasal whine.

I gave it a whole minute before I said, "Why are we watching this shit?"

"It ain't shit." She glared at me. "I'm glad somebody's talking about jobs and stopping that free trade crap. Folks are fed up. They've been fed up a long time."

"Why are you so fed up? You've got more money than God."

"Where'd you ever hear a thing like that?" she said, feigning shock, although the twinkle in her eye said something else entirely.

Rozella's still the richest woman in Shelter Valley, Mom. I admire her for it. Who else could go from deserted at twenty-three, with no money, no job skills, and a little kid to raise, to running the most successful business in town? Though she'd shut down the One Stop when she "retired," she still owned the Mobile Manor, her share of the Tastee Freeze in Diamond Lake, the land J.J.'s sat on, and that big apartment building in Kayoga. Sure, she might live like one of those hoarders on TV who spends the last week of the month eating mayonnaise sandwiches while waiting for her Social Security check to arrive, but that's just because she's tighter than Scrooge with a buck.

Yet another reason Nicki doesn't return her phone calls.

"Anyway," she continued, "We need to take back our jobs from China. We need to get back our pride, our dignity. You're too young to remember what it was like here before the mill closed, but things were better. Just ask Jim. He's a working man. He'll tell you."

I nodded and let it drop. I'd gotten used to humoring this particularly unpleasant quirk of her personality. Besides, I knew damn well the only reason Jimmy still had a job was because of all the toilet paper his company shipped to China. The world was a different place outside of Shelter Valley. For most of the country, progress wasn't a dirty word. Rozella had it all wrong: It wasn't China's fault things had gotten worse around here, because it wasn't China's fault that people in this town refused to change. The politicians on TV weren't offering up pride or dignity or even solutions, just a bullhorn for the chip on some folks' shoulders. They got themselves elected by channeling the grievances of the kind of old-time bigots who planted their fat asses on J.J.'s barstools by ten o'clock each morning and spent the rest of the day getting piss-drunk while bitching about how every problem in their lives was the fault of immigrants or the Chinese or the uppity n-words. Though Rozella never talked about people that way, I knew deep down she was just as afraid of how quickly the world had transformed around her.

Maybe that's why she'd always stayed in Shelter Valley.

"Can we watch something else?" I said irritably. "Otherwise, I'll finish my beer and go home."

She frowned. "They got a Crawford marathon on Turner Movies."

When I nodded eagerly, she flicked the channel, and the radiant black and white visage of Joan Crawford appeared. It was a rerun of *Mildred Pierce*, which we'd already watched a couple dozen times. But that didn't matter to us.

Watching and rewatching classic movies was our thing, Mom. I credit Rozella with helping me discover my taste for old melodramas and glamorous movie stars like Ava Gardener, Olivia de Havilland,

Barbara Stanwyck, and Veronica Lake. I even tried to emulate their looks a few times with my stash of Dollar Drug cosmetics. While Joan had her shoulder pads and big eyebrows, I preferred Gene Tierney's icy and pristine loveliness because she reminded me of you. She starred in *Laura*, *The Ghost and Mrs. Muir*, and my favorite, *Leave Her to Heaven*, where she played this conniving psycho-bitch who stops at nothing to hold onto her man. By comparison, Joan was an irritating dishrag in *Mildred Pierce*. She spends the entire movie sacrificing everything for her ungrateful nightmare of a daughter. Though it was hardly my favorite film of hers, it didn't take me long to get sucked into the story, and so it was a while before I noticed that Rozella had stopped watching the screen and was peering at me instead.

Our eyes locked as she muted the volume.

"What happened at the Mini Mart?" she demanded.

I took a large gulp of beer and glanced away. "I don't feel like talking about it, okay? Didn't Abe fill you in on the gory details?"

"He said a couple things, but I was hoping you'd tell me he was full of crap."

I frowned. "About which parts?"

"The parts with you and Donna's boy messing around at the Marsh Trail."

"Ah, that." I turned back to Joan, chewing the green from my thumbnail. I didn't feel like getting into this with her. Though she knew more than anyone else about what had happened with Dylan— that we'd "dated," that he "dumped" me, that I was "torn up" about it—it wasn't like we'd ever had a heart-to-heart on the subject. Besides, imagine confiding in your surrogate grandma that you'd blown your ex-boyfriend in the woods last week.

"You ain't denying it."

"No, but I wish you'd drop it. It's over now. Let's just watch the movie and chill, okay?"

I took another swig of beer.

"Alright," she grumbled, an unfamiliar edge creeping into her voice. "Maybe I was hoping you'd tell me you made the whole thing up to embarrass him in front of his buddies. Maybe I'm just a stupid old woman." Though she flicked the volume back up, I could practically hear the molecules of air sizzling on contact with her skin. She was pissed, although I didn't know why, and it wasn't even another minute before she whirled on me again, a firestorm raging in her eyes. "How many others besides Donna's boy have there been down there? Don't lie to me."

"What?"

"At the Marsh Trail. How many?"

"I dunno. A few. Why?"

"How many's a few?"

"Jesus, you want a head count?"

She stubbed out the cigarette in her ashtray and leaned toward me like a Spanish Inquisitor. "How long have you been going there?"

"Since school let out in June. So? Why are we even talking about this? It's too weird. I'm seventeen now. I'm legal in New York. Let's just drop it, okay? It's no big deal."

"You think being legal makes it okay?" She laughed bitterly and lit up again, and I could see that her hand was shaking.

This focused my mind.

"Look, puppy, you know I don't judge you. I go out of my way sometimes not to judge. You dress how you want, wear makeup, whatever. It's fine by me. You want to mess around with other boys your own age, fine, you go have fun." She jabbed the cigarette in my direction. "But this—this. Hanging out at the Marsh Trail."

"You go out of your way not to judge me?" I pushed myself to my feet. "What have you been doing all this time? Tolerating me?"

"That's not what I meant.... I'm all for live and let live. But I can't abide you.... I mean, you going down to that place ain't.... You don't belong there."

"Why the hell not?" I said, the blood rushing to my face. "You scared I'm turning into Mom?"

"Aw, Christ, this ain't about her." She slammed her fist on the arm of the recliner. "It's about you, what you're doing, who you're doing it with. I'm no idiot. I know the sort that goes to the Marsh Trail. They ain't all horny teenagers like you and Donna's boy. What if one of 'em pulls a knife on you? What if one of 'em gives you a disease?"

"Don't be so melodramatic. The guys that go there are harmless."

"Harmless, huh? Even if that were true, most of 'em have wives and kids waiting at home. Did you ever think about that? How they're sneaking around in those woods behind their families' backs? Is that harmless, too?"

I didn't answer—just glared at her.

"Look, puppy, you've got no business messing around with grown men like that. They're only using you for a good time. It'll lead to nothing but trouble, mark my words. Only you'll be the one that gets hurt."

She peered at me like she expected me to crumple, but I held firm. Rozella smoked two packs a day. I smoked married men. We all had our risky vices.

"Well?" she demanded, the blood slowly draining from her face. "Please tell me I ain't talking to the wall here." She was shaking even worse than before, and it occurred to me that our argument had cost her something.

Actually, it'd cost us both.

"I should go," I said and grabbed the magazine off the couch. "Thanks for the beer."

"Dammit, puppy! Have some self-respect. You're better than this. Why not find yourself a nice boy your own age? Go on a few dates. Fall in love."

I stared at her in disbelief. "I already tried that, Rozella," I said, pointing to the cut on my forehead. "In case you hadn't noticed, this is what it got me."

Then, I bolted for the door.

CHAPTER SIX
CRISIS MANAGEMENT

I WAS FURIOUS AS I stormed home from Rozella's place. We'd always gone to such lengths to maintain the boundaries around our private affairs. Her slut-shaming felt like a betrayal of our friendship. She was out of line.

I mean, I could've just as easily thrown it in her face that Nicki had gotten herself knocked-up at seventeen by some lowlife fourteen years her senior. Where was her own daughter's self-respect, huh? But I'd never say anything like that to Rozella because, unlike everyone else in this shithole town, I didn't shame other people for their mistakes—only for their cruelty.

Though I expected to be judged harshly by the rest of the people in my life, I'd hoped for better from Rozella. I was bitterly disappointed.

As I stepped up the front steps of our trailer, I debated whether to hike down the hill to the swimming hole to work out my anger by doing a few laps. But that plan was immediately dashed when I heard the approaching rumble of Baby, Jimmy's black '69 Camaro that he'd spent the past five years painstakingly restoring. The minute he saw me, he dropped the clutch and hammered the accelerator, spitting up a strafe of gravel from the rear tires. He screeched to a halt in the driveway beside his pickup and hurled himself out of the driver's seat.

My hand was still frozen to the doorknob.

"You alright?" Jimmy shouted as he leaped the front steps to seize the sides of my head, inspecting my face like a bruised melon.

"Don't paw at me," I said, slapping his hands away. "Why are you home already?"

He stepped back, downshifting from panic to fury, and the little vein in his neck popped like a turkey thermometer—this meant I was done.

"Donna called me at work," Jimmy growled through gritted teeth. "She said you and Dylan had a fight and that Dylan looks like he got mowed down by a backhoe. Since you turned off your damned phone, I couldn't even—you'd better start explaining."

Though my mouth began to churn, no words came out until something Rozella said popped like a flashbulb in my mind. "I... I, um, made up this crazy story about the two of us hooking up at the Marsh Trail to humiliate him in front of some girls. I said we'd been messing around down there all summer long. The Schlees and Abe heard it, too. I think they believed me." I gave a self-satisfied snicker to let him know how pleased I was with myself and added, "That obviously set Dylan off."

Jimmy gawped at me, clearly struggling to process the whopper I'd just laid on him. Meanwhile, I struggled to contain the relief breaking loose inside me. This was genius. Sheer genius. Tell him the truth, but make him think it was a lie. Now, when he heard the story from Abe or somebody else in town, he'd have a better version to believe. A version that didn't completely wreck his sanitized illusions of me.

Disaster averted, at least for now.

Jimmy rubbed the frustration from his eyes and asked in a wounded voice, "T-bird, why would you do something like that?"

"He said shit about Mom."

It was all the explanation I needed. We'd been down this road too many times with other bullies and assholes for him to fail to understand my meaning.

"Goddammit," he sighed and pushed past me into the trailer, gesturing for me to follow. "Get inside and let me look at you."

But I just stood there wishing I could fast-forward through the coming lecture and slink off to my bedroom. We didn't communicate well under the best of circumstances, but at moments like this, a stranger could be forgiven for believing we were no more closely related than chickens and dinosaurs. Years of hard and heavy labor had forged Jimmy solid and true. He was already eighteen when I was born, barely twenty-three when you died. The weight of responsibility since then had scrubbed away the last vestiges of youth from his face. With his old man Earl's keen black eyes and burgeoning beer belly, he was bull-necked, blue-collared, and as hulking as a load of cement, bearing down on life with a weary kind of tenacity, all brusqueness and persistence and as earnest as a freight train. I was nothing like him, which made living together a challenge, even at the best of times—and these were hardly the best of times.

I found him waiting for me at the kitchen table, a beer bottle in hand and the first aid kit resting open in front of him. "What the hell are you wearing?" he said as soon as he saw me. "Is that lingerie?"

"It's a camisole."

"Where did you get it?"

"Goodwill," I lied. "What difference does it make?"

"Why do you have to go out dressed like that? It makes you a target."

"Yeah, right," I said, pulling at the silky fabric covering my chest. "This is what makes me a target."

He didn't respond. Instead, he flicked open the first aid kit and gestured at the chair across from him, commanding me, "Sit."

I pointed to the bandage over my eye. "It's already been done."

"I'll take a look for myself."

There was little point in arguing with him. I set my magazine down and did as I was told, trying not to squirm while he poked and prodded at my face as if conducting a forensic examination. It went on forever, and when he finally finished, he said, "It could be worse, but maybe we should get you checked out at the clinic just to be safe."

"I'm fine." I pulled away. "You're totally overreacting. It's just a few scratches."

He reached across the table and pressed a fresh Band-Aid onto my forehead.

"When you get a call like that, see how you react. Which reminds me—why did you turn off your phone? You could've saved me half a heart attack."

My answer was a shrug.

"Fine, whatever. We'll talk about phone privileges and responsibilities later. For now, just tell me again what happened."

"Does it really matter?"

He peered at me and then took a swig of beer. I knew he was thinking the same thing I was. We'd been down this road too many times before. Only the names and places ever changed. Whether it was Dylan or Scarface or any of the other dozen assholes I'd tangled with through the years, the story remained the same.

"No, I suppose not." He eased back in his chair, pressing the cold beer to his forehead. "It sounds like Dylan's in rough shape. Rougher than you anyway." I couldn't fail to notice the satisfaction in his voice. He leaned forward, wearing just a hint of a grin. "So, you fought back this time?"

I shifted uncomfortably in my seat. "With words."

He gave me an incredulous laugh. "Aww, come on, T-bird. You must have used more than words. Donna said the whole left of his face is swollen like a balloon. When I hung up on her, she was still trying to coax him to go to the clinic, but the little punk ass wouldn't budge."

"It wasn't me," I said quietly and fidgeted with the hem of my shorts. If I ever wanted to have that beer with Gabe Fournier, I'd have to tread lightly here. I cleared my throat and added, "A good Samaritan came along and pulled Dylan off me. Maybe he slugged him, too, or whacked him on the side of the head with something. I don't really know. It's all a bit of a blur, and anyway, I was pretty out of it by then."

His expression darkened. "What good Samaritan?"

"Just some guy." I shrugged. "He was gassing up or something. I've never seen him before, but he chased off Dylan and the Schlees and then helped me into the bathroom to clean up. He left me with Abe's first aid kit and then got the hell out of there. Scarface said something about the cops, so I figured he was spooked and didn't want any more trouble."

"You didn't ask his name?"

"No, I did," I said and hesitated long enough to imply I was struggling to recall it. "I think it was, um, Gabe something.... Gabe Fournier, maybe?"

Jimmy blanched, and for a moment, I thought he would drop his beer bottle onto the floor. "Gabe Fournier?"

"Yeah, do you know him? Abe said I should ask you who he is."

Jimmy's brow furrowed, and he said distractedly, "I went to high school with him." He fell silent.

I could tell I'd dodged another bullet. There was obviously some history or hostility between Jimmy and Gabe, but like so many other subjects from the past, my brother didn't want to discuss it with me. In this case, though, I was only too happy to oblige.

He downed a couple more swigs of beer, his mind obviously racing. The moments ticked by. I was just about to ask him if we were done here when he blurted out, almost as an afterthought, "I wish you'd let me teach you how to throw a punch. I've always wanted to do that. Maybe then this shit wouldn't keep happening."

I squirmed inside but didn't reply. There wasn't any good way to answer this. It wasn't like I could learn how to fight, and even if I tried, I'd only end up disappointing him even more. It was ironic, really. When Dylan and I were still little kids, we always daydreamed about swapping Jimmy and Donna. Dylan could come live here with my brother, who'd take him fishing, show him how to rebuild an engine, and teach him to throw a punch. I'd move in with Donna, who'd take me shopping, paint my nails, and curl up on the couch with me in front of her favorite shows. It's been hard for Dylan to be her "little man" with no one around to show him how to do it the right way. It was hard on me growing up in Jimmy's shadow, never being interested in following his example. Sometimes I wondered if my brother wouldn't have been happier raising Dylan. I know Dylan would have preferred it that way. But then, that was the story of our lives: nobody ever got what he wanted.

"How's your beer?" I asked to change the subject.

He scowled at me. "So that's it then? You just expect me to drop this?"

"Nobody asked you to get involved in the first place."

"What am I supposed to do about Dylan?"

"Nothing. It's over. Let it go."

He drained what remained of the beer and sat appraising me in silence.

"Fine," he said finally, almost dejected. "If that's how you want it, I'll drop it."

Though I nodded in agreement, I couldn't help but feel a twinge of disappointment. There'd been a time, not so long ago, when Jimmy wouldn't have bothered to ask me what to do about Dylan because he would've already marched down to Donna's place and done it. He wasn't a violent man, but when he got pissed off enough to bear down on you with all 225 pounds of meat and muscle, it could scare the crap out of even the most hardened bad ass.

But those days were over now. I was no longer the blameless victim in the situations I found myself in, and after dozens of ass-whoopings and similar incidents over the years, I'd finally worn him down. Or maybe it was just life that'd done that. Lately, he seemed tired and defeated, so much older than his 35 years. Flecks of gray salted his hair. He slept poorly and ate worse. He drank too much beer and worked too many hours, pulling doubles and weekends at the paper mill, where he'd hustled his way up to foreman. It was hot, sweaty, grueling work, yet he seemed hellbent on squeezing every last dime he could get out of the place just to pad the stupid college fund I never even planned to use. I soothed my guilt a little, thinking that at least he could retire early on all that extra cash.

He'd certainly earned the right. After you died, Mom, he had no life to call his own, no dates or girlfriends or hookups, not even a buddy from the mill to catch a quick beer with after work. If he wasn't on shift, he was passed out on the couch in front of a ball game or had his head buried beneath Baby's hood. It wasn't much of an existence, and I dreaded what his life would look like once I was gone, though that wouldn't stop me from leaving.

To make amends, I asked, "You want me to fix you something to eat?"

"Naw, we've got leftovers, though I could use another beer."

Without a word, I hopped up from the chair and retrieved a cold one from the fridge, twisting off the cap with the corner of my camisole and handing it over.

"That's a good color on you," he said quietly, nodding to the silky fabric. "Too bad it's wrecked."

My heart swelled inside my chest—you could never say Jimmy didn't try—and with a dash of genuine regret, I blurted, "I'm sorry about this. I didn't mean to scare you or make you lose hours."

"I'll get over it," he said, draining half the bottle in a single gulp. "At least you're alright, though I wish you hadn't said that crap in front of all those people."

I blinked. "Wait, that's what you're worried about? That's not even why I'm sorry."

"Maybe it should be. I know you were pissed off and all, but Christ, no wonder he came after you."

I couldn't believe my ears. Abe was right: my own brother thought I had it coming, too.

"Are you seriously trying to tell me this is my fault?"

"No, but Jesus, T-bird, you can't go around saying shit like that and not expect guys to react badly to it."

"Oh, but I suppose he can say whatever he likes about Mom?"

"That's different."

"How is it different?"

"It just is, and you should know why by now." He drained the rest of the beer and slammed the empty on the table beside the first one. "I mean, shit, you really want folks thinking you're running around acting that way, too?

"Too? You mean like her? Like a slut?"

"Okay, here we go." He threw up his hands. "I didn't mean it the way it came out."

"That's exactly how you meant it, and you know it."

He mashed his face into his palm and sighed. "Look, all I'm saying is that it doesn't make a hell of a lot of sense picking fights with some kid because of the crap he says about her, and then turning around and pretending you're the same way. Why would you want people to think that anyway? Didn't I raise you better?"

"What if you didn't?" I said, fully aware that I was now skating onto perilously thin ice. "What if everything I said about Dylan and me is true?"

His eyebrows shot up and he leaned forward, his nostrils flaring. "Is it?"

I averted my eyes. "No. But that's not the point."

"What is the point then?"

"The point is, what if it were true? What if the two of us had fucked like bunnies on the Marsh Trail? What if I'd spent every afternoon this summer giving out blow jobs to strangers down there? What would you think of me then?"

He winced. "Stop this," he said, blocking my face with his hand. "You're being disgusting."

"Ah, so now I disgust you? And I suppose if I did all that stuff, you'd be so disgusted you'd wash your hands of me for good. Just like you did with her. Am I right?"

That did it.

"We're done here." He hammered the table with his fist, nearly toppling both bottles. "It's been way too hard a day for this shit. I need a shower and a nap."

He pushed himself to his feet, grabbed another beer from the fridge, and started down the hallway toward his bedroom.

I followed.

"I wish you'd talk to me for once," I said. "Make me understand why you're still so angry. If I can forgive her, I don't see why you can't at least try."

He stopped in his bedroom doorway and turned to face me, marshaling whatever reserves of patience he still possessed. "This ends now. Wake me in an hour, and we'll eat."

Then he slammed the door in my face.

"Dammit, Jimmy," I shouted and kicked the doorjamb. "You can't just throw people away like garbage when they fail you."

But even as I said it, I knew it wasn't true.

CHAPTER SEVEN
BODiES

I STRIPPED AND DIVED OFF the lichen-stitched ledge into the swimming hole. The water here was deep, plummeting through layers of green into inky blackness between the slope of Shelter Mountain and a ridge of bedrock jutting like a middle finger into the lake. The onrush of cold felt like a sucker punch, but I shook off the blow and arrowed downward, taunting the deeper currents that churned below. Though they snatched at my wrists and ankles, coiled around my chest and thighs, I grappled back toward the light, too strong a swimmer to be caught.

The blood hammered in my ears. It felt awesome to work out my anger on the water.

Goddamn Jimmy.

I burst to the surface, heaving great gasps of air like rocket fuel, and launched myself toward the shallows at the far end of the ridge. The granite formation towered above me like a fence that kept the swimming hole private from the prying eyes of town on the opposite shore, turning this secluded stretch of water into my personal fortress of solitude.

I ignored my throbbing ribs as I shredded the lake's surface like I had a grudge against it. This was the fight I'd been itching for: one I could win. I was tired of Jimmy treating your memory like something diseased and unwholesome. You weren't an infection—remembering you wouldn't make us sick. I hated that there were so many things I'd forgotten about you, so many more I'd never even known. Even the simplest details were gone, like your favorite color or food. The scent of your hair. The sound of your laughter. The few memories I had were fragments of shadows, fleeting images of you helping me cut out the models in your beauty magazines, or humming songs to soothe me when the wind roared, and the trees clawed the walls like bears trying to get inside.

I wanted so much more of you to hold onto, Mom. But Jimmy kept his own memories of you behind lock and key inside his brain. Instead of inviting me in to share the wealth, he kept slamming the door in my face. It was beyond stupid. Did he really think turning me away would force me to stop caring about you? All he ever succeeded in doing was to remind me he believed we'd come from shame. If there was anything infecting our lives, it was that.

It didn't take me long to power my way to the end of the ridge. The shoals bounding the swimming hole loomed ahead. I slowed to a halt, panting wildly as I tread water, and I threw my head back to howl out my rage at the empty sky.

But there was no response besides my echo, no other voices here, no shouts or slammed doors. Nothing but the quietly respiring wilderness that surrounded me.

My fever broke.

I caught my breath and turned back to the landing. Languid waves shimmied in the dying sunlight. Clouds of gnats swarmed the reeds along the shoreline. I licked the water from my lips, savoring the lake's mineral sweetness. Though my lungs burned, and my bruised ribs gnawed like hungry piranhas, I felt better. Lapping this lonely stretch of water always anesthetized me; it was more potent than any high I'd ever gotten off of alcohol or drugs or even cumming.

I'd been sneaking down here since Jimmy first taught me to swim. The water was the one place I didn't feel small. I'd taken to it like a salamander, spending hours a day at the swimming hole during the height of summer. Though Jimmy nagged me to join the swim team to make friends and burnish my college applications, I refused. I wasn't about to spoil swimming by turning it competitive, something I had to perform on cue in front of an audience. This was what I did for myself to shed the bullshit world from my shoulders for an hour or an afternoon.

Nobody was invited to join me here.

Nobody but you.

Not that I'd be swimming here much longer. The water would be too cold in a few more weeks, and then what? This was my last summer in Shelter Valley. Come graduation, I was out of this shithole for good. Yet, sweet as this knowledge was, it was tinged with a bitter aftertaste: I'd suffer the loss of this magical stretch of water when it was gone. There would be nothing quite the same to replace it in the city.

I closed my eyes and kicked onto my back once I reached the landing. The air near the shore was as fresh as moss, and I relished its chill on my penis bobbing unselfconsciously between my legs. Skinny-dipping always reminded me how much I loved my own body. Wearing clothes could be a kind of tyranny if you let it. Ravisha once said that what you wore told the story of who you are to the world. But that made getting dressed a huge responsibility. What kind of a story could I tell when the most fabulous things in my closet were hand-me-downs and Goodwill bargains? Sometimes it was liberating not to worry about it. At least my body was always there to tell my story to me. It was the one thing I truly owned in life, and its infinite capacity for sensation, its responses to pleasure and pain were mine and mine alone. Not even getting my ass kicked by Dylan Falcone could take that away from me.

Ah, Dylan… fuck me.

As the lake's anesthesia wore off, the slow, steady ache of Dylan's loss settled back on my heart like a weight, crushing the joy out of me. How had we come to this? I still didn't know. Last August had been a glimpse of technicolor in a lifetime of black and white: three weeks, five days, and fourteen hours when I'd been in love and believed I was loved in return.

And then he was gone.

It all began as unexpectedly as it ended, with a classic Hollywood meet-cute at the Mini Mart ice cream cooler on the hottest day last summer. A duel of rock-paper-scissors for the only Nutty Buddy— my paper won; Dylan always played rock—led to the rekindling of a connection that'd gone dormant at the start of junior high. Nostalgia for our childhood friendship soon fast-forwarded to something more, and even a year later, I still replayed memories of those days like my favorite scenes from the movie of us. The little things he said, the special things we'd done. How we'd secretly meet for matinees in the balcony of the Kayoga Cinema to smoke weed and make out. I taught him to dance (a little) while he taught me the difference between a first-person shooter and a tactical shooter. I still jerked off to the memory of our sex and dreamed of that afternoon when, with the rain hissing against his bedroom window, he told me he loved me for the first and only time. I'd actually believed I was living my happily-ever-after, Mom....

"Don't float away on your daydreams."

Gabe Fournier's voice gonged inside my head.

I thrashed onto my belly, wiped the spray from my eyes. He stood poised on the landing beside the pile of my clothes, peering down at me over the tops of his sunglasses, the remains of his six-pack still in hand.

"Didn't mean to scare you," Gabe said.

"Too late for that," I said and glowered. "What are you doing here?"

He took off his sunglasses and eyed me inquisitively, a grin teasing the corners of his mouth. "I came for a dip, same as you." He whistled a meandering tune and set the beer beside my clothes.

"How do you even know about this place? It's private."

"I don't see a 'No Trespassing' sign." He made a show of glancing around and then kicked off his boots. "Besides, this swimming hole's been around a lot longer than you. So have I."

"There's a public beach."

"Didn't pack a suit."

He began to strip.

I didn't look away.

Though I'd taken my share of locker room punches for my wandering eyes over the years, I'd come to appreciate there was a kind of power in observing what the other boys tried so hard to ignore. You could learn a lot about someone's insecurities by paying attention to how he behaved when naked. A boy might skip the showers and dress too quickly or strut around like a balls-out peacock. Maybe he'd brag too much about all the pussy he was getting or tease too loudly about those girls who never let guys score. Perhaps he'd police the gazes of the dudes around him or keep his eyes glued to his locker. Along with the tweaked nipples and slapped asses, the forced laughter and furtive glances, these tells were all a part of the same mysterious boy's code that it seemed only I had ever bothered to try to decipher, searching for clues to vulnerabilities. It'd become a way for me to quietly assert myself in a world of aggressive bro-ness, and though I occasionally still got caught looking, the satisfaction of keeping score was well worth the few hits I took for it.

"A picture'd last longer," Gabe said, smirking as he slipped out of his boxers. "Want me to hand you your phone?"

"Nothing I haven't seen before," I said and sniffed, though this wasn't precisely true. Gabe wasn't some pimply-assed teenager or one of the paunchy, middle-aged closet cases from the Marsh Trail that slobbered all over me. His body was magnificent: muscled, tattooed, and dusted all over in sandy blonde fur, every inch a burning invitation to be kissed, licked, caressed. I felt myself blush at the sight of his full-grown manhood swinging between his legs—which was enough to plump my own.

With his clothes now heaped beside mine, he flexed his toes against the smooth plain of the rock face and helicoptered his arms as if preparing to dive in.

"Nice ink," I said to excuse my gawping.

"Thanks." He drew his hand across the tattoos on his arm. "Cost a shit ton though."

"Are they tribal?"

He barked a laugh. "Dammed if I know. Never let a biker with a needle anywhere near your wallet when you're fucked up in Vegas."

"I guess not everything stays in Vegas."

If he registered the joke, he didn't let on. Instead, he swung his arms above his head and dove into the lake, surfacing a moment later a few lengths away from me.

"Feels great, doesn't it?" he asked, wiping the water from his face. "I forgot how much I missed this place."

"Shelter Valley?"

"Hell, no... I mean here. This place." He paddled towards me, coming to a stop so close I could feel his turbulence below the surface.

The sunlight caught like flecks in his hair and washed the exhaustion from his face. He was beautiful. "Kids came down here all the time when I was your age. They'd party, get stoned, mess around. They still do that?"

"Naw. I'm the only one, and I only come to swim."

"That's a shame," he said sincerely and then stifled a yawn with his fist. "I shouldn't have downed all that beer. I'm gonna need a nap soon."

I glanced longingly at the remains of his six-pack. "I see there's still a couple left."

"Go help yourself."

I wasn't about to turn down his invitation twice and swam over to the landing. I heaved myself out of the lake, grabbed a beer, and plopped down on the warm rock to watch as he propelled himself through the water in a kind of mutant breaststroke.

Beautiful or not, he was a lousy swimmer. He sploshed about lazily for a while, circling a few times before he paddled up to the landing and folded his arms over the ledge beside me.

"This feels good," he said, panting, his cheeks red. "Pass me that last one. Don't want to make you drink alone."

I handed him the bottle and said, "Glad the cops haven't hauled you away yet."

He didn't laugh. "That little prick sure did a number on you, didn't he?" He gestured to the mass that'd swollen across my ribcage. "You gonna finally tell me what that was about?"

I tensed. "Long story. Forget it."

He looked at me curiously, set his beer on the rock, and heaved himself out of the lake.

"I got time," he said, the water sluicing from his sun-golden body as he squatted beside me. "The only thing on my agenda tonight is hearing my old man bitch about the socialists ruining the country while he lies in a hospital bed the government's paying for. I'd much rather listen to you."

"Why do you even care?"

"Because we're drinking buddies now."

He tapped the neck of my bottle with his.

Though I rolled my eyes at him, I liked that he wanted to know. I polished off the rest of my beer and said, "The sweet and condensed version is that the little prick and I had a thing going on. It was cheap and tawdry and hush-hush, but I thought it was love because, well...." I trailed off. How could I explain how deeply I'd deluded myself about Dylan and me? I thought it was love because whenever Dylan called me "T-bone," the world quivered beneath my feet? Because even after he fell asleep in my arms, he wouldn't let go of me? Because whenever I was with him, I felt right with myself for the first and only time in my life?

I sighed. "Because, well, I'm stupid, that's why. And the proof of that is that once it was all over between us, he turned around and treated me like shit. I guess he was never who I thought he was."

I could feel my eyes about to betray me and had to look away.

"And the fight?" Gabe asked.

"Ah, that," I said, swallowing the sudden chalk in my throat.

"Dylan said something nasty. I called him out for it in front of his buddies. He got annoyed. With his fists. End of story."

Gabe squeezed my shoulder. "Little fucker. Wish I'd snapped his neck."

"Yeah, well, I'm glad you didn't. The cops might've hauled you away for that one."

He gave a rueful laugh and sighed. "Heartbreak's the worst. Makes it hard to trust anybody again, especially yourself."

"Exactly. I should've known better. What was I thinking?"

What *was* I thinking? More to the point, why did I still care? Once school began again last September, our teen romance abruptly turned tearjerker. Dylan shunned me in the hall and on the bus. Blew off my texts. Sent my calls to voicemail. Ignored the frantic notes I shoved into his locker. Yet, it wasn't until he started hanging out with the Schlee Posse that I finally realized our movie was well and truly over; I'd somehow missed the climax.

Maybe that was the rub, Mom, the thing I couldn't get past. We'd stopped, but we never actually ended. Only, I still didn't know why. I just wanted to know why.

Gabe tipped the beer to his lips and swallowed what was left inside before hurling the empty far into the lake. "To hell with him," he said and belched. "He's a coward and an idiot, too. You can do better than that, trust me."

"Not in this town."

"Oh, you never know." He flashed me a wink. "Besides, the world's a big place." He heaved himself to his feet and aimed his dick at the water. "Anyhow, thanks for telling me. I'm doubly glad I kicked his ass now."

"You know, people have to swim in there," I said, as I watched him piss, but he just glanced over his shoulder and smirked at me. It dawned on me then how uncomfortable this level of bare intimacy ought to be making me feel. But I liked that it didn't. After all, messing around with random strangers on the Marsh Trail was one thing. But this seemed different somehow, relaxing even. Safe.

We were just talking, and there was something liberating about that, something downright contagious about Gabe's ease in his own skin that I'd never experienced with another dude before, or at least not since Dylan and I were kids innocently comparing our bald little ding-dongs while we peed our names into the snow together.

If this was what male bonding was all about, I liked it.

"So, tell me," I said, wriggling my toes in the warm sun. "What makes you so cool? It isn't every day dudes like you are chill hanging out like this with someone like me."

"Watch it," he said and sniffed. "I may look like a redneck, but that don't mean I am one."

"Sorry. It's just, I've gotten used to people treating me a certain way. That's all."

"Well, I'm not like folks around here. There's a reason I left this town and never looked back." He finished peeing, shook off his junk, and then plopped back down on the rock to dip his feet into the very same water. "I'll tell you one thing though: I've been a lot of places and met a lot of folks, and the best ones are always like you."

"What's that supposed to mean?"

"It means the ones brave enough to be who they are without hiding behind bullshit or lies. Believe it or not, you're a rare breed."

"Um, thanks... I think."

"Trust me, it's a compliment." He lifted his face into the sun. "As far as I'm concerned, any twink going outside in lingerie and eyeliner in this town has a pair of brass cojones."

"Maybe I'm just a raging exhibitionist."

"Same here." He chuckled as he kicked at a dragonfly that buzzed across the lake's surface. "Though I shouldn't have called you a twink." He flashed me an apologetic look. "I can see you've got the equipment and all, but that don't necessarily make you a little boy on the inside."

"It's cool," I said and smiled easily at him. "I like my dick. I like boys. I like being a boy, at least some of the time. Or rather, I like to think of myself as a 'beautiful boy,' you know? A little extra sparkle and polish on the original model. I'm not trans or anything, but the clothes and makeup and stuff—well, it's complicated." I hesitated, trying to figure out what I meant to say. It wasn't every day I got the chance to explain myself to somebody who seemed interested, but honestly, I didn't have all the answers yet—I was still figuring myself out. "I guess sometimes I use it like armor. Like a barrier that keeps this shit town on the other side of me. It helps me stay grounded, in touch with who I want to be, safe on the inside even when everybody around me is hateful. But it's more than that, too, more creative and expressive. A statement about me. What I love, how I feel." A light breeze raised gooseflesh on my skin, and I pulled my knees to my chest, shivering. "I just don't care about picking sides or following gender rules or whatever. I can be beautiful in jeans and a hoodie just as easily as I can butch it up in lip gloss and a miniskirt. People get so hung up on labels, you know? But it's like what Ravisha Mann says: Why do I have to be anything when I can choose *everything*?"

"Bonnie would've loved to hear you say that."

My heart stopped cold in my chest. "You knew my mom?"

"Well, duh…. Of course, I did." He said this as if it were the most obvious thing in the world. "Everybody knew Bonnie. Best bartender J.J. ever had. A good woman, too. Generous. Smart. A hell of a lot of fun. A real rebel like you. It was tough how she…. I mean, I'm sorry you had to…. How she died and all."

I bristled. "I don't talk about that."

"Understood," he said gently. "I just wanted you to know I cared about her, too. That's all."

"Thanks," I muttered, my hands shaking. No one had ever spoken so kindly about you to me before, Mom. Not once in my life. Kindness was not something the people who knew you ever showed to me, and to be honest, I didn't know what to do with it now, especially since it felt as if Gabe had just made me the guest of honor at a pity party.

An unpleasant chill shimmied down my back. It was time to leave.

"Jimmy will be waiting for dinner," I said, hoisting myself to my feet. "I should go."

So much for male bonding.

I could feel Gabe watching me as I yanked my cutoffs over my wet hips with such haste my phone toppled from my pocket onto the ledge. When I picked it up, I saw a notification on the screen that I'd been DM'd by this random girl I knew from my A.P. European History class:

Have you seen this yet?

I unlocked the screen, swiped open the link, and was instantly greeted by my own profile pic attached to the naked body of a gay porn star spread-eagle on his back. He was taking it up the butt from another porn star who had a Dylan selfie superimposed on his shoulders. Someone had blurred out the naughty bits, and though the picture had been posted by Owen Betts, I couldn't imagine him having the brain power necessary to master the limited photoshopping involved.

This had Scarface written all over it.

The picture had already garnered over 50 likes from half the kids in my class, as well as a dozen humiliating comments, culminating in a shockingly accomplished limerick from a cute boy named Scott Keeney I'd once let cheat off my English midterm:

> *There once was a fag from the Valley*
> *Who liked to take dick up his alley*
> *Oh, Dylan! he cried*
> *Deeper in, won't you slide?*
> *But please don't get jizz on my belly!*

"Fuck my life," I groaned and jammed the phone back into my pocket.

"Everything alright, Little B?" Gabe asked. He was still watching me, only now he looked concerned. He climbed to his feet, swatting the grit from his ass, and turned to face me.

"It's fine," I mumbled, struggling to prevent a torrent of profanity from spewing out of my mouth. "I just need to go."

He cleared his throat. "It ain't Jim, is it? I hope he ain't giving you shit about being late."

"No, not this time—wait, did you just call me 'Little B'?"

"I did." He flashed a sheepish grin. "It's what I called you back when Bonnie brought you around to my old man's diner. You were a little badass even then. Get it? Little badass. Little buddy. Little Bonnie…. Shit, you're still the spitting image of her."

As he said this, Mom, I noticed for the first time just how he was looking at me.

I always recognized the men by these looks. Your men.

Like flecks of human debris from the fallout of your past, they poisoned my little patch of the earth with their quiet, radioactive stares. No matter where I was or what I was doing, I might suddenly feel a pair of strange eyes burning holes into me as one of them passed me by on the street, swung open the school bus doors, handed me my ticket stub, or unzipped his fly for me. They were your lovers and your leftovers. The one-night stands and no-named quickies. The weeknight barflies and weekend boyfriends. They were the silent ones, the secret ones, often married with kids. Total strangers who nevertheless peered at me with deeply knowing eyes, betraying hunger or lingering shame, but always with that same unspoken question: first recognizing your face in mine and then searching beyond it for any dreaded trace of their own.

All at once I felt as if I might puke.

"I really need to go," I blurted and jammed my feet into my sneakers, though Gabe seemed too lost in his memories to notice my distress.

"I've got a confession to make," he said. "I recognized you the minute I laid eyes on you in the Mini Mart parking lot. How could I not know you with that face? You look just like her."

"I've heard that one before," I muttered, not bothering to tie my laces as I stumbled toward the footpath.

"I'll catch you later, Little B?" he called after me.

"Sure thing, Gabe," I lied. "Sure thing."

CHAPTER EIGHT
WHATEVER GETS YOU THROUGH THE NIGHT

MOM, JUST TO BE CLEAR, I knew damn well Gabe Fournier was not my sperm donor.

Back in middle school, I'd discovered that this dubious honor belonged to Roy Allen Krause. Jimmy had hidden a manila envelope labeled "FOR TOBY" in his closet, right where he knew I'd snoop. Inside, he'd saved a picture of the dude—paunchy, pasty-faced, unfortunate tufts of ear and nasal hair—plus paternity test results, the order for child support, and a bunch of official documents you'd kept from family court. These provided all the detail my eleven-year-old brain could process, including the delightful tidbit that I was the result of "faulty birth control during a one-time encounter." Jimmy also thoughtfully saved a copy of the dude's obituary from a couple of years later, as well as the certified letter you got from that Albany lawyer looking for money to bury him since I was apparently his only next of kin.

No judgment here, but where did you dig up such a loser?

Finding that envelope was the only "conversation" Jimmy and I ever had on the subject. I could've badgered him to tell more, but what was the point? He couldn't even bear to talk about you, let alone one of your hookups gone awry. Besides, as I grew older, there were plenty of other people in town who were only too happy to fill me in on the gory details, like that I was supposedly conceived in one of J.J.'s booths after closing time.

Not that I cared about any of it. I didn't need Roy Allen Krause to know who I was. I didn't want his name. I didn't want his memory. He was nothing more to me than a squirt from a turkey baster. So, case closed, right?

Right, except when some creeper came along and flashed me one of those looks.

Goddamn it, Mom. For Gabe to even imagine I might be his kid, you must have slept with him when he was still my age. And I was starting to like him, too.

Nevertheless, by the time I reached home I'd resolved not to think about him ever again. I slipped in through the back slider to find Jimmy snoring on the couch in front of a baseball game, an empty plate, and a beer bottle on the coffee table. So much for waiting for dinner.

There was no beer left in the fridge, so I snagged a bottle of Pepsi and headed to the bathroom to inspect your camisole for damage. There was some blood, dirt, and a few rips small enough to mend—

nothing irreparable. I scrubbed it clean in the sink with some Woolite, and then draped it over the back of my desk chair, aiming my fan at it to dry.

Next, I grabbed the music magazine from where I'd tossed it on my bed, made myself a bologna sandwich in the kitchen, and settled into one of the Adirondack chairs on the back deck to eat and read. Although sunset was still at least an hour away, the sun had already dipped below the tree line, turning the woods behind the trailer a softly shimmering gold. Cicadas buzzed in a pleasing drone as I breezed past articles about Drake, Dandy-O and Nana Hughes, Rhianna, Gellio Suvilli, and mega-hottie Shawn Mendes, before finally settling on a lengthy exposé by this political journalist who'd traveled through a bunch of rural towns on his way from Philadelphia to the Republican Convention in Cleveland: "A Journey Through America's Heart of Darkness." It was mostly just a series of increasingly unhinged interviews the guy conducted with "seemingly normal, everyday Americans" asking how they really felt about "the commie Democrats, Blacks, illegals, and goddamned queers," as he quoted one particularly irate truck driver braying at him in some diner outside of York, PA. The tone of the piece was one of shock and dismay that there was so much hatred and bigotry bubbling up in "real America," but the only shock to me was how it'd taken a journalist so long to notice. Hell, I could hear worse than that any day of the week just shopping for deodorant in the Kayoga Walmart.

By the time I finished the article, it was getting dark, so I headed back inside, locking my bedroom door behind me. I grabbed the scissors from my desk and then surgically excised Ravisha from the Andes before climbing onto the bed, where I balanced on my tip-toes to pin my latest image of the Diva to the constellation of superstars already tacked to my ceiling.

Although Ravisha shone brightest among these heavens as the reigning queen of my musical universe, she was orbited by a coterie of New York City club divas and idols, including the sweet and sassy Peaches Viramontes, Cazwell the buff buffoon, radical visionary Miko Tika San, the slinky and curvaceous Miss Amanda Lepore, plus several other fabulous and infamous Club Kids. They'd all transformed themselves into queer icons through sheer nerve and outrageous fashion genius. Jimmy raised an eyebrow whenever he glanced up at my celestial menagerie, but I didn't care what he thought. They were my guiding stars, pointing the way through the sky of possibility that was my future. Though I doubted I'd ever burn brightly enough to be worthy of them, it didn't matter: Simply wanting to shine like that felt like the only thing lifting me up from the gutter of my life.

Once I'd affixed Ravisha to the perfect expanse of bare ceiling, I collapsed into the sheets to nurse my Pepsi. A quiet breeze eased in through the open window, carrying the piney breath of the twilit woods. I sighed, flicked on my bedside lamp, and grabbed my phone.

I couldn't avoid the inevitable any longer.

Since I'd last checked in on Scarface's prank, it seemed everyone in Kayoga County under the legal drinking age had given it a thumbs-up. I wondered if Dylan had seen it yet. I pictured him abandoned and alone, staring at his phone while the rest of the Schlee Posse was off at some kegger getting shit-faced without him. I wondered what he would do now. Though it was just a stupid meme, he didn't have my expertise at rising above public humiliation.

I'd survived far worse over the years. Homophobic slurs hurled down crowded hallways. Slaps to the back of the head that sent me sprawling. My clothes shoved into a shit-loaded toilet during gym class. It wasn't like I was the only queer kid around. There were others, too. Drama nerds and uber-goths. A debate champion. A cheerleader. Even that spooky Willa Mars girl from Little Tip that everyone said munched bush when she wasn't seeing ghosts.

But they all steered clear of me. I was a target that attracted too much heat, and nobody wanted to get burned in my proximity. I didn't care, though. I didn't need them. I was better off alone. Besides, if I'd learned anything from dealing with bullies my whole life, it was to keep my head high and repeat to myself over and over that no matter what they did to me, I'd be just fine. It would eventually be true if I said it enough times. Self-deception is an excellent life-preserver. But Dylan didn't know that, did he?

Hey. You okay?

I hit send on the text and waited, but of course, he didn't respond.

Instead, I heard Jimmy stir in the living room. The TV went quiet, and a moment later, he shuffled past my door without even knocking to see if I was alright. He was still pissed off about our fight, but I had too many other things on my mind to worry about that now. Tonight would hardly be the first time we'd gone to bed with anger poisoning the air between us.

I waited until I heard him flick on the TV in his bedroom before I texted Dylan again:

I'm sorry, okay? Just let me know you're alright.

But as soon as I hit send, I regretted it. This was stupid. Why would he respond now when he hadn't answered a single text in nearly a year? After today, he probably hated my guts.

I only wished I could return the favor.

I reached over to my nightstand and snagged the slender plastic figurine that had stood vigil over my bed since Dylan gave him to me nearly a year ago: Vergil from *Devil May Cry III*. A shock of silver hair. An elegant blue satin cloak. A sleek Katana in hand with an ornate ebony hilt. This was one of Dylan's two dozen or so collectible action figures from his favorite video games. He'd been saving up to buy them online for years and kept them all displayed behind glass in a tall case in the corner of his bedroom. When he'd given this one to me, he'd explained that Vergil was the twin brother of Dante, the demon-hunting star of the series, and Dylan's all-time favorite gaming character. He said the two brothers were linked together by forces more powerful than nature, their fates forever intertwined.

"Kind of like ours," he'd said.

It was only later that I discovered they spent most of their time trying to kill each other, but that didn't matter to me. I knew what he was trying to say.

It was his version of a broken heart necklace.

Vergil was the best gift I'd ever received, only now, I wondered if he regretted sacrificing him for me. Maybe he'd already replaced this one with a newer Vergil. Maybe he'd forgotten it was gone. I fingered the action figure's cold, lifeless form and then slammed him back on the nightstand. I should hate Dylan for breaking my heart, just like any normal, self-respecting person would. I should be glad I'd finally made him pay for ghosting me. For choosing them over me. For making everything that came after him feel so awful and empty and pointless and gray. But no, Mom. Here I was again, a whole year later, still hoping against hope that he would, just this once, please God, answer a single, goddamned text.

Sometimes I wondered how I'd ever let myself become so pathetic.

I grabbed my earbuds and hit play. Ravisha began to purr "Burn This Mother Down" from MANNtastic. I swiped open my browser and slammed my finger on the first bookmark. A bus ticket from the Kayoga Wal-Mart to the Port Authority Terminal was still $75. Same as this morning, yesterday, last Friday. I had almost $800 in cash hidden in my closet from the bribes Jimmy paid me for every A, plus what I'd filched from the housekeeping fund. I could do it if I really wanted to. Just pack up and go. Melt into the wild and wondrous city and leave all this backcountry melodrama far behind me.

If only....

The phone rang. My heart nearly leapt out of my chest, until I realized it was Rozella's number.

"Hey," I said, picking up. "What is it?"

"You're missing Jack Palance chase poor Joan through the streets of San Francisco."

In the background, I could hear ominous violins playing over the grinding whir of Rozella's air conditioner. "You're watching *Sudden Fear?*"

"Yeah, come over and catch the ending with me." She sounded drunk and a little maudlin. "I've got bananas and chocolate sauce. I'll fix us sundaes."

This was her way of making amends for earlier.

"Sounds like fun." I faked a yawn. "But I'm going to bed."

"Okay." She fell silent. I heard her lighter strike, followed by an intake of breath, a slow exhale. "How's Jim?"

"I dunno. Asleep?"

"Good for him." Another puff. "So, did he ask about what happened down at—"

"He knows all he needs to know. He won't know the rest unless you tell him."

"I ain't a snitch," she said and sighed. "I get that I ain't your babysitter either, and it's not my business what you do, but would'ya please not go back there? That's all I'm asking. Call it a personal favor."

"Why do you even care?"

A long pause, followed by another puff, another exhale. "I just do."

"Alright, fine." I flipped the bird at the phone. "I won't go back, okay? Feel better?"

We both knew this was a lie, but we also knew it was the best she would get out of me.

She took a sip of what was presumably beer and said, "We won't talk about this again, deal?"

"Deal."

Another puff, another exhale. "So, you coming over?"

Ice cream and a movie would be just the ticket to distract me from obsessing over Dylan the rest of the night.

"Naw," I said finally. "I'm tired."

"Will I see you tomorrow?"

"Sure. Maybe. Unless you have stupid errands for me to run."

"No promises." She snorted and then paused for another round of puffing and exhaling before asking with surprising sincerity, "You sure you're okay, puppy?"

"I'm fine," I assured her. "But thanks for asking." At least somebody gave a shit.

Once we'd said our goodbyes I checked my messages again. Still nothing from Dylan.

The temperature had dropped outside, so I shut the bedroom window. I confirmed that your camisole was dry and then turned off my fan before fishing into the back of my closet to retrieve the haggard cardboard box I've kept hidden there for years.

As soon as I unfolded the lid, I found you just as I'd left you, smiling up at me from the prison of your shiny silver frame. It was the only photo I'd managed to salvage from Jimmy's purge a few years after you died, and I was pretty sure it'd been taken long before I was even born. An autumn scene at the public beach, the mountainside in the distance stitched in blazing patches of orange and gold. Falling leaves swirled in the sky behind you as the wind played havoc with your hair.

Mom, you were laughing. You looked happy. You looked like me.

The other mementos I'd rescued from the garbage bins years ago were packed neatly beneath the picture frame. Pieces of your cheap costume jewelry. Empty perfume bottles I'd long since used up. Your hairbrush with a few precious blonde strands intertwined in the bristles. Your silver-plated hand mirror with the crack in the glass. The shiny brass crucifix that once hung above your bed. Beneath these items lay a thick pile of your neatly folded clothes, including jeans, skirts, tee-shirts, lingerie, and blouses, none of which still smelled like you. Not even the camisole did anymore.

Now, they all smelled like me.

I carefully folded up the camisole and laid it on top of the rest of your things. Then I closed the box and returned it to its hiding place in my closet. I flicked off the lights and climbed into bed with my phone. There were still no messages from Dylan, so I scrolled to my favorite playlist. Louie B's RAZOR'S EDGE remix of Ravisha's "Whatever Gets You Through the Night" began to sizzle in my ears. I lay there staring into the darkness, grateful that at least Rozella had called. It occurred to me that being alone and feeling alone were two different things, and as Ravisha sang about the pleasures of one-night stands, I nuzzled into my pillow. Maybe the Diva was right: sometimes just knowing you didn't have to be alone was enough to get you through the night.

I hoped you knew that wherever you were, Mom.

I hoped Dylan knew it, too....

I must have dozed off after that, because when the text alert buzzed in my ears hours later, a gibbous moon shone brightly through my window, bathing the room in ghostly light.

The message on the screen was brief. Only two cryptic lines:

Meet me at the Marsh Trail in the morning.

We need to talk.

CHAPTER NINE
A DIRTY LITTLE AFFLICTION

BAM... BAM... BAM...

Distant thudding roused me in my dreams. Though I'd been playing with a box of kittens a moment ago, the bams had transformed into the paws of a hissing mama cat batting the sides of my face.

"Hello? Anyone in there?"

I jerked open my eyes. The room was dark, although eerie light streamed in through an ice-encrusted window, bathing me in a sickly green glow.

But that wasn't my window. This wasn't my bed. No. No. I was lying at the bottom of a... a bathtub?

Sheets and a thin blanket had been laid across the tub's cold porcelain surface for me to sleep on. A bare pillow rank with sweat was wedged beneath the faucet. The faucet had leaked, soaking the pillow through, and the back of my head was wet, icy.

I shivered. I sat up and began to whimper. "Mommy?"

Bam... Bam... Bam...

"Open the door, please."

A man's voice, a stranger.

Frightened, I called out for you again, but you didn't respond. Where were you? I couldn't remember coming here, wherever here was, but I did remember you yelling on the phone—an argument? And then you were crying.

Had you left me here all alone?

"Mommy!"

I clambered out of the tub, my bare feet sinking into a sticky bathmat. I was naked except for my Underoos, which I'd peed sometime during the night. A toilet glugged hungrily in the corner. On the floor beside it, a rusted vent hissed lukewarm air that smelled of pee and mildew. MOTEL blazed through the window above the sink like a neon green demon. Seeing it filled me with such bone-deep dread that I began to tremble.

I scampered across the frigid tile toward the slightly ajar bathroom door and pulled it open to peer into the next room.

Bam... Bam... Bam...

The TV was on, tuned to the late show. A woman in a slinky black dress sang a Christmas carol. "Santa Baby." A length of dusty red garland snaked around the screen. Tinsel and satin balls. The room stank of mold and cigarettes and—used diapers? It was lit by a single lamp without a shade, its bare bulb so harsh I had to squint just to see.

Bam... Bam... Bam...

"Open the door, ma'am…. It's the police."

When my eyes adjusted, I saw you on the bed. Laid out in your panties and bra, your skin paler than a fish belly, the needle still speared into the fold of your arm, your eyes wide and glassy and staring straight at me.

Mom, that's when I screamed.

"JESUS, WAKE UP!" JIMMY POUNDED on my door with such force it shook the bed.

I sat up, eyes wide, drenched in a cold sweat. "Alright, I'm up. Stop banging."

I wiped your afterimage from my eyes and sat up on the edge of the bed. The stale air in the bedroom reeked of perspiration. The motel sign was gone, replaced by the glaring sun. My head throbbed. My body ached like a fist I'd clenched for hours.

Jimmy whacked the door again. "Open up. We need to talk. Don't make me late."

I grabbed the sheet I'd kicked loose during the night and wrapped it around my shoulders. Then I pushed myself to my feet and shuffled past the door, unlocking the knob on my way to the window.

Jimmy threw open the door and cursed as soon as he stepped into the room. "It stinks like a flophouse in here."

"If you don't like it, get out," I said and slid the window open to inhale the woodsy morning air. "What do you want anyway? I'm up. Go to work."

"I want to talk about your applications.... Would you look at me?"

I pulled the sheet tighter and whirled around to glare at him. He'd taken up position in front of my bed clutching an armload of the SUNY view books he'd been amassing practically since the day I graduated kindergarten.

"Here," he said and dumped the pile onto the bed. "I want you to start making some decisions. You've had plenty of time to do your research. You can't put this off any longer. Your counselor said you need to pick at least five schools, so pick them. Today."

"Why do we have to talk about this now?"

"Because the summer is nearly over, and I'm sick of waiting. If we're going to visit campuses, I need to put in for the time off, and you need to tell me where we're going."

I opened my mouth to argue, but the look on his face made me think better of it. I didn't have it for another knock-down-drag-out with my brother.

"Fine," I said. "Anything else?"

"No." He turned for the door. "Just get it done."

As soon as he was gone, I bent down to finger through the dreaded view books. Each was glossier and more vacuous than the last, featuring a smorgasbord of well-scrubbed collegiate types in Gap sweaters and ironed khakis strolling purposefully across leafy quads bathed in autumnal light. If I had a lighter and some gasoline, I would have torched the smug-faced lot of them right there on my bed.

Of course, Jimmy was right that I couldn't put off the inevitable much longer. I would have to tell him soon that I wasn't going to college. But not today.

I waited until I heard Baby roar out of the driveway before I grabbed my phone to check for messages. I'd texted Dylan a dozen times after his cryptic midnight missive, but he hadn't responded to any of them.

Meet me at the Marsh Trail in the morning.

We need to talk.

Well, duh. We'd needed to do that for a whole year. Still, this was better than nothing, and since Dylan hadn't bothered to specify what time he wanted to meet, I'd have to hurry my ass up if I wanted to catch the early bus.

I darted into the bathroom to drain my raging bladder, the image of you on that bed still fresh in my mind. I hadn't shaken off the nightmare yet. Sometimes it took a while, Mom. Jimmy hadn't bothered to ask if I was okay, although I was pretty sure he'd heard me cry out in my sleep. But then, he'd stopped acknowledging I even had these dreams when I was still in middle school, and the child psychologist made the mistake of suggesting we seek counseling together.

That was the last time I saw any counselor.

I distracted myself from the afterimage of you in that bed by assessing the damage from my eventful yesterday in the mirror. The swelling on my bottom lip had gone down, and the scratches on my forehead were scabbed over. The bruise on my torso had begun to purple. Though it still ached when I breathed or turned sharply, all in all, it could have been worse.

I showered and dressed: black thong, blue onion-skin hot pants, my pink Converse high-tops, my vintage Scissor Sisters concert tee, cherry lip gloss, and for luck, your silver wrist bangle. It took me longer than expected to select an outfit that Dylan would find irresistible but was subdued enough for the general public, and when I glanced at my phone, I realized I'd have to run down the hill to J.J.'s if I wanted to catch the bus.

FORTY-FIVE MINUTES LATER, THE SUN-DRENCHED asphalt of the Dollar Drug parking lot warmed the soles of my sneakers. The doors of the K-CAT #2 squealed shut behind me. I hopped the curb and loitered by the entrance, pretending to check my phone until the bus disappeared into the traffic on Route 10B. Then I scanned the lot for busybodies. Seeing no one, I skirted along the shady side of the building and emerged a moment later in the narrow service lot at the rear.

This lot lay empty save for a couple of junkers belonging to the Dollar Drug's minimum wage staff. Beyond were the cool Marsh Woods where Dylan hopefully awaited.

I paused to wipe the beads of sweat from my brow. I inspected my hair and face in my phone. I breathed into my hand and sniffed: hardly minty fresh, but not dog food either.

I bolted across the pavement toward the tree line.

The Marsh Trail has changed little from what you might remember, Mom. Officially called the Kayoga Creek Marsh Nature Preserve Trail, it still begins five miles to the north, where the creek empties out of the mountains onto a meandering plateau of swampy marshland and pine forest. Since the state built a fancy new visitor's center at the mouth of the marsh, the Preserve has become a popular destination for naturalists and photographers. But the sightseers rarely venture down by the Dollar Drug, where the woods turn dense, and the marsh peters out into little more than a smattering of mucky pools.

I slipped into the woods past a rusted blue sign warning of plainclothes police officers patrolling the premises. Though I'd never spotted any cops here, whenever I saw that sign, I felt a thrill of danger at the possibility. Thick, moss-covered maple and hemlock irised closed behind me, muffling the world beyond. The light fell differently here, faceted by the leaves and branches into dazzling shafts that shifted in the breeze. The air felt different, too: cooler, wetter, almost slick, a kind of greasy mist that gathered on the hairs of my arms and face. Something charged radiated up from the ground here, teasing my senses with the murmur of the foliage, the aroma of the soil, the shadows that lingered a moment too long.

I'd spent half my adolescence fantasizing about the hookups I'd someday have in these woods. Since junior high, I'd heard whispers about the perversions that went on at the Marsh Trail, rumors of men doing things with other men not even their priests would absolve.

The reality had not disappointed.

Ironically enough, Dylan dumping me gave me the courage to visit that first time. After ten wretched months of feeling rejected without him, I'd been desperate to be wanted again, even if just for a few breathless minutes by a total stranger. Though Jimmy probably considered the Marsh Trail some kind of unholy trinity of Sodom, Gomorrah, and San Francisco, whenever I came here I stopped feeling lonely.

Roughly fifty yards from the parking lot, the trail widened into a small clearing where most of the action took place.

No Dylan.

I checked my messages again, and finding nothing new, I blasted off a quick *I'm here... Where are you?* Then, I leaned against a tree and surveyed the woods. Nobody seemed to be around, though it was still early. I usually came in the afternoon, when lunch hour traffic swelled on 10B, and random dudes stopped by the Dollar Drug to snag their Lipitor prescriptions and a quick slice of relief around back.

Rozella had been right about one thing: the men who came here kept secrets, including some of Jimmy's coworkers at the mill, sperm donors of kids I knew at school, and even one of my old bus drivers. I'd hooked up with about a dozen so far, and except for Dylan, they'd all been the wife-and-family type, sneaking back here to do things they'd probably rather die than have revealed to the world. Part of me relished the idea that no matter how average they might seem in their public lives, in private, we shared the same desire for encounters that were nameless and brief, with no promises or illusions, no emotional ties or regrets.

Just sex: hard, anonymous, pure.

I know you'd understand if you were still alive, Mom, though trying to explain it to anyone else seemed pointless. What was it about us and sex? Just something we had to do, some random glitch in our

DNA that'd skipped over Jimmy. A dirty little affliction that, owing to the local prevalence of small minds and limited selection, we'd each been forced to sweat out on the down low in our own risky situations.

My phone pinged in my hand with a new message from Dylan:

Down by the marsh. Come find me.

Hardly a warm and cuddly invitation, but at least it got to the point.

I pushed off the tree and followed the trail deeper into the woods, where it narrowed, branching off into private cul-de-sacs littered with condoms and cigarette butts. The blazes soon faded as the trail became overgrown, but I finally spotted him through the brush ahead. He was hunched on a log beside a pool of reedy water skinned in algae, the remains of a campfire smoldering at his feet. He looked as if he'd just been rolled. His shorts and Adidas were caked with mud. Flies swarmed a nearby puddle of vomit. Wedged against the log beside him lay a mostly empty bottle of cheap Canadian whisky.

I called out to him.

He lifted his head slowly, turning to look at me. It was obvious he'd been crying. Dried tears reddened his cheeks. His lips were swollen, and the entire left side of his jaw had turned an angry purple.

"About time—you showed up," he slurred as I came up beside him, his whiskey breath reeking like a sewer.

"What the hell happened to you?"

His eyes narrowed with confusion. "You did, T-bone," he said, the name twisting my stomach up in knots. "You did."

Then he bent forward and began to weep.

CHAPTER TEN
THIS IS WHAT YOU CAME FOR

IT TOOK DYLAN A WHILE to calm down, but when he finally quit blubbering, he glanced up at me and said, "Why did you text me last night?"

"I was concerned. Obviously, with good reason. When did you get here?"

He shrugged. "Before Mom got home from work."

"You spent the whole night out here?"

"Here and in the car. So what?"

"Alone?"

"Yeah, alone." Dylan flashed me a bewildered look. "You jealous?"

"Would you care if I was?"

"I might," he said as he pawed clumsily at the log beside him. "Sit. Talk to me."

"Now you want to talk?" I snorted. "Why should I listen?"

"Because I've got nobody left, T-bone."

I flinched as something hard wrenched out of shape inside me.

"I'm sorry," Dylan moaned. "I shouldn't have said those things about your mom. I shouldn't have hit you. I don't know what I was trying to prove."

"If you want me to stay, please stop." I surprised myself with how bitter I sounded. I didn't want this sniveling display of remorse. It felt obscene witnessing him grovel, like being trapped in an elevator when a little kid shits his pants. The only appropriate response was to look away, pretend you didn't smell it, and let his mommy deal with it. And I wasn't Dylan's fucking mommy. "Let's not do apologies, okay? I didn't come here for that."

I settled on the end of the log as far from him as I could get.

He wiped the wetness from his face and said, "Why did you come here then?"

I didn't answer him, although it was a fair question. If I were honest with myself, I would admit that what I came for was my chance at that climactic scene in the movie of us. The ending I never got. The one I'd been rehearsing in my fantasies. The one where words proved unnecessary, and we'd say everything with our eyes. He'd only need to look at me to know the pain he'd caused me, and then it would melt into nothing because it would be nothing now that we were together again, him and me against the world. He'd brush an errant lock of hair from my forehead. I'd tenderly caress the bruise on his jaw. The violins would swell as he told me what a fool he'd been, and then he'd sweep me into his arms, kiss me and kiss me and kiss me.... Roll credits.

Or something pathetic like that. Only this was way too real for that. The thought of kissing Dylan as he was made me ill.

"Well?" he said, peering at me intently. "Why did you come here?"

I couldn't seem to spit out the truth, so I picked at the hem of my hot pants and said nothing.

"See, that's what I thought." He hung his head between his legs. "You don't know either."

"Jesus, what do you want me to say? That what you did to me sucks? That how you treated me sucks? That despite it all, I still feel like shit for outing you and ruining your life? That I'm a pathetic loser who still cares about you? That's why I texted, asshole. That's why I'm here."

He stared at me as if I'd spoken ancient Greek, which only pissed me off even more.

"Don't you get it? Don't you know this already? Or did you really ask me to come all the way out here just to apologize? Do you really think I need your worthless apology?"

He scowled. "What do you need then?"

"I need an explanation. How about giving me that?"

Dylan smashed his head into his hands and groaned. "It's all going to sound so stupid now. You'd never believe me."

"Try me."

He glanced at me pleadingly, but when he saw I wasn't letting him off the hook, he cleared his throat and said, "Labor Day weekend last year. Mom came home from work one night and told me this messed-up story about these two gay guys she waited on down at the Lamplighter. Old dudes, like in their seventies. She said they looked like they were there on a first date, only it wasn't going well. They were clearly a bad match. One of them was this redneck farmer. Dirty overalls. John Deer cap. He ordered a Coors and drank straight from the bottle. The other was this prissy, librarian-type with glasses and clear-painted fingernails who nursed a Shirley Temple the whole time. She said they tried to make chit-chat, but it was painful to watch, especially since all eyes in the lounge were on them."

Dylan paused to swat a mosquito slurping from his ankle and wiped the bloody remains on the log between us.

"She said a couple of the guys at the bar started laying bets on whether these old geezers would get a room upstairs. They were laughing about which would be the 'man' and which the 'woman,' and soon the regulars had all joined in, too. Mom said the whole place was buzzing with whispers and jokes about these two old-timers looking for love in all the wrong places."

He hesitated, glancing over at me.

"I'm listening.... So?"

"So, that's when Mom looked straight at me and told me that it was the most heartbreaking thing she'd ever seen. Two tired old dogs with nothing to show for their lives. No family or grandkids, and there they were, just trying to mind their own business and stave off the loneliness for a night. But instead, they ended up the butt of the joke for every drunk in the shithole Ramada lounge. She said she couldn't bear to think about how empty life must be for them. For any man like that."

I aimed my finger at my temple and pulled the trigger. "I know she's your mom, but where does she get off? Maybe they're perfectly happy. Maybe they're in love."

"That's not the point."

"What is the point?"

"The point is that my mom knocked on my door at one o'clock in the morning to tell this story to me. To *me*, T-bone. To my face. Like she was warning me. Like she knew about me, about *us*, and it scared her. Like she was saying, Please, Dylan, don't make this mistake. Don't end up like that."

"*That's* what this is all about?"

"Maybe." Dylan shrugged. "I don't know. I told you it was stupid, but it got me thinking. Haven't you ever wondered what your life would be like if you weren't so—different?"

"You mean if I didn't like dick?"

"No, I mean, if you weren't different. Like, what if, besides liking dick, you totally fit in around here? You played video games, wore flannel, got lousy grades, listened to Country instead of that EDM crap, and got shit-faced at keggers like everybody else."

"You mean, what if I were like you?"

"Yeah, I guess."

"Well, that would suck," I said and laughed. "Being me is the best part of being me."

"Exactly."

"Exactly what?"

"Don't you see?" Dylan clenched the sides of his head like he was trying to squeeze out the right words. "You get to be who you are and still like dick, because those things—go together. Like wine and cheese, you know? But it doesn't work that way for me. Liking dick and being me don't go together at all. It's like wine, and I don't know—Doritos or something."

"Seriously? How drunk are you?"

"Don't be an asshole. I'm trying to be upfront here. You think you have it so rough because you're different from everybody else. But at least who you are and what you want, they, like, line up. They make sense together."

"And they don't for you?"

"I don't know." He shrugged again. "I mean, the whole thing got too real that night. I started thinking about all the stuff I was going to have to give up if you and me were together. Like how I couldn't just be regular anymore, like everybody else. One of the guys."

"Like one of the guys at that bar making fun of those old dudes? Is that what you want? To be a bitter asshole hiding in the closet for the rest of your life?"

He shook his head. "I just don't want to be *you*. I don't want to be different, to stand out. I want to blend into the woodwork and be, like, normal, and have a normal, boring life, just like everybody else." Dylan grabbed the bottle of whiskey and chugged a mouthful as if it were Gatorade. He gasped through the whiskey burn.

"So that's why you ghosted me?" I said. "So you could fit in?"

"Was that so wrong? I mean, let's face it, we were always as bad a match as those two old dudes. We stopped being compatible in sixth grade, T-bone. We only got together again because there was nobody else."

I winced, dying a little inside. Okay, sure, Dylan was Carhartt, I was Chanel. That wasn't going to change. And to be honest, I hated playing video games with him. I hated his friends too, the music he liked, the insipid superhero flicks he forced us to watch. Sometimes, I even hated being called T-bone, as if I were nothing more than a slab of meat.

But still, I'd always believed we shared something deeper than a mutual liking of dick. Call it history if you like, a connection, understanding.... *Love?*

What the hell did Vergil mean if not that?

But maybe he was right. Maybe I had to step back and at least entertain the possibility. What if none of what we'd shared was real, just a matter of convenience and proximity, the fond memories of childhood confused by adolescent hormones and late-summer boredom?

What if we'd never been anything more than a bad match?

If so, then I'd wasted the past year deluding myself about us, when the only thing we shared was the high school equivalent of what I could get on the Marsh Trail any day of the week.

"Christ, fine, whatever," I blurted, more angry with myself than him. "It's your life. If you want to be normal, it's on you. But you could've told me all this a year ago and saved me a ton of grief. You didn't have to quit me like cigarettes. I deserved a goodbye text, at least."

"I thought it'd be easier this way." Dylan downed another swig of whiskey. "Clean break. No temptations or backsliding."

"Easier for you, asshole."

He flashed me a sheepish grin. "You sure you still don't want me to apologize?"

"Fuck that apology shit. This isn't a break-up song."

"Okay, okay." He wiped the mouth of the whiskey bottle with the corner of his shirt and offered me what was left. "Here, kill it. You'll feel better."

I eyed the contents warily.

"Don't worry," Dylan said. "There's a whole unopened bottle in the car. Mom got a case of it from work."

"That's not what I was worried about."

Though the lingering stench of his puke remained a potent deterrent, getting shit faced suddenly seemed like the best idea I'd had in forever. I tipped the bottle to my lips and braced myself. As expected, the flavor was heinous, like swilling old, charred cardboard. But though I grimaced as the whisky scalded my throat, there was something satisfying about throwing back with Dylan for old time's sake, even if I wasn't about to admit it.

"Tastes like ass," I gasped and hurled the empty bottle into the trees, where it landed with a squelch somewhere in the mire. I wiped the sides of my mouth and eased into the pleasant warmth pervading my body. I felt better already. Less anxious, less angry. Maybe it was good to clear the air between us, even if it hadn't gone as I'd hoped.

"You know," I said, "Jimmy thinks I made this whole thing up to embarrass you. As payback for what you said about Mom. There's no reason that can't be the story for everybody else."

Dylan regarded me like I was an imbecile.

"Come on, man. We both know nothing sticks around here like the truth."

I thought about arguing with him, but he was right. Some genies couldn't be shoved back into the bottle. I'd robbed him of his chance at normal. The meme was only the beginning. From now on, we'd both have to live with the consequences of what I'd done.

I was debating whether to offer an apology of my own when I noticed him gazing at me.

"What is it?" I said.

"Nothing." He flushed. "It's just, your face looks like shit." He scowled as he leaned in to inspect the damage. "Can I at least be sorry about that?"

"It doesn't look half as bad as yours."

His eyes went wide.

"Whoa, dude. Who was that guy, anyway?"

"My guardian angel."

I glanced down and toed at the dirt, hoping he wouldn't ask me anything more about Gabe.

But I didn't need to worry, because Dylan blurted, "God, I'm so sick of fronting. Shad and Owen are cool, but Eddie, man. It's too much work." He grimaced. "Maybe it's a good thing this happened. Maybe I can finally relax." He laughed before adding in a sly voice, "Besides, last week with you was nice. Brought back fun memories."

"It was nice," I muttered.

An uncertain smile tugged at the corners of his mouth. "Thanks for coming, T-bone. Being alone out here really sucked." He reached over and squeezed my shoulder.

I smiled. "You never had to be alone, asshole."

Our eyes locked, and for one brief, wondrous moment I thought I heard those violins swell.

But then Dylan grabbed me by the sides of my head like some face-hugger alien and planted the most revolting kiss of my life on my lips. It was like being smothered by slabs of rotten liver. His body reeked of onions and dirty feet. His breath tasted of booze and puke and sleep mouth.

It was all I could do to keep from gagging as I wriggled free. "Hey—don't," I stammered, my hand planted on his chest to push him away. "You're drunk. Let's not do this."

I laughed to let him know things were still cool, but he didn't seem to notice.

"Don't be a tease, man," he said. "We both know this is what you came for." Then he seized the back of my neck and jammed his tongue down my throat.

Fuck! I tried to shove him from me, but even drunk, he was way too strong. When I tried to squirm free, he shifted his weight, and I tumbled off the log, landing with a thunk on my back.

He pounced on top of me, bearing down his full weight. His arms and legs writhed like tentacles around mine, his hands everywhere at once, squeezing into my flesh, ripping at my clothes, his mouth suctioning the air from mine, his hard-on jabbing like a beak between my thighs.

But when his tongue strayed between my teeth, I chomped down hard.

"Ulgghhh!" he howled and lurched off of me, rolling onto his back in the mud.

I scrambled to my feet and hurled a furious kick to his balls. "Fucking asshole!" I screamed and spit my bloody saliva in his face, rubbing the inky taste of cheap booze and sick from my mouth with the back of my hand.

For an instant, I thought he would try to get up and come after me. But instead, he just curled into a fetal ball and began to cry, heaving once, twice, and then puking up all over himself.

I just stood there dazed, watching in horror as the last shreds of Dylan Falcone's dignity disintegrated before my eyes. I didn't know what else to do. Seeing him like that made my heart ache so badly... I feared it might explode.

I had to back away.

"I'm—*sorry*," he stammered between unquenchable sobs, blood and vomit glossing his lips. Despair twisted his face into such unspeakable ugliness it took my breath away. "Don't go, T-bone. Please! I was—a mistake."

But I couldn't not go. There was nothing left to do to make this right. I had to escape that dirty, wretched scene in the woods that had suddenly made me hate everything about him. And myself.

So, I ran, Mom. I ran.

CHAPTER ELEVEN
RESPECT IN THE STRAIGHT WORLD

I HAD TO GET CLEAN.

That was the only thought hammering inside my brain as I bolted into the Dollar Drug men's room, quaking with an overflow of adrenaline. My mouth was streaked with Dylan's blood, my eyes wide and hollowed out. Mud saturated my clothes. He'd torn the seam in my crotch in his frenzy to get into my shorts. The collar of my tee shirt was stretched halfway down my chest, and Mom, your poor silver bangle was bent into a pretzel around my wrist.

I still smelled Dylan on me. In my clothes, between my fingers, up my nose. His sweat, his puke, his booze breath. His stench had soaked into me like cheap cologne. I wanted to peel off my skin and toss it into an industrial washing machine with a gallon of bleach. Instead, I had to make do with a cracked sink and a nearly empty soap dispenser.

I must have spent fifteen minutes scouring my skin until it glowed red. At some point, a store employee with a beard and a dirty Dollar Drug smock wandered into the bathroom to relieve himself. He stood at the urinal, smirking in the mirror, and then flashed me a knowing wink when he zipped up and left without even washing his hands.

As soon as Smock Guy was gone, I faced myself in that mirror to see what he saw standing there.

It wasn't pretty. I was a hot mess, another silly faggot who'd gotten what he had coming on the Marsh Trail. I wondered how many others like me that dude had found wrecked in this very bathroom over the years. When had I become such a cliché?

I tensed as the door squealed open again.

In walked Gabe Fournier.

"Little B?" he said, recognizing me in the mirror.

Dammit.

"Hey," I muttered and wiped the wetness from my eyes. I spun around, fixed my gaze on the floor, and tried to slip past him out the door, but he pushed it shut, barring my exit.

"Whoa, hold up a minute," he said.

"Are you following me?"

"Just came in to take a leak." He lifted the plastic Dollar Drug bag dangling from his wrist. "They been calling all week to pick up my old man's prescriptions. He's on enough painkillers to knock out a grizzly. Can you believe the government pays for it all? Who knew getting old was the cheapest way to get high?"

He laughed.

I didn't.

"I need to catch my bus," I said and tried to shove him aside, but he leaned his weight into the door.

"Not so fast," Gabe said, his eyes widening. "What the hell happened to you this time?" He reached to touch my cheek.

I slapped his hand away. "Get the fuck off me! You're not my father."

He put his hands up and slid away from the door. "Whatever. Didn't mean to freak you out."

"Thanks," I spat and hurled myself out of there, rushing down the hair care aisle and back into the sunlight.

Once outside, I collapsed against the sunbaked wall and checked my phone. It was at least an hour until the next bus home. Shit. I could slip inside, grab a Pepsi, and hang out in the beauty aisle until the bus showed. But I desperately wanted to jet before I ran into Dylan again.

I scanned the lot and spotted Donna's blue winter rat parked near the dumpster, where I'd missed it when I arrived. Damn. He'd see me standing here the minute he came out of the woods.

I spun around to duck back into the store just as Gabe emerged from the entrance.

"Don't take off on me again," he said, holding out his hands. "Sorry I tried to touch you. Didn't mean nothing by it. You just look like you could use a friend."

"Why do you care? You hardly know me."

"Maybe I want to get to know you better."

"Why? What's so interesting about me?"

"You remind me of somebody."

"Who? Mom?" I gave a bitter laugh. "You do realize you're not the first dude she ever slept with to notice how much we look alike. Most have the decency to shut their mouth and leave me alone."

His lips curled into a frown. "Me and Bonnie? Shit, I'm younger than Jim. Trust me, she and I were just friends."

"Okay, fine. Just friends. Whatever."

His back stiffened. "I got nothing to explain to you, okay? You don't want a ride, fine. But I'm guessing you'd rather not be stuck hanging around here all morning long, am I right?"

I eyed him warily and glanced over my shoulder at Dylan's car.

"Jesus," he said. "Relax, it's just a ride."

I hesitated a moment longer before giving in. "So long as we don't have to talk."

"Whatever." He zipped his lips. "Mum's the word."

He gestured across the parking lot, and I followed him to where he'd parked Harold's ancient Silverado. He unlocked the passenger door and held it open for me, apologizing that the AC was busted before he slammed the door behind me. As I rolled down the window, he slid into the driver's seat and fired up the engine.

A blast of cock rock erupted from the speakers.

"Sorry," he mouthed and lowered the volume. "I can turn it off?"

"It's fine," I said, since it made it harder to talk.

I buckled in and waited, but he didn't shift into gear. Instead, we sat there idling. My ass began to sweat on the vinyl upholstery. Thunderheads had gathered on the horizon. A tarry breeze wafted into the cabin, swaying a golden crucifix on a chain around the rearview mirror. I caught a whiff of Gabe's musky deodorant and squirmed in my seat. The singer on the stereo howled about heads exploding while my own brain beat against the insides of my skull.

And still, we didn't move.

"Jesus, can we go?"

He flicked off the music, squeezed the steering wheel, and said reluctantly, "You need a doctor or something? Maybe a cop?"

I sucked in my breath. "Hell no. I'm fine. Can we just go?"

"Look, I know what goes on back there." He nodded toward the Marsh Woods. "If some pushy bastard went too far—"

"I knew this was a mistake," I said and reached for the seatbelt.

"Wait, forget it." He threw the truck into gear before I could jump out. "A deal's a deal. I won't say nothing more, I promise."

"You'd better not," I said, struggling to keep my voice from shaking. "Because I am none of your fucking business."

I slammed my head against the seat and glared out the window as we pulled into traffic.

We drove in silence. Soon, the forest expanded on either side of the road, dark and impenetrable even in the high summer sunlight. The state land went on for miles along this stretch of highway, with an occasional road sign or deer carcass to break up the monotony. The ride home from Kayoga always felt oppressive. No matter how routine it became, it was like a permanent reminder in distance and wilderness that I was not a part of the civilized world but belonged to someplace separate, someplace cutoff and dead-ended. The notion left me despairing, not least because Dylan belonged there with me. But when I squeezed my eyes to wipe him from my thoughts, all I could see was his stricken face as he flailed in the mud like a suffocating guppy.

I caught Gabe watching me out of the corner of his eyes. Though he didn't say a word, I knew what he was thinking as plainly as that Dollar Drug asshole in the men's room. He'd already jumped to all the obvious conclusions. He felt "sorry" for me, the poor little faggot who'd gotten what he had coming messing around with grown men who wouldn't take no for an answer. But who was he to judge me?

Just friends, my ass. I didn't believe for a second, Mom, you two hadn't hooked up. I could picture him in the Kayoga Unified locker room bragging about it afterward to all his buddies, their eyes wide and eager, nobody quite believing him, yet wanting so badly for it to be true. Shit, he probably got treated like a conquering hero all over town, with pats on the back and free beers from all the horny old losers delighted for a vicarious thrill, imagining their own teenaged selves getting it on with their own fantasy Mrs. Robinsons.

Of course, you would have been the only one called a slut for it. And that was just a part of what made it so infuriating. If getting laid by an older woman was the gold standard of conquests for every straight kid on the planet, why should the flip side be any different for me?

The rules were fucked up for beautiful boys.

Maybe Jimmy was right. Maybe being an upstanding Disney gay was the only way to get any respect in the straight world. But that didn't make it fair.

Fuck Gabe Fournier and all the hypocrites like him. Fuck the fear and shame they tried to hang around my neck like a noose.

No wonder Dylan was so messed up.

When we pulled up to our trailer, I unbuckled the seat belt and offered Gabe a mumbled thanks for the ride.

But before I could slip out, he said, "Do me a favor and pass me your phone."

"Seriously?"

"Yeah. Unless you want Jim to hear about today."

I gasped. "What makes you think I won't tell him myself?"

"Because I know him," he said simply and held out his hand.

"You're blackmailing me?"

"Call it a friendly nudge."

I was too stunned to argue, so I handed over my phone, watching in silence as he punched in a strange number and held it up to his ear.

"It's ringing," he said, as his jeans pocket began to jangle. "Now you've got my number, and I've got yours." He hung up and tossed me the phone. "When you get bored, give me a call. Anytime, day or night. We'll shoot the shit. I bet we've got a lot to talk about."

I peered into his eyes, looking for judgment or pity, but all I saw was playful curiosity.

I shook my head. "I don't get you at all."

"That's alright. You don't need to get me. I get you."

I hopped out of the truck and was halfway to the front door when he called after me.

"Hey, take a hot shower. You'll feel better." He gunned the engine. "And just so you know, it ain't Bonnie you remind me of—it's *me*." He floored the accelerator and peeled off in a shower of gravel.

CHAPTER TWELVE
POSTER CHILD OF NO CHOICES

GABE WAS RIGHT ABOUT ONE thing: the shower helped. So much so, I ended up taking three more in between counting out my savings, cleaning out the housekeeping stash, and checking and rechecking the next day's bus schedule.

There were no options left: I had to leave town. How could I face Dylan again, day after day, month after month, until graduation? Although the showers had cleared my head, they hadn't rid me of his smell. He still lingered in the air, his voice murmuring in the hum of the cicadas, the funk of his breath coating my mouth like postnasal drip.

From now on, he would live in the faces of everyone I knew.

This had become inescapable. Sometime during my second shower, another meme—this one of "me" spread eagle on the hood of a car while a hairy-chested "Dylan" hammered sweatily into my ass—

materialized online, garnering a stream of hateful new comments. The situation had spiraled beyond my ability to rise above it. This wasn't going away. In less than a day, we'd become a community joke, sure to generate laughs and whispers the rest of our miserable lives here. Just like you, Mom.

I couldn't face another year of this. I had to get out now.

By the time Jimmy got home from work, I'd made peace with my decision. I even fixed him dinner while he showered—a box of spaghetti with jar sauce and a hastily assembled salad—and set out a chilled six-pack and five of the view books on the table, ready, for the evening at least, to humor his college daydreams as a sort of parting gift.

"What's all this?" he said, emerging from the bathroom with a wet towel draped around his shoulders. He slumped into his chair, twisted open one of the beers, and surveyed the table, sliding the stack of view books closer and rifling through them as he drained the bottle dry. "These the ones, then?" he asked, covering a belch with his fist.

"Yep." I grabbed his plate and smothered it with spaghetti.

He said nothing—just watched me suspiciously.

"What?"

"So that's it? Just like that, and you're ready for college?"

"Duh? Isn't that what you want?"

He shifted in his seat. "Sure, it's what I want. I just didn't expect—never mind."

"You were right this morning," I said, passing him the salad. "The summer's nearly over. I can't keep putting off my future."

He stared at me as if he couldn't quite believe his ears.

"I guess not." He eased back into his chair with a satisfied sigh. "This is great, T-bird. Really great. I'm proud of you."

Then he smiled, Mom. He actually smiled.

I didn't eat much, just pushed forkfuls of pasta around my plate while Jimmy regaled me with his plans for my big college adventure. I couldn't remember the last time I'd seen him so happy. He was thrilled with the colleges I'd picked at random, even admitting in a rare moment of reflection that a couple had made his own shortlist when he was still daydreaming of going away to school himself. Between gulps of beer and mouthfuls of spaghetti, he rambled on about dorms, majors, and financial aid, smiling and laughing and hardly noticing how quiet I'd grown. It helped that I oohed and ahhed in all the right places, nodding like a simpleton while privately debating whether or not to ditch my phone so that he couldn't track me in the city.

I checked my notifications again when he got up from the table for a bathroom break. They'd posted another image—this time of "me" mounting "Dylan" doggy-style—followed predictably by a slew of new comments. When was somebody going to shut down Owen's account? Not that it mattered anymore. Scarface's handiwork had gone viral, or at least as viral as anything could go in the social dead-end of Kayoga County. I wondered if Dylan was okay, had sobered up yet, and had seen the latest installments in our slow-rolling mortification.

Then I wondered why I even cared.

By the time Jimmy polished off his meal and two more beers, he'd set a firm plan of action: five schools in five days, starting with the University of Albany next week. He'd make all the arrangements.

We'd treat it like a little vacation. He'd even let me drive if we took the pickup. All I had to do was nod and smile. What could be easier?

Soon enough, he'd passed out in sated bliss in front of a ball game, leaving me to clear the table and wash the dishes. I listened to him snore over the blare of announcers calling plays and tried to ignore how much I hated myself for what I was about to do to him.

Jimmy was the poster child of lost dreams. I was his last shot at living the life he never got to live, and now I was going to take that away from him, too. But then, I was the poster child of no choices. Nothing in my life had gone the way I would've wanted had anyone bothered to ask me. Not the way you lived and died, Mom. Not being saddled with Jimmy's dreams and regrets. And certainly not growing up in this freak show of a town, where I was the star attraction that everyone loved to poke through the bars with a stick.

I stared out the kitchen window at the gathering mountain dark, trying to picture what came next. Hopping a Greyhound to the Port Authority Terminal was the easy part. Things grew murky after that, as reality set in like the shadows encroaching outside. I had no idea what life would look like in the city. I knew what I *wanted* it to look like, the movie I'd daydreamed, but I wasn't so naive as to mistake that for a plan. Where would I live? How would I eat? What would I do to support myself? These were questions I'd never dwelled on before, always assuming I'd have plenty of time to answer them. But time had run out, and with it all of my blithe self-assurance that everything would fall into place.

The truth was, Jimmy had taken care of me my whole life. He earned the money, paid the bills, made all the big decisions. I'd never spent a single night away from Shelter Valley without him. I didn't have a bank account, a credit card, or my senior driver's license. I'd never even held down a summer job. With no skills and zero experience, how could I earn a living in a city where I knew nothing and nobody?

I did the math in my head. With what I'd lifted from the housekeeping stash today, I had just over $800 in cash. That wouldn't last long in New York. Even a shitty room at the YMCA cost $75 a night. I could maybe hold out for a week or so, and then what? I honestly had no clue. I couldn't begin to think that far ahead. When I tried, all I could see was how I'd end up slinking back to Jimmy once the money ran out.

But if that were the case, what was the point of leaving?

Maybe I should try to make myself invisible until graduation. Put my head down, disappear into the closet, mute the volume on being me. I'd watched Dylan melt into the background often enough to learn the technique. You just needed to crumple your true self into a ball and shove it in your pocket until the coast was clear and you could smooth yourself out again.

I could do that if I needed to. If they'd let me, maybe.

But they never would.

When I'd dried the last dish, I slipped out through the slider onto the back deck to clear my head. The moon had barely risen above the cusp of the mountain. Though three-quarters full, it had enough wattage to spear long, jutting shadows across the silvery walls of the trailer. The storm that'd threatened all day had never materialized. The sunset cooled things off from the earlier swelter. Fall was coming.

I could smell it on the air, like a whiff of mildew when cracking open a cellar door. Summers blazed through their lives in these mountains.

My phone buzzed with a text from Gabe.

You okay?

I stared at the pulsating words on the screen, wondering how this stranger kept appearing at my most vulnerable moments.

I'm fine. Thanks for checking.

I'm down the hill at JJ's having a beer. Wanna meet?

I felt myself smile.

JJ's isn't my scene.

There was a long pause, followed by the words *No, not here,* and then the little ellipses danced for what felt like an eternity as he seemed to struggle with what to type next.

Somebody showed me a picture. I thought you could use a friend tonight. I have beer at home. Pot too. Or we could hang at the lake.

Of course, he'd seen them. Like everybody else. That was the way of things around here. I imagined a small crowd down at J.J.'s gathered around somebody's phone laughing their asses off at Dylan and me.

It wouldn't be much longer before someone sent them to Jimmy. Fuck my life.

Yet, I felt a twinge of disappointment. Maybe I'd hoped Gabe wanted to talk about something else. He'd been lurking in the back of my mind all afternoon. I'd begun to wonder if I'd gotten him wrong. I couldn't shake that playful look in his eyes, how he'd said I reminded him of himself.

Oh, that? I typed. *It's nothing. I'm used to it. No worries.*

More dancing ellipses.

I know what it's like to be different, Little B.

My heart raced. *Do you really?*

I do. We should talk. You don't have to be alone tonight.

I felt the blood rush to my face. Why did talking to him always leave me feeling like I'd taken one more step onto thinning ice? I needed to get a grip here. He was, at best, an intriguing footnote I didn't have the time to write.

Still, my fingers trembled as I tapped out my reply. *Thanks, but I'm visiting a sick friend. Another time? Good night.*

I switched off the phone before he could reply. Then I hurled myself down the back steps and tried to swallow the pang of regret caught in my throat.

CHAPTER THIRTEEN
BEER AND SYMPATHY

TURNING OFF MY PHONE DIDN'T shut Gabe out of my mind. As I sat planted on Rozella's couch an hour later, nursing my third Utica Club in front of a rerun of *The Birds*, I found my thoughts creeping back to his final text.

We should talk. You don't have to be alone tonight.

The message was both explicitly vague and vaguely explicit. It irritated me. I didn't like how easily he'd read me, especially while he remained so inscrutable. Every time I thought I had him pinned down, he slipped away. It was frustrating, to say the least. But worse, it made it hard for me to trust my instincts about him.

After all, Dylan had already obliterated my self-confidence in my own judgment.

I polished off my beer, eager for the birds to start pecking people's eyes out. I'd screwed things up royally today. Why had I agreed to meet Dylan at the Marsh Trail? Why had I put on those skimpy hot pants, that cherry lip gloss? Why had I shared a drink with him, refused all his apologies, listened sympathetically as he had the gall to tell me we'd been a bad match from the beginning? A bad match! As if that erased the past year of misery he'd put me through. I should have turned around and clawed his goddamned face off for that. Instead, I tried to see his point. No wonder he thought he could hump me at will. I clearly had no self-respect. I might as well have worn a fucking tee-shirt that read MOUNT ME TIGER, I'M YOURS!

Okay, so obviously, he hadn't meant for things to go that far. Just like he hadn't meant what happened at the Mini Mart either. He was weak, confused, easily cornered, and—at the Marsh Trail, at least—very drunk. Even after every shitty, selfish thing he'd done and said, I could still come up with theoretical reasons to excuse him. I hadn't handled him carefully. I'd been reckless, self-absorbed, too caught up in the movie in my mind to reckon with the very real, very scared, very horny boy sitting right in front of me.

So then, why couldn't I just forgive him and move on? Maybe because I couldn't forgive myself.

"I need another beer," I announced and crushed the empty can in my fist.

"Whoa, pace yourself there, puppy," Rozella said from her recliner. "I don't need Jim bitching at me tomorrow about your hangover."

She was one to talk. She'd forgone beer for a plastic tumbler full of sherry and was already three sheets to the wind. She often got smashed in the evenings, usually when we had the most fun. I liked her best at least a little bit drunk. That's when she let her guard down and turned funny and rambling, or weepy and maudlin. Unlike Jimmy, who just got more tight-assed and tightlipped the more he drank until he eventually passed out.

"You know," she slurred blissfully before downing another swig from the tumbler. "I got a green suit just like the one she's wearing." She gestured with her cigarette at the TV, where Tippi Hedren was trapped inside a phone booth, getting battered by a flock of bloodthirsty seagulls. "Wore it when I got married. It's packed away somewhere. Wool, it was, with tiny silver buttons."

"You'll have to show me sometime."

"It'd look good on you with your coloring," she said, stroking the blue paisley kerchief wrapped around her wig-less skull. "I wish I was a natural blonde like you. I bet Tippi ain't."

"Probably not," I agreed, though I was having a hard time paying attention. I kept stewing over Dylan: What I would do tomorrow? Should I hop on that bus. I wished somebody would just tell me what to do.

"Hey, Rozella. Can I ask a question?"

"Shoot, puppy."

"Why didn't you ever leave Shelter Valley?"

She gave me a double take. "What?"

"I mean when Duke ran off. Or when Nicki flew the nest. Why did you stay in this shithole town all these years? Nothing's keeping you here."

"Where am I supposed to go?"

"I don't know." I shrugged. "Somewhere different. Somewhere better."

"Somewhere like the city?"

"Yeah, maybe."

She exhaled a billow of smoke into the air. "A wise woman once said wherever you go, there you are. Remember that."

"What the hell's that supposed to mean?"

"It means you take your troubles with you, puppy. Changing the scenery don't change nothing." She grabbed the tumbler and took another sip. "And anyway, it's a hell of a lot cheaper to be miserable here than in some city." She stifled a belch with the back of her hand. "Why are you asking this? You plan on hitting the road soon?"

"Maybe…. Always." I forced a laugh. "Just daydreams."

"Yeah, well, you just cool your jets. It's a hungry world out there. It'll eat you alive if you ain't ready for it. Just ask Jim." She peered at me through her sherry haze and then eased back in the recliner. "Besides, who's gonna fetch my beer when it's too hot for me to get in the car? Speaking of, go grab another one if you want. I know you're having a rough patch."

I wasn't about to turn down another beer. I pushed up from the couch and wandered into the kitchen. Though she hadn't mentioned the memes, I figured she'd heard all about them. Otherwise she would have cut me off by now.

"Fix yourself something to eat, too," she called out. "Soak up some of that beer."

But I was too preoccupied for food. Maybe she was right. Maybe running away wouldn't fix anything. Maybe I'd just trade one set of troubles for an even bigger one.

And maybe that's why I'd come here tonight: to let Rozella talk me out of leaving.

I wasn't ready for New York. A bookmarked bus schedule and a memorized subway map didn't constitute a plan for the future. I needed a better one, a real one, not some last-ditch, half-assed scheme that would leave me panhandling in Central Park or running home with my tail tucked between my legs. Maybe Jimmy was right, and college was the answer. I needed someplace to start. College was as good a way as any to get out of Shelter Valley. Maybe I could even test out of senior year and take some classes at the community college. A few credits in something practical like accounting might be enough to land me a job in the city.

And at least it would get me the hell away from Dylan.

I cracked open the last Utica Club in the fridge and leaned against the counter to check for more memes. But as soon as my phone powered up, it bleeped with a new text from Gabe:

You still there Little B?

"You ever seen Tippi Hedren in *Marnie*?" Rozella called from the living room. "Weird picture. She plays a thief. Sean Connery forces himself on her on their wedding night. I never could stomach him after that."

"Who?" I said while I debated whether to answer Gabe.

"Connery… Mr. James Bond himself." She snorted. "Always strutting around, bedding beautiful women like he thinks he's God's gift. And then he rapes poor Tippi on her wedding night. Rat bastard."

Yes, I'm here, I typed, keeping it simple. I sipped beer and watched the movie while the little ellipses danced.

Is it Jim? Is he why you can't see me?

No. I told you, I'm with a friend. What does Jimmy have to do with it?

"I never liked those James Bond movies. Even after they got rid of Connery and hired that English fella. He left a bad taste, you know?"

He came to see me this afternoon. Warned me to stay the hell away from you.

My stomach bucked like a bull at a rodeo.

"Now, Rod Taylor here," Rozella said, nearly sloshing herself in sherry as she waved at the hottie on screen who'd just pulled Tippi to safety. "He's my kind of man. A real gentleman. He'd never force himself on nobody. They should've made him James Bond instead."

My fingers trembled as I typed, *Did you tell Jimmy what happened today?*

Hell no. That's between us. Besides, he didn't give me a chance to say anything.

Jesus Christ. What the hell was Jimmy's problem?

What's he got against you anyway?

You'd have to ask him that yourself, Little B.

That sure as hell wasn't going to happen. But maybe I could ask somebody else.

Brb, I typed and muted the ringer. Then I plopped back down across from Rozella.

"Hey," I said. "Can I ask you something?"

She flashed me a bleary grin. "What is this tonight, twenty questions?"

"No, just one: What do you know about Gabe Fournier?"

The grin avalanched off her face. "You mean your knight in shining armor?" She batted her hand at my look of surprise. "Yeah, I heard about that, too. Is he the one you're tap, tap, tapping to on that phone of yours?"

"Naw," I lied, shifting in my seat. "But I'd like to know more about him. Jimmy won't tell me anything. I don't think he likes him much."

"No love lost there," she said and rolled her eyes.

"Why? Is there a story?"

She gave an irritable sigh, and I thought she would tell me to mind my own business. But instead, she muted the TV. "Yeah, there's a story. There's always a story. How much have you heard already?"

"Nothing really. Just that Gabe is Harold's son. He said he and Mom were friends."

"Friends, huh?" she said, eyebrows raised. She lit another cigarette and then peered at me. "Is that all you heard?"

"What else is there?" I said, bracing for the worst.

"You know how people talk. Always trying to make more out of a thing than there is."

"Well, what is there? If you've got something to say, spit it out."

"Fine, fine." She waggled her cigarette at me before downing another gulp of sherry. "It all started when that Fournier boy was around your age. He was a scrawny kid. Kept to himself. Got picked on a lot. Kind of like you, as it happens." She paused to flick a precipice of ash into her ashtray. "I guess he and Bonnie got to be friendly down at the Grill. She used to pull extra shifts waiting tables for Harold. Maybe she felt sorry for the kid. I don't know. But whatever it was, one day she comes over to tell me that Harold's kicked him out and that she's moved him into your place so he don't have to sleep in the woods."

"Wait. Gabe lived in our house? With Mom?"

"Not for long. A few weeks, maybe a month. Then his mother sent him off to California to live with her relatives." She took a long draw off the cigarette. "It's a shame you didn't know Nance. She died when you were little. Good Christian woman. Why she married that asshole Harold, I'll never know." She exhaled with a violent cough and took another swig of sherry. "Anyway, Gabe lived with Bonnie until he hopped the bus out west. Didn't show his face around here again until a few years later, when Nance got the cancer, and he moved back home to help out at the Grill while she was doing her chemo. After she passed, he took off again. That's the last I saw of him. He and Harold—they've always been matches and dynamite together. I'm surprised he's come back to look after the old bastard this time. Connie's the one Harold mostly gets to wipe his ass."

"Wait," I said, my head spinning. "I'm still trying to wrap my mind around the part where he lived in our place. Where was Jimmy?"

"Oh hell, that's a whole other story, puppy. Didn't your brother ever tell you how he ran out on your mom his senior year?"

"Of course not. He never tells me a damn thing."

"Typical." She scratched the bridge of her nose before stubbing out the remains of the cigarette. "The two of them used to fight like cats and dogs. About money. Her lifestyle choices. You name it. When he told her he wanted to go away to college, they had some kind of blowout, and he packed up and went to sleep on Earl's couch down in Kayoga. It wasn't too long after that when Bonnie moved Gabe in."

She fished out the last of the cigarettes, crumpled the empty pack into a ball, and tossed it on the couch beside me. "Throw that out for me later?" She lit up again without missing a beat. "Now, like I say, people talked. They always do. They whispered Gabe and Bonnie had some kind of *Tea and Sympathy* thing going on. But I never believed that. She felt sorry for him, is all. No different than if Jim kicked you out and I took you in. Besides, that kid didn't have it in him to do anything like that with a grown woman. He'd have shit his pants if she said boo to him. He was younger than her own son, for Christ's sake. Bonnie might have been a basketful of trouble, but she wasn't like that, you hear me? Which is why I'm telling you this story. You don't need to be getting your head full of dirty lies from the filthy-minded gossips around here."

"Then they were just friends?"

"Sure... friends." She looked at me with a curious expression. "I never really thought of it like that before."

"Why not? We're friends, aren't we?"

She raised the tumbler in a kind of salute. "Fair enough, puppy," she said and downed another swig.

"Why didn't you tell me any of this before?"

She snorted. "You never asked."

"But what about Jimmy? What's he got against Gabe?"

She pursed her lips. "Aww, you know your brother. How do you think he'd feel about some guy half the county believes slept with your mom?"

"Ah, I see your point." I slumped back into the couch cushions. Of course, Jimmy didn't want me to have anything to do with Gabe. Gabe had your name written all over him, Mom.

I took a gulp of beer and let my mind graze over the details of Rozella's story as the pieces fell into place. It all made a comforting kind of sense: why Gabe had saved my ass at the Mini Mart; his kindness in cleaning me up afterward; that strange look he'd flashed me at the swimming hole; the creepy, almost fatherly way he kept inserting himself into my life.

You were the reason, Mom. You were Gabe's Rozella. It was kind of sweet when I thought about it.

I noticed Rozella had gone quiet and was staring at me.

"Is there something more?" I said.

"Why'd you want to know about Gabe Fournier all of a sudden?"

"He saved my life yesterday. Wouldn't you be curious?"

"Is that all there is to it?"

"What else would there be?"

"Well, I don't know, puppy." She flicked another ash into the ashtray. "You know how it is around here. People talk is all."

She didn't need to explain what she meant. I could read it on her face. We'd been spotted, Gabe and me. At the Dollar Drug, or maybe when he dropped me off at home this morning. The rumor mill must already be churning if news had gotten to Rozella. If it hadn't already, it'd probably get to Jimmy soon enough.

As if on cue, my phone began to vibrate with a new call from my brother. I froze, staring at his name on the screen. Was he checking up to see if I was with Gabe? Fuck my life.

As soon as I answered, Jimmy barked, "Toby!" Even Rozella jump.

"Jesus, what do you want?"

"Where the hell are you?"

"Watching movies with Rozella. Where did you think I was, huh?"

"Are you drunk?"

"Naw. No, I'm just—"

"Listen, I don't care right now. Just come home."

"Don't get your knickers in a twist. I'll be home later. We're watching *The Birds* and—"

"Now," he demanded. "Get your ass home. It's urgent. Donna Falcone's sitting here in front of me. She needs to talk to you about Dylan."

CHAPTER FOURTEEN
WHEN IT HITS THE FAN

IM SO SORRY MOM... SO SORRRY

Tell Toby Im sorry about this morning too

I love you

I scanned the text. It was terrifying. I scanned it again. It was even worse.

We were all thinking the same thing from the looks on Jimmy's and Donna's faces.

Jimmy had been hovering around the living room since I sat in your old rocker, Mom. He was still in his boxers and wife-beater. His knuckles were raw from biting, and his eyes vibrated with such undisguised alarm that I could barely look at him.

Donna teetered on the edge of the sofa across from me, her eyes hollowed out by worry. She still wore her bawdy-wench uniform from the Lamplighter Lounge, although she'd at least changed out of her work clogs into a pair of pale blue Keds. She tugged absently at her split ends and sucked on a freshly lit cigarette like an oxygen mask. Jimmy, who normally never allowed smoking in the house, had rustled up one of your old ashtrays for her to use. It was the one from Lake Placid in the shape of the Olympic rings, and it sat on the coffee table beside the three full-color printouts she'd brought of the memes Scarface had posted online.

I didn't feel drunk anymore, just sick.

"He sent that text while I was at work," she said, her hand trembling as I passed back her phone. "I tried calling and texting back, but he wouldn't answer." She gestured with the cigarette at the pictures. "When I got home, I found those in an envelope in my mailbox marked 'From a friend.' That's when I called my friend Karl from the lounge. He works for the sheriff's department. I'm waiting to hear back from him, but I was too frantic to sit still." She squeezed her phone and held it up to Jimmy like Exhibit A. "I'm not overreacting, am I? This doesn't sound right, does it?"

"I—I don't know, Donna," he said warily. "But I'm guessing he'll be home soon. Why don't I take you there? We can wait with you."

"I don't think he's coming home tonight," she said and turned to face me. "Please, Toby, tell me what's going on? I tried calling his buddies, but none of them would speak to me. Why would they post these awful pictures? Did you see him this morning like he says? Did you boys have another fight? You two used to be such good friends. I don't understand what's going on with him anymore. Lately, he's so different. Distant. Withdrawn."

Jimmy had moved behind me and was squeezing my shoulders so hard it hurt.

"Let's hear it," he said, tightening his grip. "And no bullshit this time. Just tell us straight what's been going on."

I glanced down at Dylan's smile on the topmost meme and grimaced.

I was on my own now.

"It's kind of a long story," I said.

"Cut to the chase."

I took a deep breath and said, "I saw him this morning… We didn't leave things on the best of terms."

"Where was this?" Donna asked.

I gulped. "At the, um—at the Marsh Trail."

Jimmy's hands flew off my shoulders. "What the hell were you doing there?"

"I told you, it's a long story."

"What time was this?" Donna interrupted. "Was he hurt? Was he upset?"

"I dunno. Maybe 9:30 or 10:00. Dylan wasn't hurt, but he was very upset when I left. He'd been drinking. Like, a lot."

"Goddamn it, Dylan," she said and jumped to her feet. "I need to call Karl." Then she hurried onto the back deck, slamming the slider behind her.

Jimmy came around the chair to face me. "What the hell is going on?" he said. "Why were you at the Marsh Trail? I thought that was just a story you made up to embarrass him in front of some girls?"

"Yeah, well, it wasn't, okay? It's true. All of it's true."

"All of what's true? What are you talking about?"

I eased back into the chair and shut my eyes. I couldn't bear to look while I told him.

"Dylan and I had a thing last summer, okay? We fooled around for a few weeks in secret. Nobody knew. It was stupid. I was stupid. I thought we were in love, but as soon as school started, he ghosted me and turned into a complete asshole. I didn't... I didn't want you to know." My voice caught in my throat as waves of heat pulsated off my face, burning away the last calloused layers of deceit I'd hidden for the past year. I was helpless, naked, exposed before my brother. "I didn't want anybody to know, okay? I was hurt... humiliated... I never said anything to anyone about it until yesterday, when he pushed me too far."

"And the Marsh Trail?" Jimmy pressed unsympathetically. "How does that figure in?"

"Seriously? Does it matter?"

"Of course, it matters!" He leaned forward and pushed down on the arms of the rocker, forcing my face into his. "This is serious." He glanced at the slider and lowered his voice. "You saw that text. You know what it sounds like. The time for fucking around is over. I want the story straight, and I want it now. No more lies or bullshit, or I swear to God, you won't live long enough to regret it."

"Okay, fine," I spat, meeting the fire in his eyes with flames of my own. "I've been cruising the Marsh Trail for dick all summer long. How's that for being straight? Last week I ran into Dylan there, and we, well... figure it out. Afterward, he blew me off again and then had the nerve to say all that shit about Mom. That's what started this whole mess."

"Was he the only one you were ever—*with* down there?"

"Jesus, what do you think?"

"Oh, Toby." He blanched and backed away as if I were contagious. "Why were you there today?"

"To talk about this—this shit!" I grabbed the pictures from the coffee table and hurled them at him. "He asked me to meet him there. He said he wanted to talk. So I went, and we talked, and it seemed okay. But then, I don't know, he got the wrong idea or something, because he got handsy with me, and I had to leave. End of story."

"What do you mean he got handsy? Did he hurt you?"

"Not at all. I'm fine."

"Tell me the truth."

"I am telling the truth. I'm fine, okay? Can we please just focus on what's important? And don't say anything about the handsy part to her, will you?" I gestured at Donna, still on the phone, pulling at her hair and pacing the deck. "She's got enough to worry about."

Jimmy nodded gravely. He circled the room several times, and then whirled back on me and demanded, "Who else knew about this?"

"Nobody."

"What about Rozella?"

"I said nobody."

"I don't believe you." The cords in his neck shot livid with blood. "I don't want you hanging out over there anymore, do you hear me? She's a bad influence. Just look at you. I can smell the stink of beer on your breath from halfway across the room."

"Fuck that shit!"

I leaped out of the rocker, but he grabbed me by the arm and whipped me back so hard the whole thing nearly toppled over sideways. I was too dumfounded by the violence of it to react. He'd never laid a finger on me like that before. Never.

"I'm not done with you yet," he growled, crushing my arm in his grip. "What about Gabe Fournier? You ever meet him down at the Marsh Trail?"

"Are you for real?" I said aghast. "Hell no!"

I tried to wriggle free of his grasp, just as Donna rushed back through the slider.

"They found him!" she announced, her hair transformed into an abused mass of fright curls. "Karl said a deputy spotted the car pulled off the road halfway to Sacandaga. He was passed out in the backseat with an empty liquor bottle. He's on his way to the hospital with alcohol poisoning. They're not sure he's going to make it."

After this last bit, she let out a gasp and then exploded into tears.

Jimmy was unprepared for this. He let go of my arm and stood there gawping at her like she was an alien life form, until common decency broke the spell, and he gently pulled her into his arms.

"It'll be okay," he said soothingly. "I'm sure they found him in time. He's young and strong. He's going to be fine. I know it."

"Will you take me?" she said, sobbing into his shoulder. "I can't drive like this."

"Of course I will. Just let me grab some pants."

He peeled himself away from her and retreated to his bedroom.

I watched, paralyzed, as she hugged herself and continued to weep. She reminded me of Dylan, how I'd left him alone, desperate and floundering in the mud. I didn't know what to say to her either. I wanted to apologize, to tell her that this wasn't her fault, or even his. I wanted to reassure her and reassure myself that he was going to be fine, just fine. But I couldn't speak, could barely breathe as the sheer voltage of despair short-circuited my heart.

My God.... What if he died?

Something in me sparked and sizzled, and then I went cold inside. Numb. My vital components fried. The networks of receptors and neurons melted. What remained was an empty husk in the shape of a boy who could move and think but was no longer human. I said nothing, just rocked in place, staring at the floor so she wouldn't look at me.

Jimmy came rushing back into the living room a minute later in sweatpants and a rumpled shirt, his bare feet jammed into untied boots. He took Donna by the arm and led her to the door, but before he ushered her outside, he glared at me with a face so white with fury he might as well have been the walking undead.

"If you leave this house or go see Rozella, I swear to God, I'll—" But he slammed the door behind him before he could finish the threat.

PLENTY OF BLAME

CHAPTER FIFTEEN
ZOMBIES CAN'T SCREAM

JIMMY BURST THROUGH THE FRONT door just after dawn, startling me awake on the couch. He went straight for the fridge and cracked open a beer, guzzling the entire bottle before coming up for air. He belched, opened another bottle, and wandered into the living room, where he collapsed against the wall and peered at me with exhausted, empty eyes. The worst of his anger had burned off during the night; a cold, hard shell remained.

He barely mustered a sympathetic grimace as he updated me on Dylan's condition. "He died," he announced as if describing a faulty car battery. He didn't even register my gasp. "Once on the way to the hospital, and once on the table in the Emergency Room. Bad seizures. He stopped breathing, but they managed to bring him back both times. Now he's on life support in a coma. They don't know for how long or if he'll come out of it. There may be permanent brain damage. Only time will tell."

When he'd finished, Mom, I only wanted to curl up into a little ball and die myself.

But that didn't happen. Instead, the hours and days that followed were like being trapped inside a remake of *The Night of the Living Dead*, pursued by the relentless, unblinking horror of Dylan's coma. Only, in this movie, I was the zombie, so I couldn't even scream. Instead, a subtle humming buzzed in the back of my head like static. Everything seemed remote and unreal as if I were observing myself through the filmy lenses of undead eyes. I was a sleepwalker shambling through an unending nightmare, yet it was all happening. I knew it was real not because I could feel any of it, but because I witnessed what it did to my brother.

I watched Jimmy fall to pieces right in front of me.

When he'd finished that second beer, he called in sick for the day—the first time in six years, as he bitterly reminded me. He dragged me to the Planned Parenthood in Johnstown for an excruciatingly invasive STI screening. He demanded the full battery of tests. They asked question after intimate question about my sexual history and took enough blood, urine, and saliva to paint an abstract artwork entitled Toby's Body Humiliation #1. But I didn't complain. I let them poke and prod me and pick apart my sexual secrets right in front of my brother. I let them take whatever they wanted from me, and I didn't utter a single grumble.

We waited forever for the preliminary HIV results to come back, and Jimmy audibly gasped when the nurse announced "negative."

I didn't react at all.

Yet, my brother's relief turned out to be short-lived. The very next day he got a call that I'd swabbed positive for gonorrhea of the throat and would need an industrial-strength antibiotic to cure it. From the look on his face when he told me the news, you would've thought I'd been the one who died in that ambulance ride.

Perhaps for him I had.

Things unraveled between us after that. Our conversations turned monosyllabic, if they occurred at all, and with each passing day Jimmy became more and more like a caged animal, brimming with pent-up rage.

For one thing, he didn't know how to punish me. He was my brother, not my father. This had always made the meting out of discipline more or less a meeting of the minds between us. For minor offenses, he might yell or lecture me, withhold my allowance, or make me do crappy chores like scrub the grout in the bathroom with a toothbrush. But for the bigger stuff, I'd always respected the boundaries and feared disappointing him enough not to cross them. At least in theory.

In return, he held the reins more loosely than I cared to admit. He turned a blind eye if I stole a beer or two from the fridge. He never policed what I did online. Though I might complain that he nagged and checked in on me too much, he let me go where I wanted, wear what I wanted, and stay out as late as I wanted, so long as I got up for school and kept my grades solid.

What he mostly did was trust me because that's all he could do. But now that I'd nuked that trust, he was floundering in the fallout. It wasn't a pretty sight.

He wouldn't hit me. Grounding me was pointless when he was gone all day long. Taking away my phone was counterproductive since he used it to keep tabs on me. Even lecturing me seemed unbearable to him, when he could barely bring himself to say out loud what I'd done.

Still, his eyes were always on me. I'd look up from my dinner plate to find some unsettling mixture of rage, confusion, and raw-to-the-bone hurt glaring back at me. It was like he was struggling to figure out what he'd done wrong, where I was broken, how he might salvage whatever was left. But he refused to talk to me about it. If I tried to apologize or explain myself, he cut me off or left the room.

Soon he stopped eating, skipping breakfasts and barely touching dinners. Worse, he couldn't fall asleep unless he passed out drunk. By the end of the week, he was downing a six-pack a night. He spent the whole weekend tinkering under Baby's hood, listening to the country station as he polished off beer after beer. By late Sunday afternoon, he was chasing the beers with swigs of bourbon, and the next morning, I practically had to light firecrackers in his nostrils to wake him for work.

The more he drank, the more erratic his moods became. One evening he got so furious that I'd forgotten to wash a cereal bowl, he smashed it on the counter, only to rush into my room five minutes later and bear hug me to death. Another night, I thought I heard him sobbing in bed, but when I knocked to see if he was alright, he pretended to be asleep.

The only thing that hadn't changed between us was the planning for our college visits, which he pursued with the do-or-die intensity of a priest prepping for an exorcism. Campus tours were scheduled, websites consulted, and routes checked and rechecked at least a dozen times.

When he was home, I tried to stay out of his way, absconding to my bedroom to listen to music and stare at the walls. I stayed off social media as much as possible. As the news about Dylan spread, the very same people who'd taken such delight in Scarface's handiwork fell into deep and profound mourning for him. They shifted all their outrage to me. I was the obvious villain and an easy scapegoat for collective guilt, and things turned ugly for me online. So much so that I deleted some accounts and stopped checking my email, although most of what they said about me seemed fair enough. I was a monster. The walking undead. The one who shouldn't be walking.

Rozella stayed away. I didn't know whether this was because Jimmy had told her off, or because she was disgusted with me for breaking my "promise" not to go back to the Marsh Trail. I didn't much care either way. Though I could've called her or walked over to beg for forgiveness, I didn't bother. Zombies can't apologize.

I blew off Gabe, too, ignoring the increasingly concerned texts he kept sending me:

I heard what happened, Little B. I'm real sorry.

How's Donna's kid? How are you holding up?

I've got plenty of weed and beer. If you can sneak out, we should talk.

At least let me know you're okay.

Eventually, even these stopped, and I was glad to be left in peace.

I spent my days in a fog of busywork and minutiae. I YouTubed new makeup techniques. I waxed my legs and pits and switched nail colors a half-dozen times. I cleaned like a housewife on Xanax, mindlessly sanitizing the refrigerator, oiling the paneling on the living room walls, and vacuuming our carpet so many times I wore tracks in the pile. I cooked us fancy dinners we didn't eat. I washed our winter coats. I even polished our funeral shoes.

Whatever might channel my energy and keep my hands preoccupied.

The nights were harder, though. As soon as I shut my eyes, that staticky hum in the back of my head grew louder, and all I could see was Dylan. Balled up in the mud at the Marsh Trail. Convulsing in the back of some blaring ambulance. Strung up like a hydroponic vegetable by the tubes and wires keeping him alive. Or, worst of all, ten years old and beaming at me on the beach as I struggled to tie some ridiculous fishing lure to his line.

The pills came in handy. Though Jimmy hoarded the beer and bourbon for himself, the medicine cabinet was mine for the plundering: Benadryl, NyQuil, and a third of a bottle of his expired Percocet from when he'd broken two ribs colliding with a pallet of hand towels at the mill. I'd never been reluctant to self-medicate, only now it felt more like self-preservation. Anything to hold back the horror of the void, to keep me numbly sedated when there was no other escape from dwelling on the nightmare that inched closer and closer, step by ruthless step.

What would I do if Dylan's coma finally caught up with me? What if I never even got the chance to say goodbye?

I knew Jimmy spoke to Donna on the phone every day, but whenever I asked him about Dylan's condition, he only ever answered "the same." I'd wanted him to take me to the hospital to see Dylan that first morning, but he refused, and he kept on refusing as the days wore on and reports of Dylan's condition remained the same, the same.

I would only make things worse, he said. Nobody wanted to see me there, least of all Donna. The kindest thing I could do was to stay out of her sight and leave her to grieve in peace. Hadn't I done enough harm already?

When he said these things to me, I'd simply nod and choke down the guttural sound that'd crept its way up the back of my throat. What else could I do, Mom? Zombies can't weep. Instead, I'd go off and polish the silverware or chug some more cough syrup. Anything to channel my grief and keep my dread preoccupied.

It was a week to the morning from when Dylan's coma began that the nightmare finally broke through my zombie daze. I could feel its breath on my neck as I dipped my toes into the frigid water of the swimming hole for the first time since that sultry evening with Gabe. White stars still dotted the cobalt sky. Dawn approached but hadn't yet arrived. Neither had sleep. A deep restlessness stirred within me. What'd begun as a subtle humming days before was now a low, thrumming roar in my ears that not even a handful of pills had quieted.

I held my breath and slipped naked into the lake. My muscles seized as needles of ice pierced into my flesh, but I swallowed back the pain and kicked off, the weight of gravity releasing me as I tread smoothly into the cold, dark water. My strokes were even and measured. The surface parted before me like ripples in a bolt of black silk.

Though I hadn't slept all night, I'd still dreamt of Dylan, of the last time I'd shared the swimming hole with him. That summer before seventh grade. A warm evening in July. We were still friends then, maybe best friends, though we'd already begun to drift apart from the pull of forces we were too young to understand.

My longing…. His fear.

We'd been at the lake for hours. I'd taught him how to do the breaststroke, sort of, and as we sat on the ledge together, kicking at the water, we laughed and joked about what a lousy swimmer he was, and tried our best to ignore the fact that he would be leaving in the morning to spend the rest of the summer with his cousins in New Jersey. The sun was poised to slip behind the mountain. Our laughter quieted, and though I still don't know why I did it—maybe I didn't want him to go, or maybe I just wanted him to take a piece of me with him—I leaned over and kissed him hard on the lips.

To my surprise, he kissed back.

Or at least he did until he shot up like a startled bunny and bolted for home. I was too shocked by what I'd done to go after him. I didn't see him again until school began that September, but by then it was too late, and everything had changed between us.

That was when I vowed never to bring another boy to the swimming hole. But now Dylan was here with me again, strapped to my back, just like he would be for the rest of my life.

Just like you, Mom.

All at once that roaring restlessness inside me broke free.

I stopped dead in the middle of the lake and screamed screamed screamed. I screamed until I thought my voice would bleed. I screamed until there was no air left in my lungs, until I pictured myself sinking like a weighted corpse to the bottom of Shelter Lake.

But I didn't sink, and the stillness that followed my screams only mocked me. There would be no solace for me at the swimming hole, no anesthetic strong enough to numb my roaring rage.

I swam back to the ledge, got dressed, and stalked up the hill for home.

Jimmy's alarm was blaring when I finally slipped through the slider. I stormed breathlessly into his bedroom and nearly shoved him out of bed to wake him. He staggered into the bathroom without saying a word, and I heard the pipes groan as he turned on the hot water and stepped into the shower. Then I retreated to the kitchen, where the timer on the coffee maker had brewed us a fresh pot. I poured myself a mug and settled at the kitchen table to think.

One thing was for certain: I didn't feel like a fucking zombie anymore. I was too furious for that. Furious with Dylan. Furious with you. You'd done this shit to me, too, Mom. Taken the easy way out. Chosen to leave me behind to shoulder the burden of your exit. Who pumps her veins full of smack in some cheap motel room with her four-year-old tucked into the bathtub, nice and cozy? Yours was no accidental overdose. It took intention. Planning and preparation. Execution. Jimmy and I both understood this, though the word "suicide" had never passed our lips. But I knew what you'd done. Just like I knew you'd brought me there for a reason, even if you'd left it up to my guilt and self-loathing to figure out what that was. You'd turned me into your suicide note, like my very existence in the room with you that night was both the cause and the explanation for what you'd done. And now Dylan was doing the same damn thing to me.

I was the cause. I was the explanation.

He'd chickened out of having to deal with all the pain and bullshit that went along with being boys like us—just like he'd done last summer, just like he'd done that evening at the swimming hole all those years ago. Instead, he left it to me to answer for whatever happened. I'd have to answer to Donna. I'd have to answer to myself for the rest of my fucking life. Just like I'd been answering for you every day for the past thirteen years.

Goddamn him. Goddamn him to hell.

Jimmy's phone buzzed on the table across from me. Concern overtook my anger when it buzzed a second and a third time, and I flipped it over to check.

The texts were from somebody named Theresa:

The doctor talked to Donna last night about signing the DNR.

It may not be much longer.

I understand why he doesn't want to come, but would you please ask him again? It would mean so much to her to see him here. She thinks it might help Dylan, too.

I read the messages again. By the third time, I was scared, and by the fourth, I was furious again.

"Who's Theresa?" I demanded when Jimmy finally rushed into the kitchen.

"What?" he grumbled, still hungover. He looked like death warmed over: hair sopping wet, sallow cheeks, eyes sunken in whorls of puffiness.

"Theresa. Who is she?"

He glanced at his phone and then back at me.

"She texted you about Dylan."

He grabbed the phone, scanned the messages, let out a dispirited sigh.

"She's Donna's cousin, up from New Jersey to help out. You know damn well not to read my private messages."

"What's a DNR?"

"We'll talk about this later. I'm late."

"Just answer me."

He wiped the moisture from his brow and said grudgingly, "It's a Do Not Resuscitate order. If Dylan's heart stops again, Donna's given permission for the doctors to let him go."

My own heart stopped. "Why would she sign such a horrible thing?"

"She hasn't, not yet anyway. But sometimes it's kinder not to keep people going on machines forever. Besides, it's not like she has insurance to pay for any of this."

"You mean he really might—*die?*" Though my voice was barely a whisper, it felt like I'd just screamed the word. But at least I'd finally said it out loud: Dylan might die.

Jimmy hesitated before answering long enough to tell me what he thought. "It's not looking good."

"Why have you been lying to me then?" I slammed my fist on the table so hard I tipped over my mug, spilling coffee all over the floor. "If Donna wants me there, we need to go. She thinks I can help him."

He drew his lips into a tight line. "I don't care what Donna thinks," he said coldly. "I don't want you going, and that's all that matters. You need to focus on your future, on college, what's important. Trust me, you start wallowing in this kind of guilt and it'll poison the rest of your life. You need to push through this. We both do."

"Are you fucking kidding me? I've been staggering around this house like the walking dead all week. You can't even stand to be in the same room with me without getting drunk. How are we pushing through anything?"

"Enough." He shoved past me to grab a wad of paper towels and squatted down to mop up the spilled coffee. "I'm sorry for Dylan, I really am. But I'm not letting you get sucked into this any deeper. This isn't your fault. He's not your responsibility, and neither is Donna. In time you'll see that I'm right."

"All I see is that you're a liar."

"Yeah, well, it runs in the family."

I grabbed him by the shoulder. "Please, Jimmy. I need to go— Please."

"I said no." He tossed the sopping towels into the garbage. Then he snatched his keys from the counter and strode to the front door.

I watched him go, hating him, wishing he would burst into flames. "Mom turned me into her suicide note," I blurted when he opened the door. "I won't be Dylan's, too. I need to see him. I need to see Donna. I need to do that before he… before I… before—" I stumbled. I didn't know what I meant. I didn't know what good seeing Dylan would do. Maybe Donna was right and it could help somehow. Maybe I needed to say goodbye. Maybe I wanted to hold his hand and tell him all the things I never got to say to you, Mom. Maybe that might exorcise his unquiet ghost before it haunted me for the rest of my life.

Maybe.

All I knew for certain was that I had to go.

"You can't stop me," I finally said. "I won't let you."

Jimmy stood frozen in the doorway, his shoulders as stiff as rails. "No, I guess not," he said quietly, and for a moment, just a moment, I thought he might try to understand how I felt.

But no. Instead, he walked out into the sunlight, calmly shutting the door behind him.

"You could at least slam it!" I screamed and hurled the empty coffee mug after him, but it merely bounced off the wall and thudded onto the carpet without so much as a fucking chip.

CHAPTER SIXTEEN
FRIED MEATS AND DEFEAT

THUNDERHEADS MASSED ABOVE THE LAKE as I crossed J.J.'s parking lot, a storm of my own gathering within me. I'd spied the white Silverado parked next to the building while I waited for the bus. If Jimmy wouldn't take me to the hospital, maybe Gabe would.

A rush of anticipation stole my breath as I pushed through the heavy front door. Inside was shadiness incarnate, like the cantina from Star Wars, only with less attractive patrons and the latest Toby Keith rouser twanging from the juke box. The stink of fried meats and defeat leached from the walls. A yellow glow emanated from the skylights in the vaulted ceiling. Red booths lined the walls beneath beer advertisements buzzing in half-defunct neon while the bar itself slouched in the back corner, hemmed in by a U of vinyl stools.

Ever since the Sunset Grill shut down, J.J.'s started opening early to accommodate the "breakfast crowd," which meant that a half-dozen of Shelter Valley's finest were already getting sloshed at the bar. Pale faces turned to gawp at me as soon as I slipped through the door. The whispers and sniggers of the Greek chorus of barflies meant word would quickly get back to Jimmy that I'd been here. My eyes adjusted to the dimness, and I heard a voice say, "If it ain't one half of Shelter Valley's new Internet sensation," while another mumbled, "Hell of a lot of nerve showing his face after what he done to Donna's kid."

J.J.'s wife, Bev, was the only one who bothered to be civil. A large woman too fond of her hair spray and lipstick, she flashed a businesslike smile and waved a shiny menu at me.

"Looking for breakfast, hun?"

"No thanks." I nodded at Gabe, who sat in a booth facing the kitchen, a half-eaten plate of Italian greens and eggs in front of him. "I'm here to see him."

At the sound of my voice, he glanced over his shoulder and shouted, "Little B! Where the hell you been?"

"Hey," I said, marching past the withering stares and slipping into the seat across from him. "Sorry, I've been incommunicado."

"Understood." He swallowed a wedge of buttered toast. "How's Donna's kid?"

"Not great. That's why I'm here. I was hoping you could give me a lift to the hospital."

"You're timing's perfect." He took a sip of coffee. "I'm heading over there as soon as I'm done. Want something to eat?"

"I'm good, thanks."

"Have a cup of coffee, at least."

Before I could stop him, he called to Bev for a refresh. He looked like he needed it, too: His eyes were bloodshot, and his whole body sagged over his plate.

"Is everything okay? You look like you haven't slept."

He rubbed his face and sighed. "That obvious, huh? It's been a tough few days with my old man."

"What happened?"

"He had a couple small strokes in the hospital." He prodded at the greens on his plate before stabbing a cherry pepper and popping it into his mouth. "Lost the use of his right hand. They say it's temporary, but I don't know." He drained his mug and added, "I wish he'd lost the use of his fucking mouth. He's been bitching up a storm. Says he wants me to bring him home so he can die in his own bed. But I didn't sign up for that. It's bad enough schlepping back and forth to see him. Talking to doctors. Taking care of all the bills he forgot to pay. Arm-twisting my damn sister to come up before it's too late. Family shit: it's a real pain in the ass, you know?"

Bev appeared at our table with the coffee before I could agree. She refilled his mug without looking at him and then slapped one in front of me and began to pour.

"Your brother know you're here with him?" she said, as if Gabe were a child molester or a big city liberal. "I bet he don't."

"I bet it ain't your business," Gabe replied with a wide grin and politely thanked her for the refill. "We were just in the middle of a private conversation," he added, and though she clucked her tongue in disapproval, she took the hint and shuffled back to the bar.

A groan of thunder rumbled through the walls as fingertips of rain drummed against the dirty skylight above us. Gabe sipped more coffee and glanced at our little audience. He flashed them all a smirk, raised his mug in a chummy salute, and turned back to me and grumbled, "Fucking losers. I can't wait to get back to the city."

"You live in the city?" I said, surprised. "New York City?"

"The one and only. Why?"

"No reason." I shrugged. "It's just, I heard you went out west."

"Who you been talking to? Jim?"

"Not bloody likely," I said and gave a rueful laugh. "No, it was Rozella Ames. She told me about you. About Mom, too. How you stayed in our place for a while in high school. How you two were, um…" I hesitated. "Just friends."

He smirked at me. "So you believe Rozella, huh?"

I shrugged.

"Glad you trust somebody around here." He swallowed another forkful of greens and covered a discreet belch with his fist. "After I busted out of Shelter Valley, I landed with Ma's cousins in California. Got my GED out there and worked a bunch of crap jobs. Washed dishes for a while. Painted houses. Drove a delivery truck. Even mucked the stalls on a dude ranch in Nevada. Ended up line-cooking in this rat hole on the Vegas strip until a buddy of mine talked me into going to culinary school in the city. So, I moved back east. The school thing didn't pan out, but the city stuck. Been in Washington Heights ever since."

"Doing what?"

"This and that. Nothing exciting."

"Are you still cooking?"

"Yeah, sure."

"That's not much of an answer."

He laughed. "How much do you need?"

Something about the way he said this made me uneasy, so I decided to drop it.

"Tell me about the city then. What's it like to live there?"

"Expensive as hell. Hot. Dirty. People are mostly selfish pricks and users. You can't trust no one. Everybody's got an angle to run, but then that's the truth no matter where you go. You just learn to roll with it. Adapt. Play the game." He took another swig of coffee. "Why do you care?"

"I plan on moving there when I graduate. Though everything's kind of up in the air right now, you know?" My stomach clenched as I flashed on Dylan lying in his hospital bed, clutching onto his last threads of life while I was sitting here shooting the shit.

Gabe considered me as a small frown crept onto his lips. "You wanna talk about it?"

"Naw." My skin crawled at the notion. "You almost finished?"

He arched an eyebrow as if about to argue with me but then seemed to think better of it and simply said, "I'm getting there."

He returned his attention to his plate.

We were quiet for the next few minutes as Gabe polished off his breakfast. I gripped the warm mug before me to keep my hands from trembling, trying to ignore the glares and titters coming from the bar. It was always unnerving being in J.J.'s, Mom. Though I mostly avoided the place like the plague house it was, occasionally, I found myself stopping by to pick up Rozella's rent check or grabbing take-out for dinner. Each time I did, your presence seemed to vibrate off the walls. Though I'd been too young to actually remember you working here, over the years, I'd imagined you often enough, hovering behind that bar, the center of both attention and scorn, slinging drinks for shitty tips to the same assholes that dragged you behind your back. All those old rumors still held their sting whenever I set foot in the place, sending a lifetime's worth of accumulated gossip coursing through my veins like venom, poisoning my thoughts of you.

I couldn't help myself, Mom: I scanned the booths again. I always did when I was in here, trying once more to guess which one you and Roy Allen Krause conceived me in. There were only eight, so it wasn't like I had a huge number to choose from. Maybe it was even the one Gabe and I were sitting at now. Not that I'd ever know for sure, though the sudden image of you spread eagle on the table before me with that fat, grunting bastard plowing into you like a pig in heat made me want to retch.

No wonder I hated this fucking dump so much.

I took a sip of coffee to calm my stomach, but it was too hot and too bitter.

"You alright?" Gabe said, glancing up from his plate. "You've gone awful pale."

"I'm fine. You done yet?"

"Almost," he said, stabbing a final hunk of egg and shoveling it into his mouth. "Hey, Bev, can I get the check?"

"Tell me something good about Mom," I blurted, before I even knew what I was saying.

He arched that eyebrow again and said, "What do you want to know?"

I thought about it for a moment. I didn't know what I wanted to know. Something nice, I supposed. Something innocent and blameless.

"Tell me the just friends stuff," I said. "Something fun that only a real friend would know."

He sighed, not unkindly, and said, "There's probably not a hell of a lot I can tell you that you ain't heard already."

"You'd be surprised what I haven't heard."

A flash of recognition passed over his face. "Jim, huh?"

I nodded.

He shook his head with disgust and grumbled, "Some folks never change."

"Fuck him," I said, and took another sip of bitter coffee. "I don't want to talk about him. Tell me about her. Whatever you can remember. Start with… I don't know…. Her favorite color? If you knew it."

He didn't hesitate. "Burnt orange. Like the sunset."

"Oh," I said, surprised I'd gotten an actual answer. "How about her favorite food?"

"Cinnamon ice cream. She used to treat herself to a couple scoops up at the Tastee Freeze in Diamond Lake."

"Um. Okay. Well." This felt weird all of a sudden, like I should be taking notes. "What about her, um, favorite candy?"

"Red Hots—no, wait. She liked Red Hots, but she went nuts for black licorice. Only the good kind, you know? The expensive kind. The stuff that comes from Europe, not that cheap Twizzler crap they sell at Wal-Mart."

Okay, okay, I thought. Deep breaths.

"And her favorite song?"

"Aww, that's easy." He beamed at me. "Dolly Parton, 'Light of a Clear Blue Morning.' She used to hum that tune all the time."

A lump formed in my throat, and I asked, almost whispered, "What did she sound like when she laughed?"

"Shit, she laughed like a horse: big and throaty and loud." He closed his eyes and smiled as if he could almost hear your laughter.

A strange warmth glowed inside me. Though there was something deeply unfair in having to learn these precious things about you from a dude I barely knew, I wanted more, so much more.

But that feeling passed just as quickly as it arrived.

"You boys need anything else before we settle up?" Bev asked, just as a crack of thunder shook the floorboards. The sky burst open, unleashing a downpour onto the roof. She slapped the check onto the table.

CHAPTER SEVENTEEN
PANTOMIME OF LIFE

THE LOBBY OF KAYOGA GENERAL resembled the hospital set of a soap opera from the 1980s. Nothing had been updated in decades, Mom. Not the curved front desk beneath silver letters shouting WELCOME VISITORS. Not the chrome and pink vinyl benches in the waiting area. Not the dusty plastic palms nor the speckled terrazzo floor that had been waxed so often it shined like Plexiglas. It was all strange and unpleasantly retro.

Though I knew I'd been here once before, the smell was the only thing familiar: stale piss mixed with Clorox and a note of something sweetly-sour that could've been the funk of a clogged drain, a bouquet of wilted flowers, or a whiff of the morgue wafting up from below.

"Dylan Falcone?" Gabe asked the young woman at the front desk. He'd been so sweet on the drive into town, not prying, giving me distance, letting the silence hold between us without making me uncomfortable about it. I was grateful for that.

The woman directed us to the elevators that led to the ICU. We passed through a set of automatic doors that emptied onto a long, white corridor lit by flickering fluorescent lights.

It was the lights that did it.

All at once, I was back to that night. Jimmy carrying me in his arms down one of these same hallways. Where had he come from? Had the police brought him to the motel? I didn't know, but I remembered crying, screaming in fact, clinging to his neck and clawing not to be let go when he tried to lay me down on a steel table in a white room. He held my shoulders as the doctors examined me. They thought you'd hurt me, or neglected me, or—

I didn't want to know what they thought.

When we reached the elevators, Gabe pressed the up button and stepped back. "My old man's this way." He gestured with his thumb down the hall. "I'd go with you, but I doubt Donna wants to see me."

"No worries."

"Meet you in the lobby when you're done?"

"You don't have to wait. I can catch the bus home."

"Naw," he said as the elevator doors opened. "I'll be waiting. Take your time."

"Thanks, Gabe."

I gave him a weak smile as I stepped onto the elevator.

"You'll be okay, Little B."

"Thanks," I said again as the doors slid shut between us.

The ICU was on the third floor. Stenciled in red letters across the glass-partitioned entrance read: ONLY STAFF AND IMMEDIATE FAMILY BEYOND THIS POINT. A small blue sign with a picture of a cell phone exed out hung from the adjacent wall. I turned off my phone and peered through the glass. Six rooms surrounded a central desk, where a nurse in lime green scrubs typed into a laptop. The rooms were walled off in glass, though some had large green curtains drawn across, so I couldn't see inside.

It was now or never.

I pushed through the doors. It was like entering an arcade on mute. Lights flashed on strange machines that made low, whirring noises. The air smelled of ozone. The few patients I could see were all unconscious, their visitors looking on with stricken stares. Nobody paid attention to me as I hurried along the left side of the ward.

Dylan's was the third room in. Although the curtain was drawn, "D. Falcone" was scrawled in red marker on a little whiteboard mounted outside. The door hung open. I sucked in my breath and slipped through the curtain.

The empty chair in the corner by the window was the first thing I saw. A blanket lay crumpled in the seat, a pile of magazines littered the floor.

Then Dylan caught my eye, and I lost my breath.

He looked dead already. His body had melted into the mattress like a candle left in the sun too long. His eyes were puffed shut, and he stank of alcohol swabs and baby lotion. A blue plastic tube taped into his mouth led to a large white ventilator that inflated and deflated his lungs with a loud mechanical hiss. They'd taped electrodes to shaved patches all over his chest, and both of his arms were pierced with IV's. Looming above him, a bleeping screen monitored his vitals via thin green lines that rose and fell, rose and fell. It was a scene straight out of every medical show I'd ever watched, but it still punched me square in the gut.

Jimmy was right: I never should have come here.

"Fuck—*Dylan*," I stammered, tears already streaming down my cheeks.

"Toby?"

A hand touched my shoulder.

Startled, I spun around and found Donna smiling wretchedly at me from the doorway. Before I could say anything, she gathered me in a gigantic hug and began to sob.

"Thank you," she said. "Thank you…. Thank you."

I stood there dumbly and let her cry.

When she finished, she wiped her tears with the cuff of her sweater. "Sorry," she said, embarrassed by her display. Her face was lined with worry. Her nose and lips were chapped raw, and she seemed shrunken somehow as if her whole body had tried to crawl inside itself to hide from what was happening to her son. She ran her fingers through her unwashed hair and slumped into the chair. "I'm glad you're here. None of his buddies visit except for Shad."

"The sign says nobody but family's allowed."

"That's not why," she said, her lips trembling angrily. "I asked for special permission for his friends to come. Shad said he'd get the word out, but nobody's bothered to show up."

I wondered if she really thought Scarface or Owen would have the balls to show their faces around here. It was shocking enough that Shad had come, although I kept that to myself.

"How's he doing," I asked instead.

"About the same. Sometimes, he kicks in bed or curls his fingers, and I swear I can hear him struggling with the breathing tube. But then I realize it's just my imagination. The doctors say he could wake up at any moment. They promise me there are still signs of brain function, and he's strong and young, so... I'm hopeful. I'm really hopeful."

Though I nodded like I agreed with her, when I turned back to face Dylan I couldn't see any reason to be positive. Without the pantomime of machines pretending there was still life inside his body there was nothing left of him. I thought I'd prepared myself for the worst, but this was far beyond what I could have imagined. His presence didn't even feel like it was in the room with us.

She might as well sign that DNR. Dylan was already gone.

I turned away. I couldn't bear to look at him anymore, and so I focused on the bedside table, where she'd set up his entire collection of video game action figures. I quickly scanned the lot of them and realized they were all there, Master Chief and Razorback, Lara Croft, Handsome Jack, John Marston... Dante.

The only one missing was Vergil. Dylan hadn't replaced him. Only now, he never would.

I couldn't hold back any longer, Mom. I sank to the floor at his bedside and bawled.

I don't know how long it took until I finally cried myself out. Maybe

I would have gone on like that forever had Donna not touched me on the shoulder and handed me a wad of damp tissues to wipe my eyes.

"Thanks," I said quietly.

"It's good sometimes to cry. I've done it a lot. I hope you feel better now."

"I guess so."

She leaned back in the chair. "Jim's been apologizing for you all week. He tells me how sorry you are this happened but that you've been too upset to come see us."

"He lied to you," I said, not bothering to conceal my bitterness. I clambered to my feet and walked back to the bedside table, where I picked up Dante by the devil sword slung over his shoulder and gently cradled him in the palm of my hand. "I am upset," I added quietly. "But that's not why I didn't come."

"Oh, I know that," she said, not unkindly. "If the situation were reversed, I would've probably kept Dylan away, too. That's why it means so much that you're here. You followed your heart. I know Jim thinks he's protecting you, but he was wrong to apologize for you. We're the ones who owe you an apology. The world's ugly enough for our beautiful boys without us making it uglier. If I'd thought about that before, maybe my son wouldn't be lying in this bed."

For a moment, I held Dante to my chest before carefully replacing him among Dylan's plastic army of imaginary warriors. "He's not here because of you," I whispered and forced myself to sigh to expel the sob in my throat.

"Isn't he though? What kind of a mother lets her child go through his whole life and never sees such a big part of who he is? I feel like I don't even know him."

I shrugged. "Maybe he didn't want you to know him."

"Why not? I'm his mom. What was he scared to tell me? Did he think I wouldn't accept him?"

"Maybe he wasn't ready to accept himself."

I thought of Dylan's story about those two old men at the Lamplighter Lounge and wondered if she even remembered telling it to him. What if she hadn't meant it the way he assumed she had? What if a simple heart-to-heart between them that night could've prevented all of this from happening? The whole thing felt so stupid, clumsy, and arbitrary, with bad luck and miscommunication leading to wrong assumptions and worse decisions.

If there was a guiding hand controlling our fates, it belonged to a fucking bastard.

A thin line of drool oozed from the corner of Dylan's mouth. I reached down and wiped it away with the balled-up tissue. He didn't flinch. I could probably jab my finger in his eye, but he wouldn't react to that either. I wondered if he could even hear what we were saying. If so, did he regret downing that second bottle of whiskey? Had he really been trying to kill himself, or was he just hoping to forget? Nobody knew for sure, and now we never would. A life ended like this left behind so much damage and blame, so many unanswered questions.

I knew that better than most.

"I found the letters and notes you sent him," Donna said quietly. "You loved him very much, and he hurt you, didn't he?"

"He saved all those?" I said, genuinely surprised.

She watched me a moment, watched for my reaction. "Something happened at the Marsh Trail, didn't it? That's why he did this. Why he apologized in that text. Did he hurt you again?"

I looked away. "We hurt each other."

I wanted her to be angry with me, to see this was my fault. I wanted her to fly off the handle and hit me, to scream and yell and spit in my face. Anything to shift the burden of hating myself onto somebody else's back for a little while. Instead, she blew her nose into another tissue and said wistfully, "You boys have known each other such a long time."

I deflated. "Since we were little kids. Our whole lives, really."

"Do you still love him?"

I stared at Dylan's chest as it rose and fell with the jerky rhythm of the ventilator. I remembered falling asleep there, my head resting just above his softly beating heart.

"I care about him very much." I reached out to stroke the soft, dark hairs on the back of his arm. But his skin was cool, and I yanked my hand away.

"Does he love you?"

I hesitated. "I don't know."

"Well, I hope he does," she said. "But only because I'm a selfish woman. I want him to come back to me, but he needs reasons to do that. I hope you can be a reason, Toby. That's why I kept asking for you to come. For his friends to come, too, for Eddie and Owen and some of the other boys from school."

The thought of Scarface showing up here to gloat turned my stomach.

"Why aren't you angry with them?" I said. "For that matter, why aren't you angry with me? None of this would've happened if I hadn't—"

She cut me off with a wave. "It's like I told Shad: There's plenty of blame to go around. But I don't care about that right now. Maybe I'll get angry after he wakes up, but I need your help. He needs to hear more voices than just mine. He needs his friends."

Friends—what a fucking joke. She'd be better off paying total strangers to read to him from the phonebook. Not that it would make any difference now. She should just sign that DNR instead of dragging this out any longer. I could cope with going back to being a zombie myself, but I couldn't bear the thought of Dylan lingering undead in this hospital bed. Would she hold out until his poor body shriveled up like dried fruit?

It was too late for friends, too late for hope. It was just too late. He deserved to rest in peace.

"I'm going to leave you boys alone for a little while," she said and got up from the chair. "I need some coffee, plus I have to call down to the lounge to see if they'll give me more time off. I can't afford to lose my job right now, but I can't bear to leave him alone in case he wakes up."

She retrieved her purse from beneath the chair and shuffled listlessly to the door, turning back to look at me as she pulled aside the curtain.

"Sit with him while I'm gone. Talk to him. Let him know you're here, that he needs to come back to us. Tell him how much you miss him, okay?"

"If you think it'll help," I said weakly.

"I do," she said and smiled. "I really do." Then she walked out the door, sweeping the curtain closed behind her.

If I wasn't such a coward, Mom, I would have yanked all those tubes and wires from his body the minute she left the room. I would have ended it right then and there. But instead, I tried to do as she asked. I settled on the edge of the bed and grasped his cold, lifeless hand. I cleared my throat and said, "If this is what it takes to be normal, count me out." Then I forced a pathetic laugh.

Silence.

"Seriously, though, I'm sorry this happened. What I said. What I did. But you've got to fight now. Your mom needs you…"

Silence.

"I need you."

Silence.

"Maybe we are a bad match, asshole, but that doesn't mean I don't get to love you."

Silence silence silence.

"Fuck this shit," I grumbled and wiped the moisture from my eyes. This was ridiculous. I felt like a bad actor in a B-movie, faking it for the camera. He wasn't going to answer me. He never had, he never would, and no matter how hard I tried, I couldn't answer for him.

"I'm tired of holding on for you, D," I whispered and released his hand. "I can't do this anymore. It hurts too much. I'm so sorry—goodbye."

CHAPTER EIGHTEEN
BEND IN THE RIVER

BY THE TIME I GOT back to the lobby, another storm had torn open the sky. There was no sign of Gabe, so I wandered into the waiting area, grabbed a copy of Popular Mechanics, and huddled in the corner to avoid eye contact.

The minutes ticked slowly by.

Thunder brayed through the plate glass windows like a stampede of wild horses. I tried to read, but it was obvious that learning how to DIY my own composting toilet could not compete with the lingering image of a comatose Dylan. The TV was on, tuned to CNN, and so I suffered through an update on the election and a feature on a new treatment for ovarian cancer, before they finally switched to the entertainment segment.

Ravisha Mann materialized on screen.

She looked radiant in full homage to Whitney Houston wearing the white silk suit and matching white fedora from the "I'm Your Baby Tonight" video. The interviewer lobbed a few softballs about the new album and juggling the logistics of the Manntasia World Tour, and then they segued to a preview of the upcoming closing show at Terminal City.

It felt like a slap in the face. The world hadn't stopped turning because of what happened to Dylan. Nor would it stop for me. Like the thunderstorm raging outside, the whirlwind of life just kept on blowing beyond the sad little confines of my guilt. Concerts and world tours. Crises and wars. Elections and murders and cancer and babies and even DIY composting toilets. Nothing had ended the moment I entered Dylan's hospital room.

Nothing, except my hope.

This was what death did, Mom: it changed you, not the world. It was a sharp bend in your river, forcing the onward flow of your life onto violent new rapids that might or might never again return you to peace. I could turn eighteen, move to the city, and begin a new life. I could meet and even marry Ravisha Mann and become the world's most famous kept boy, and still, Dylan would be lying in that bed upstairs, plugged into baffles that inflated his lungs, while nurses wiped his ass and fed him mush through a tube.

That is, if he weren't already planted six feet under.

I slammed my head back against the wall and shut my eyes. I hated this. I hated the stupid, fucking unfairness of it. I hated its open-endedness, its disinterest in everything I wanted from my own life. I hated being forced to change, to become this new person who couldn't even sit through an innocuous promo on TV without unbearable bleakness creeping in.

But most of all, Mom, I hated my own selfishness.

Because no matter how heartsick I felt for Dylan, there was still a part of me that raged at the way his miserable fate had clamped a deadweight around mine. How on earth could I spend the rest of my days dragging Dylan Falcone behind me, too? Weren't you enough?

"About time you showed your face around here, Ryerson," said an all-too familiar voice.

Shad Schlee plopped onto the edge of the bench beside me, his jeans and tee-shirt soaked through with rain, a dripping plastic grocery bag dangling from his wrist.

"Um, hey?" I said and sat up to scan the lobby. At least there were other people around.

"Relax," he said. "I'm not looking for trouble." He leaned forward to shake out his hair, sending water droplets sailing everywhere. "You been up to see him yet?"

"Yeah. Just now."

"Donna, too?"

I nodded.

"Good," he said and wiped his brow with the hem of his shirt. "She's been asking after you all week. I would've come looking for you myself, but I figured I wasn't high on the list of folks you or your brother'd wanna see right now."

"You figured right." I shifted uneasily in my seat. "What do you want, anyway?"

"I brought him this," he said and tossed the wet shopping bag onto my lap.

Inside, a blonde elfin action figure wielded a sword at my face.

"It's Link. From Zelda. For D's collection. I got it off a guy I know owes me a couple favors. It's stupid. He's not a little kid anymore, and it's not like he'll even see it."

"It's not stupid," I said, surprised by what a thoughtful gift it was. "He'd like it." I closed the bag and handed it back to him. "But what I really meant is what do you want with me?"

"I know what you meant." He set the bag on the floor and leaned back, sighing while he surveyed the waiting area. "Not too busy today. You should've seen it Saturday. Place was packed, like it was coupon day or something." He cracked a grin at his own joke and turned to face me. "You heard the cops are sniffing around? Talking harassment charges, cyberbullying. Ed and Owen are in some deep shit over this."

"Am I supposed to feel bad about that?"

His grin twisted into a scowl.

"Naw. Just letting you know."

I glanced at the clock above the front desk. Where the hell was Gabe?

"You'll understand if I don't lose sleep about it," I said and picked up the Popular Mechanics again. "Whatever they get is what they deserve."

He ripped the magazine out of my hands. "And what do you deserve?" he said coolly.

I tensed. "I thought you didn't want trouble."

"It's a simple question. What does Ryerson deserve for what he did?"

"Fuck off."

I tried to stand up, but he shoved me back into the seat.

"Hear me out," he said, his hand planted firmly on my chest. "I'm not trying to make excuses for Ed. He's always been a hot head. No impulse control. Never thinks things through. That's why Dad used to kick the crap out of him, but he never learned. What he and Owen did was some serious shit, but neither of them meant for it to go this far. They might've been busting D's balls for lying to us, but they didn't want him hurt, not really. Not like you did."

"Ball busting?" I squirmed against his grip. "Try gay bashing, asshole."

"You think if I cared about D being gay I'd be here now? It might surprise you to know most people don't give a rat's ass what two dudes do with their dicks in private. We're not all backwoods hicks."

"Tell that to my life. Tell it to every fag joke and beating I've taken since I was a kid."

He laughed and yanked his hand from my chest. "Um, newsflash dumbass: that was never because you're gay. It's because you think your shit doesn't stink. You and your brother. You strut around here like you're so much better than the rest of us. Even when we were kids you didn't want to have anything to do with anybody else. Always keeping to yourself, turning up your nose at everyone, what we liked, how we dressed, what we listened to. Calling us stupid, low class. Making jokes about us behind our backs, or did you forget who first started calling Ed "Scarface" back in fifth grade? You knew how that would stick even then, just like you knew how it would stick when you outed D in front of everybody at the Mini Mart."

"Are you for real? You're actually trying to pin this on me?"

"Not at all." He folded his hands behind his neck and stretched out his legs like he owned the world. "Like Donna says, there's plenty of blame to go around. But if the cops get their way, Ed and Owen are going to pay for what they did. Dylan's already a vegetable, and Donna's lost her only kid. But what about you? That's what I can't figure out. What's any of this gonna cost you? Or are you just going to skip off into the sunset feeling sorry for yourself like always, with your tight-assed brother chasing after you to clean up your mess?"

"Are you done?" I jumped to my feet. "I have better things to do than listen to this crap."

He sniggered as I stumbled over his legs and lurched toward the exit. "Must be nice to walk away from all this," he called out. "Too bad Dylan can't."

The automatic doors whooshed open.

With nowhere to go, I dashed for the leaky clamshell of the K-CAT bus shelter, though the downpour quickly soaked through to my skin.

A better person might have felt chastened by what Shad said, but I was too pissed off for that. This was why I hated Shelter Valley. This shit. This gaslighting. This making me feel like I always had it coming for having the audacity to be different. For not being a braindead dude-bro throwing back brewskis and pissing into the bonfire with the guys. For wanting more out of life than busting my ass through some crap nine-to-five just to get to J.J.'s in time for happy hour.

If that's what it meant to think my shit didn't stink, then my shit was Chanel #5.

God, I hated Shad Schlee and every asshole like him in my life. It was just like a bully to play the victim when he held all the power. Or maybe he'd forgotten that the minute before I'd endowed his psychopathic brother with the moniker "Scarface," Eddie had called me a sissy and shoved me face-first into a fence post, busting open my lip and getting blood all over me. So what if I struck back? It was my right to defend myself. When I had weapons, I used them. Mercilessly. Just because I refused to blend in around here so people could feel better about their own pathetic life choices, didn't mean they could use me as their punching bag whenever they felt like it, let alone condemn me when I stood up for myself the only way I could.

I wasn't weak like Dylan; nobody would browbeat me into being normal.

By the time the familiar white Silverado cruised to a halt in front of me, I was almost grateful to Shad for getting me so angry I'd nearly forgotten why I'd come to the hospital.

Gabe reached across the passenger seat and threw open the door.

"Get in before you catch your death," he commanded. He waited until I'd climbed inside before adding, "You're lucky that little blonde at the front desk saw you walk out. I told you I'd meet you in the lobby."

"I needed air," I said, buckling in. "Sorry."

His expression darkened, though not with anger. He pulled the truck up to the curb and parked before turning to face me.

"How's Donna's kid doing?"

"He's dead," I said and slammed my head back against the seat. "Or he might as well be."

"Jesus, is it that bad?"

I nodded.

"How's Donna taking it?"

I gave a bitter laugh. "She still thinks he's gonna pull through. She wanted me to sit there and chat him up like a houseplant."

He hesitated before asking quietly, "You want to talk about it?"

"Nope." I shot him a warning glance. "I'm done talking about Dylan. He's dead. I'm not. There's nothing more to say." My stomach knotted, and I felt like retching. Time to change the subject. "How's your dad?"

His shoulders stiffened.

"Same old bullshit. We got into it over my sister again."

"What about her?"

He rolled his eyes and waved me off. "It don't matter."

"No, tell me. I want to know."

He sank back in the seat and drummed his fingers against the steering wheel.

"He's still pissed I'm the one here babysitting him instead of Connie. The sun rises and sets on her as far as he's concerned. I'm just the hired help. Same as always."

"That really sucks."

He snorted. "That's just me and Pop." He reached out and fondled the golden crucifix dangling from the rearview mirror. "We've never been close, not like me and Ma. I hoped he'd mellow with old age, but he's only gotten meaner."

He gently lifted the chain off the mirror and draped it around his neck.

"But you dropped everything to come home and take care of him," I said. "Doesn't that count for something?"

"Nothing I do counts. Let's just say, he don't approve of my lifestyle choices. Until they plant his ass six feet under, he's never going to let me forget how much I disappoint him."

"I know the feeling." With some slight variation, Harold and Gabe's story sounded an awful lot like Jimmy's and mine.

"Anyway, I talked to Connie this morning. She's flying up tomorrow night to take over here. Then my sentence is done. He'll be happy to see the back of me. That makes two of us."

Something in my chest squeezed up tight. "You're leaving already?"

His eyebrows shot up. "What? You disappointed?"

"Maybe, yeah." And I was. I'd sleepwalked through the entire week hiding myself from the world, when I could have spent some of it with the only person I'd ever met who had a kind word to say about you, Mom. Only now he was leaving. Fuck my life.

Gabe peered at me, and I could see the gears behind his eyes working something out. "I've still got that beer and pot back home," he said playfully and flashed me a sly little smirk. "What's say you come over, and we get seriously fucked up?"

CHAPTER NINETEEN
A LITTLE SEDUCED

THE FOURNIER HOMESTEAD WAS A slouching workhorse of a frontier Victorian set in a swamp of un-mown grass at the foot of Shelter Mountain. I followed Gabe inside, leaping up the broken porch steps through a waterfall overflowing from the busted rain gutter. The foyer of the old house stank like a musty attic. Lit by a bare bulb that dangled at the end of a knotted silver cord, the room wore its gloom shabbily, with peeling paisley wallpaper, wide-plank floors slathered in dirty footprints, and shoes heaped on water-stained newspapers by the door.

Gabe leaned back against the staircase railing and wrenched off his boots.

I shut the door behind me and kicked off my wet sneakers.

"Go sit," he said, gesturing to the living room. "I'll be back soon." Then he disappeared down a hallway to the rear of the house.

The living room reeked of cigars and congealed cooking grease as if Harold had spent the years since he closed the Grill shut up alone in here, waiting for God. Thick mauve curtains were drawn across the windows. An ancient console TV dominated the corner by the foyer. Directly across from it, the swaybacked couch hunkered against the far wall, swathed in a vinyl slipcover stained yellow from eons of smoke. In front of the couch, a cheap coffee table teetered on uneven legs, its surface littered with dirty dishes, empty beer bottles, and two overflowing ashtrays.

I flicked on a lamp and sank into the couch, the slipcover crinkling noisily beneath me. The pipes clanged deep in the belly of the walls as Gabe turned on the hot water for what sounded like a shower. Hail pelleted the windows outside as the storm intensified, and a chill seeped through my wet clothes like rot spreading up the bones of a derelict building.

The drive back from the hospital was a revelatory one, Mom. Gabe did all the talking, spewing a steady stream of unsolicited stories about you. He told me how much you hated gossip, but never missed an opportunity to cuss; how your favorite movie was *Pretty Woman*; how you'd drag him onto the back deck on hot summer nights to dance with you under the stars. He told me how you liked to nickname your new boyfriends "Jake" in case you forgot their real names; how J.J.'s had regulars who drove from all over the county just to flirt with you over a beer; how you'd give them kisses if they filled your car with gas or left a twenty as a tip. He told me how the two of you snuck whippets together in the Grill's walk-in cooler during Sunday rushes;

how you'd taught him to do shots and mix Long Island Iced Teas; how, though you were afraid of silly things like ghosts and aliens, he once watched you chase a three-hundred-pound black bear out of our backyard with nothing but an empty vodka bottle.

It was mesmerizing, to say the least. I listened raptly as deeper and deeper shades of you came into view through the warm afterglow of Gabe's remembrances. In time, I saw him reflected back in that same golden light. I could understand how you'd been drawn together, like Rozella and me, a pair of loner outcasts finding comfort in each other's company.

Still, I couldn't shake the feeling that all of his storytelling was meant to distract me from Dylan. To loosen me up. To set my mind at ease with pleasant memories of you. Not that I could blame him: My miserable mood was obviously a buzzkill.

A few minutes later, he returned, padding barefoot from the dining room wearing only tattered blue boxers and a towel draped over his shoulders. His hair was damp and matted to his skull. The golden crucifix from the rearview mirror hung around his neck, nestled in the downy fur between his pecs. In one hand, he slung two beer bottles by their necks; with the other, he dangled a gallon Ziploc bag containing enough weed to get half the county baked.

He tossed me the towel and offered to throw my wet clothes in the dryer. But since I wasn't ready to get naked again just yet, I declined, though I gave my hair a quick once-over before ditching the towel on the floor. There was plenty of room on the couch to spread out, but Gabe collapsed right beside me. His body heat felt like curling up with an electric blanket. I inched closer. Beneath his shampoo's floral sweetness, I detected his body's lingering tang.

"Why do you have so much pot?" I asked.

"Would you believe I'm holding it for a friend?"

"Not really."

"Does it matter then?"

"No, I guess not."

He twisted open one of the beers and handed it to me. "There's more in the fridge if you want. I could make you a sandwich, too."

"I'm cool," I said and took a hard gulp from the bottle. I hadn't eaten anything since dinner the night before, and the beer hit my stomach like turpentine. I belched, tasted bile, and then washed it back with three more gulps before slamming the empty onto the table.

So much for being a buzzkill.

"Take it easy," he warned, opening the other beer and taking a miserly sip.

"It's alright. Weed gives me a headache if I'm not a little buzzed first."

"Well, ain't you an old stoner."

He chuckled as he leaned forward to unzip the bag of pot. From inside, he retrieved a smaller baggy that held a lighter, rolling papers, and an empty Altoids can. He popped open the can, set it on the edge of the table, and then peeled off a square of paper and nestled it within the lid. He began to root through the weed, plucking out the fatter buds and delicately arranging them on the paper.

"Watch and learn," he said, beaming. He gingerly lifted the edges of the paper, careful not to spill any of the precious bud, and rolled it into a tidy joint that he licked sealed and proudly displayed for my approval.

"Not bad," I said.

"Not bad? It's damn good. A woman of many talents taught me how to do this. Now, I pass on the knowledge to her son."

Then he reached for the lighter.

The first toke was a revelation, Mom, like inhaling velvet or concentrated bliss. Though I'd smoked with Dylan before, the weed we'd gotten off the propane delivery guy was as harsh as burnt plastic. But this—this was the real deal. I'd never experienced anything like it before: smooth, aromatic, crazily potent. The chill in my bones vanished in just a few puffs, and I began to sweat. My toes tingled, and my whole face vibrated as my body heaved a sigh of relief. It felt like falling through a sultry cloud onto a warm mountain of downy pillows.

"Whoa," was all I managed to say.

"I know, right?" Gabe exhaled a milky puff. "Best shit available. I get it off a guy I know who's got a little hydroponics setup in his barn on Long Island. He owns some vineyards, too, makes his own wine."

For some reason, he laughed at this.

"It's hot in here all of a sudden," I said, peeling off my shirt. I leaned back into the sticky slipcover and shut my eyes as waves of delicious heat permeated my body.

"Your bruises are almost gone." The backs of Gabe's fingers grazed my torso. He exhaled slowly, hungrily. "You're good as new."

I felt myself blush, but before I could think of anything to say, he took his hand away.

"We need music," he announced, and lurched to his feet, stumbling back through the dining room with the lit joint still pinned between his lips.

I took a deep breath and tried to clear my head. Something was going on here. Something more than just stoner camaraderie. That hard-to-pin-down feeling I'd gotten from his explicitly vague texts came rushing back. I wasn't sure what to make of it yet, but I wasn't turned off by it. Maybe it was just the drawn curtains with the rain beating down outside, but I felt cocooned inside this sleepy old house. We were all alone here, cut off from the world and all the misery we'd left behind, nestled in our own private Marsh Trail. I wasn't sure if Gabe knew what he wanted from me yet, but I could tell he wanted something. He'd brought me out here for a reason. Plied me with beer and pot and stories of you. I wondered if he sensed the same sparks I did and just didn't know what to do about them.

Not that I knew either.

He returned with a bag of chips and his phone blaring an annoying cock rock song.

"Don't take this the wrong way," I said, "but you've got the straightest taste in music."

He plopped onto the couch nearly on top of me and tossed the phone in my lap. "Play whatever you want then."

It took me a minute to find what I was looking for, but when Ravisha's voice finally began to purr her rendition of The Mary Jane Girls' "Candy Man[n]" off of *MANN 'O War*, he glanced at me with his brow furrowed and said, "Shit, she's all they play in the clubs anymore. I didn't think I'd have to hear her up here, too."

"Clubs?" I waggled my fingers for him to pass me the joint. "Which clubs?"

"All of them. Evolution... Pomp and Circumstance... Terminal City."

"Those are all gay clubs," I said and took a hit.

"How do you know so much about the club scene in Manhattan?"

"I do my research," I said exhaling. "Ravisha's going to be at Terminal City in a couple of nights. I've been daydreaming about going for months."

He grabbed his phone from my lap. "Hold on," he said and began scrolling through texts. "My buddy Lon's a floor manager there. He's been texting me all week about the crazy shit they're setting up for that show. It's out of control—here, he sent me a pic."

He traded me his phone for the joint.

The image was of a gigantic, five-tiered wedding cake made entirely of aluminum bars and twinkling LED lights. At the top was a podium on which I'd seen Ravisha perform an encore of "Mann of My Dreams" in a bootleg clip from her show in San Francisco.

I handed him the phone back. "It's cool that your friend works there. Will he get to meet her?"

"I doubt it. He mostly just corrals drunks and keeps the peace."

"Tell me about Terminal City. What's it like?"

"Not much to tell. Just another meat market with watered-down drinks. Used to be an old shipping terminal or something until they converted it to a club. Nothing but a big ugly box with lights and a dance floor. They're all the same, really."

"Why do you go then? To dance?" I flashed him a little smirk. "Or just to hook up?"

He groaned self-consciously. "Do I look like I dance?"

"You said my mom made you dance."

"Against my will."

"Poor baby." I patted his thigh. "But you still haven't answered my question."

He shrugged. "It's just business," he said and took another hit. "I go there for business."

I supposed I could have pressed him to tell me more, but what was the point? Even baked, I wasn't stupid. Nobody carried around a gallon bag of pot for personal use. It was obvious what his business was, although I couldn't have cared less by that point. I took another toke and shut my eyes as swirls of light danced behind my lids. I exhaled slowly, letting the smoke pour from my mouth like kissing the air. I couldn't remember the last time I felt so relaxed.

Gabe managed to get a couple small puffs out of what was left of the roach before pinching it off and dropping it into the Altoid can. "I'll roll that into the next one," he said, and then settled back into the couch to ride out his high, throwing his arm over the cushions behind me.

I folded my legs beneath me and laid my head against his shoulder.

"You want some chips?" he asked dreamily. "Weed makes me hungry."

"It makes me horny." I giggled, adding too quickly, "It did with Dylan anyway."

I winced. I didn't want to think about Dylan. I just wanted to be high and flirt and forget.

Gabe hesitated, as if he sensed the rawness that lurked below my surface. I could feel the weight of his unspoken attraction shift and settle onto a new center of gravity a little bit closer to me. He cleared his throat and asked, almost coyly, "Was he your first time?"

"Yeah, he was," I said quietly.

"And is he the only one you ever——?"

I gave him an anxious laugh. "Hardly. You found me at the Marsh Trail, remember?"

"That I do." He chuckled lightly. I felt his hand slip onto my shoulder. "I had my first time there when I was your age."

A jolt of electricity sizzled up my spine. "Really? Tell me."

He flashed me a sheepish grin. "He was a long-haul trucker. Flannel and jeans. Big and meaty. A beard as thick as a Brillo pad and breath that tasted like chaw. It was over so quick, I barely knew what hit me. But I was hooked after that. Down there a couple times a month. I'd skip the bus after school and walk the two miles from Kayoga Unified. Went on like that for a while before my old man caught on."

I jerked my head from his shoulder. "You got caught?"

He smirked at the look of horror on my face. "Ma knew something was up with me, that I wasn't going to the library to study or whatever bullshit excuse I'd fed to her."

"What happened?"

He laughed bitterly. "I showed up there one afternoon to find him waiting for me with his belt in his hand. Dragged me home kicking and screaming. Whipped the living shit out of me right in front of Ma and Connie. Then he made me pack up my stuff and kicked me out that very front door." He nodded to the foyer. "Said he didn't want to see my face again until I learned how to be a real man."

"Holy shit. Is that when Mom took you in?"

"Yup. Thank God for Bonnie, too, otherwise I don't know what I would've done."

I paused to soak it all in. It was a hell of a story. No wonder he said I reminded him of himself. I wondered why it'd taken me so long to see it. Maybe my gaydar was busted, or I'd just gotten too distracted by his swagger, his self-confidence, his easy comfort in his own skin. These were not qualities I'd ever associated with anyone like me before, certainly not Dylan nor any of the Marsh Trail's closet cases. Gabe had sure as hell learned how to be real man.

"You know," I said, "when I met you, I figured you were straight."

"Yeah, well, you're not the first."

"How come I've never heard about any of this before? Even Rozella didn't mention it. At least, not directly."

"Pop sure as hell wasn't bragging all over town about it." He snorted. "Besides, you'd be surprised the kind of secrets people can keep when they need to. It helped that Bonnie was fine with letting people's dirty minds draw conclusions about us. Made things easier on me. Maybe not so much for her, though."

"Wow," I said and dropped my head back onto his shoulder. "Mom was your beard." I laughed at myself for how badly I'd misjudged him.

We fell silent. The air tingled with anticipation. I could feel us teetering precariously on a knife's edge. One of us had to make the next move, to push things forward. I sensed Gabe was holding back, still waiting for me to signal what I wanted, so I took a deep breath, marshaled my nerve, and said, "So, your buddy Lon. Is he your boyfriend?"

"Naw. We just have fun together sometimes. I don't have a boyfriend."

"Good," I said and began to stroke his belly with my fingertips. "I like fun, too, you know?"

That was all the signal he needed. The muscles of his abdomen tensed beneath my touch, and he reached over and grasped me by the chin, carefully tilting my face to meet his. Our eyes locked, and then his lips fell into mine, suddenly, eagerly, my mouth flooding with his salt and smoke and molasses, my own hardness pulsating between my legs as my fingers slipped beneath the waistband of his boxers to caress his—

His head jerked backwards.

"Whoa—shit." He blinked as if startled awake. "What are we doing?"

He prized my hand from his erection and gently pushed me off of him.

"We're making out. Don't tell me you didn't like it."

"But you're not sober, Little B, and I'm—"

"I'm not your Little B anymore," I said firmly. "Stop calling me that."

I smashed my mouth against his, but he pushed me away again.

"I don't want to take advantage here."

I laughed. "Don't worry. We're both taking advantage."

Then I kissed him again, Mom. Only this time, he didn't push me away.

CHAPTER TWENTY
THE OTHER SIDE OF NOW

GABE PULLED ME CLOSER. His tongue swirled around mine, his hands frantic for me. All at once he hoisted me into his arms. I cinched my legs around his waist to hang on for dear life as he hauled me up the stairs to his bedroom, tossing me onto the musty sheets like a bag of dirty laundry. He yanked off my Daisy Dukes and cinnamon panties so roughly I thought they would tear. He groaned something about my "beautiful ripe peach" and then his hands and mouth were everywhere at once, smothering me until it seemed like I would drown beneath him.

Sex had never felt this urgent before. With Dylan—and even the strangers at the Marsh Trail—it had always been more hesitant, slower, skittish. Plus, I'd always been the one in control. But this was happening so fast, too fast, like I was strapped to a runaway train and there was no stopping it now. Gabe knew exactly what he wanted from me, and since I couldn't begin to keep up, I let myself go limp and just surrendered to him.

When his face slid between my thighs, seismic waves radiated up from my core.

My heart spasmed. My eyes rolled back in my head.

A condom soon materialized from a gym bag on the floor, and I heard myself mutter, "No, I trust you," even though I wasn't sure I did.

"Who says I trust you?" he teased, and then added before I could respond, "Never trust any guy with your life—never."

He slipped the condom on and then flipped me onto my stomach, hocking a couple of loogies onto his dick before jamming himself inside of me.

I won't sugar coat it, Mom: it hurt. Like, *crazy* hurt. When Dylan and I experimented with anal sex the first time, we were so scared of it hurting we used half a bottle of Donna's olive oil as lube and kept stopping every few minutes just to check in on each other. But Gabe was getting the job done with nothing but spit and elbow grease. It was all I could do to keep from yowling and squirming out from under him.

Instead, I bit the back of my arm, squeezed my eyes shut right, and rode out the pain.

When it was over, Gabe spooned his sweat-slicked body around mine like I was his comfort pillow. We listened to the rain patter against the window. This had always been the best part with Dylan. The part I missed the most. The closeness of it. The not-aloneness. Only with Gabe I couldn't shake the feeling that I'd done something wrong, somehow disappointed him. I'd been so reactive, so meek, so overwhelmed, and clueless. Maybe he thought I wasn't any good.

Maybe I wasn't.

He kissed the back of my head and whispered, "You smell like blueberries."

"It's just the dandruff shampoo Jimmy buys."

"I like it."

"That was something else, wasn't it?" I said, fishing for a compliment or at least some kind of acknowledgment that he'd had a good time. When none was forthcoming, I added, "You sure know how to melt a boy."

He chuckled. "I do my best."

I closed my eyes and mumbled, "Was I, um, any good?"

He hesitated just long enough for me to get my answer. "You were fine. Was that your first time?"

I felt my face burn. "No, Dylan and I did that before."

"I mean your first time with a man…. Somebody who knew what he was doing?"

"I guess."

He nuzzled the back of my neck with his chin and said, "You'll learn to relax eventually. It takes practice."

It also takes lube, I nearly spat but held my tongue.

I must have tensed, too, because he gave me a little squeeze and laughed. "Aww, come on, beautiful. Couldn't you tell how much I enjoyed myself? You're amazing. That was amazing."

"You don't have to say that."

"I'm not just saying it. It's true."

The knot in my chest finally loosened a bit, and I nestled closer to him. "Ha. I bet you tell that to all the boys."

"Hardly."

"I don't mind if the others were amazing, too."

"What makes you think there are so many others?"

"Uh, you're a grown-ass man."

He let go of me and rolled onto his back, folding an arm beneath his head like a pillow. "I'm no saint if that's what you mean. I get plenty. But that don't make this, or you, any less special."

I flipped over to curl myself around his torso. "There must be other special ones, though. At least a couple."

"Nope."

"Oh, come on."

"It's the truth. Dudes are users. Selfish pricks who split as soon as they cum. If they stay, it's only because they want something more. A second helping of your ass, maybe. Money. Drugs. A place to crash for the night."

"You're still here. Does that mean you want something more from me?"

He pretended to think it over. "Maybe I'm just holding out for seconds."

I swallowed hard and said, "I'm ready."

He laughed again. "Give me a few minutes, okay there, Tiger?" He reached down to swat my ass. "I ain't a teenager anymore."

I smiled and nuzzled my cheek against his skin. In truth, I was in no hurry. My ass still burned like hell, and besides, this was too nice to rush. I wanted to hold onto it for as long as I could. I fiddled with the crucifix between his hairy pecs and said, "You don't strike me as the Jesus type."

I felt him tense beneath me.

"I'm not. Ma gave that to me as a Confirmation gift. I thought I'd lost it years ago but found it buried in a drawer my first night back. She was the religious one. Believed in the whole peace, love, and forgiveness thing till the day she died. I'm glad to have it back. It reminds me of her."

"Tell me about her."

"Why do you want to hear about that?"

"Because she was your mom."

He hugged me closer. "See, this is why you're special. Nobody ever wants to talk about Ma. Not even my old man." He plucked up the crucifix and gazed dreamily at the wall across from us. "She was a quiet woman. Always busy with her hands. Always looking out for her family. She worked her ass off her whole life, at the Grill, raising two kids, dealing with my old man's bullshit. But she never complained, not once, not even when the radiation cooked her insides so bad she couldn't swallow a sip of water. Dragged herself to church three times a week until the very end. Dragged me and Connie, too, kicking and screaming. She wasn't a strong woman, though, especially when it came to my old man. She couldn't stand up to him. It was hard on her the way he used to come at me. With his fists, his belt. Shit, once he even broke a chair over my back. But she could never get between us to stop him. I had to learn to do that on my own, but by then I was out the door, and out of her life, too."

He dropped the crucifix, his hand drifting onto the sheets beside him.

"I know it ate her up inside, me leaving home so young. But she never made me feel guilty about it. Never blamed me for being who I am, no matter what the church and my old man had to say about it. I was her boy, and she loved me. She's the only one who ever will."

"She sounds awesome," I said. "I can see why you miss her."

"Best woman I ever knew. You would've liked her, and she would've gotten a kick out of you." He sighed as if unburdened of a weight he'd just hauled up a mountain. "Anyway, thanks for asking about her. I—I appreciate it."

"Nothing to thank me for." I gave him a sad smile. "Remembering is the only gift we can still give to the dead."

He looked almost startled as if he'd just seen me for the first time. Then his hand slid behind my neck, and he pulled me in for another kiss. This time, his lips trembled against mine with something more urgent than arousal. He rolled me on top of him and wrapped his thighs around my hips, his body yearning for mine, surrendering to me. I'd broken through to what was soft and vulnerable inside him, and he was opening himself to me, inviting me to go deeper. So, I took charge.

We went slower this time. I kissed and tasted every inch of Gabe, practicing some tricks I'd learned with Dylan. Eventually, I managed to fish out another condom from the gym bag, but before I slipped it on myself, I muttered, "I can't use spit. Got anything else?"

After a grunt and a few moments rifling through the gym bag, he produced a wrinkled packet of Astroglide. While I was pissed that he hadn't bothered to dig it out to use on me, let's just say, Mom, I was way too "in the moment" to let that stop me....

When we finished, he snuggled beside me and drifted off to sleep. But I was too wired to follow. I debated slipping out of bed to watch TV, but I didn't want to wake him. I couldn't reach my phone without waking him either, so I just laid there, not moving, barely breathing, trapped and increasingly mortified as the reality of my situation sank in.

What the hell just happened?

This wasn't five minutes of heaven at the Marsh Trail. This wasn't meaningless head or an inconsequential hand job.

Not counting Dylan—oh God, *Dylan*—I'd been with seven other men in my life, and though I could recall every moment of our encounters in forensic detail—the precise fall of the light, the aroma of their skin, the music of their bodies as they came—not one of them had even said my name, let alone kissed me or fallen asleep beside me. Gabe had at least treated me like a human being instead of a sex doll, but that didn't make this alright, did it? A few hours ago, I'd been bawling at the deathbed of the only boy I'd ever loved—*still* loved, despite how much I didn't want to anymore—and yet here I was now, naked and spent in the bed of some random dude I barely knew, and it felt obscene to be this, this—*happy* about it.

Maybe I'd been a zombie for so long that it just felt good to be alive again. Maybe I was a selfish asshole, like Shad said. Maybe I really was a slut.

I tore into my knuckles with my teeth and glanced around the room for something to distract me from hating myself. There wasn't much. The space was cramped and stark. The wall at the foot of the bed was sloped like the roof, with a narrow, grimy window set into an arched dormer. The other walls were barren, their ancient white paint scuffed and nicked from decades of abuse. There wasn't even a closet, and Gabe's clothes were strewn in heaps across the floor. Atop a small wooden dresser in the corner sat the only remaining artifact from when this had been a teenage boy's bedroom: a lamp in the shape of a NY Jets helmet. If the room had once held other clues to the boy Gabe had been, they were long gone now.

I noticed that the rain had tapered off outside, leaving in its wake an oppressive heaviness in the air. I caught a glimpse of sunlight through the window, but it only reminded me that Gabe's sister was coming home tomorrow. Then he'd leave me behind and all of this would become little more than a bewildering memory, and I would go back to being a lonely zombie waiting for "the call."

I wasn't ready for that. I didn't want to face what came next. I didn't want what was waiting for me on the other side of that window. On the other side of now. I shut my eyes and willed myself to hold onto this moment for as long as I possibly could....

I AWOKE HOURS LATER. GABE was propped up on his pillows beside me smoking another joint and checking messages on his phone. The storm had revived itself while I slept. Rain pummeled the roof, and gusts of wind sent ominous rumbles through the floorboards. I glanced at the clock on the dresser and realized it was well past dinnertime.

Jimmy would be at home waiting for me. He would be fuming.

"Shit." I disentangled myself from the sheets. "I should go, but I don't want to."

"Then don't. Stay here with me." He stroked the inside of my thigh, sending gooseflesh gushing down my leg.

"I have to face Jimmy. He'll be pissed that I went to see Dylan today."

He took a hit off the joint and said, "Why the hell should he care?"

"You'd have to know my brother."

"Oh, I know Jim," he said sharply. "He's the same fucking bully he always was."

He offered me the joint, but I refused. I didn't want to reek of pot when I got home, although it was probably too late for that. I reached for my panties at the foot of the bed and said, "I don't get it. What do you two have against each other anyway?"

He flashed me his teeth. "How about this?" he said and leaned forward, craning his neck to show me a jagged scar at the base of his skull that vanished beneath his hairline. "A gift from your brother."

"Jimmy did that? When?"

"High school." He sank into the pillows to take another hit. "He and a couple of his buddies cornered me in the locker room. Said he didn't want some faggot checking him out in the showers. Then he slammed my head into one of those porcelain sinks by the urinals. Cracked the sink. Cracked my skull. Blood everywhere. Took twelve stitches to sew me up. Nearly got his ass expelled for it that time."

"That time? You mean there were others?"

His lips curled into a sneer. "So, 'ole Saint Jim never told you what an animal he was in high school? Shocker." He took one last hit and pinched off the joint, dropping it into the Altoids can. "I was an easy mark back then. Skinny. Quiet. Kept to myself. Plus, once the rumors started flying about Bonnie and me, it hung an even bigger target around my neck. He stopped kicking my ass for being a faggot and started kicking it for being the faggot everyone thought was banging his mom. Not that it mattered why. He just needed somebody to punch, and I was available."

"That doesn't sound like Jimmy at all."

"Yeah, well, you didn't know him back then." He climbed out of bed and began to root through the clothes on the floor.

I pulled my knees to my chest. I felt sick to my stomach. The idea that my Jimmy, Beast to my Belle, had once been a certified gay basher was too much to take. It went against everything I knew and loved about him, and I tried to rationalize it away. What did I really know about Gabe? Maybe he was leaving out important details. Maybe he was an asshole back then.

Maybe he had it coming.

I winced to myself remembering Abe's words about me and snapped, "What am I supposed to do now?" not wanting to know any of this about my brother. "I'm having a really hard time picturing Jimmy acting that way. He's not like that."

Gabe shimmied into a pair of clean boxers and turned to face me.

"Look, I'm not trying to stir shit up. You asked. I don't expect you to take sides or apologize for him. It was a long time ago. We were kids. People change. But I ain't making it up. It happened. Ask him yourself."

"Maybe I will," I said without conviction. "Though I'm not sure how I'd explain how I found out. I'm not supposed to talk to you."

He slipped into a black wife-beater he pulled from the gym bag and said, "See, this is what I'm talking about. Just tell him the truth. He ain't your father. You don't owe him explanations or excuses. Maybe it's time you stood up for yourself. Told him what you really want."

"Who says I don't?"

He flashed me a smirk and kneeled on the edge of the bed. "I'll bet you another kiss against that whole bag of Long Island's finest that he don't know a thing about your little plan to move to the city after high school."

I flipped him the bird.

"Yep, that's what I thought," he said, falling into me with a self-satisfied smirk.

Though I let him kiss me, I pushed him away as soon as he finished.

"Aww, don't be like that," he said, brushing the bangs from my forehead. "Look, I get it. I grew up under the thumb of a bully, too. You love him, sure. You can't help yourself. But you always gotta act a certain way around him. Think a certain way. Be a certain way or else. And no matter what you do, it ain't ever good enough, and you always end up feeling bad about yourself, what you want, who you are. But it don't have to be that way if you don't let it."

"Jimmy's no Harold, okay? He may have his hang-ups, but he's never a laid a finger on me. He gave up everything when Mom died to take care of me. I don't know what he was like when you were kids, but that's not who he is now."

"If he's such a great guy, why can't you tell him the truth?"

"Fuck this shit," I said, and tried to scramble away from him, but he grasped me by the sides of my face and dead eyed me with his killer stormy blues.

"Let me tell you something, beautiful. Not all bullies use their fists. The smart ones push you around without ever laying a finger on you."

I yanked free and leapt out of the bed. "Mind your own fucking business." I snatched my panties from the sheets and jammed myself into them while he watched.

"And now you think I'm pushy."

I grabbed my Daisy Dukes from the floor. "I need a shower. Then I'll take off."

"Bathroom's down the stairs at the back of the kitchen." He moved toward the door as if intending to show me the way.

"I can find it myself," I said, storming down the stairs, cursing him the whole way.

CHAPTER TWENTY-ONE
A BETTER MAN

GABE INSISTED ON DRIVING ME home, and since the mobile manor was three miles away along twisty mountain roads, I didn't put up much of a fight.

Still, I was too upset for chitchat. I didn't believe what he'd said about Jimmy. There must be things Gabe left out. Jimmy was no monster. And even if it were true, my brother had changed in the years since. Your death changed him, Mom. He was a different man now. A better man. A good man.

But what Gabe said still stung. He was right that I couldn't stand up to Jimmy. Not in the ways that mattered. I snuck around behind his back, lied to his face. My brother wasn't a bully; I was a coward.

When we pulled up in front of the trailer, all the lights were blazing inside. Baby was parked askew in the grass out front, a sure sign that

Jimmy had been out looking for me. I nearly told Gabe to haul ass back to his place, but he'd already parked and turned to face me.

"Listen, I've got no business talking shit about Jim to you. He's family. I'm nobody."

"You're hardly nobody," I said, my remaining anger deflating. "Anyway, it's done now. Let's forget it, okay?" I reached over and squeezed his thigh to let him know he was forgiven. I realized we'd just made up from our first and probably last fight. The thought was remarkably bittersweet.

"I had a great time today," he said, grinning. "You really are special. I hope you know that."

"You're special, too."

He looked away, almost bashfully, and drummed his fingers against the steering wheel before asking, "Can I see you again?"

"Um..." I glanced at the front door. "Aren't you leaving tomorrow?"

"Yeah, that." He slammed his head back against the seat. "Connie's flight lands in Albany tomorrow night. I was planning to be gone by then. I've got to visit my old man in the morning, but maybe we could meet up after that? I could pick you up here. We could head out to Diamond Lake for cinnamon ice cream or something?"

"I'd love that." I stole another glance at the front door. "Just text me first."

We both stared out the windshield. Neither of us wanted to go. How do you say goodnight when there's no future beyond goodbye? Tomorrow he would return home, and that would be that. Maybe we'd see each other again whenever I moved to the city, but that was still a lifetime away. It was hard to imagine how the little spark we'd ignited here could stay lit without oxygen.

Another relationship fail to add to my growing list.

Out of the corner of my eye, I thought I saw the living room curtains flutter. "I should go before Jimmy sees us," I said, unbuckling my seatbelt. Thanks for the ride. I'll see you tomorrow."

When I reached for the door handle, Gabe grabbed my wrist.

"Why don't you come back with me to the city?"

I looked at him as if he'd lost his mind. "Yeah, right." I almost laughed. "Don't make offers you don't mean."

"I'm dead serious. Call it paying off my debt to Bonnie if you want. But I like you. A whole lot. Besides, we both know there's nothing left for you here. I've got ears. I can hear how people are talking. They blame you for what happened to Donna's kid. They smell blood in the water. You know how it's gonna be from now on. But you don't have to deal with that shit. Come with me. You want to move to the city anyway. Why wait? I'll show you off to New York. Hell, I'll even take you to Manntasia."

I rolled my eyes at that one. "I'm only seventeen. They'd never let me into that club."

"I've got connections, remember?"

I laughed at him again. "Stop teasing me. I don't even have my GED. What would I do to earn my keep?"

"We'd figure something out," he said and smirked lasciviously.

"Oh, I see. You think I'm always this easy?"

"Naw, I just know you're too sexy to resist."

He pulled me in for another kiss. It was a good one, Mom, certainly among the top-three for the day, only just as things got going, the passenger door flew open behind me and Jimmy's fingers taloned into my shoulders.

He heaved me out of the truck and hurled me onto the wet grass. "What's wrong with you?" he howled, grabbing fistfuls of my shirt and yanking me back to my feet. "Right out here in front of the house like some goddamned—"

"Get your fucking hands off me!"

I tried to slap him away, but he held me fast and began sniffing my clothes.

"Is that weed?" he said, his own breath reeking of bourbon as he peered glassily into my eyes. "You're high? Are you out of your mind?" He began to shake me. Hard.

"Hey," Gabe barked. He was already out of the truck and storming around the hood towards us. "Let him go."

Jimmy tossed me onto the ground and turned to Gabe, hate shattering across his face like a broken bottle. "Fournier," he snarled. "I told you to stay away from him."

He launched himself at Gabe, throwing a hard right to Gabe's chin before he could react. Gabe tried to parry but was caught off guard. The punch landed like a sledgehammer. Gabe's head snapped back, and he buckled, collapsing ass-backwards onto the gravel. Blood spurted from a crack in his lower lip, and his eyes swam as he tried to shake off the blow.

Jimmy circled for another volley, but I hurled myself at him and latched my arms around his bicep.

"Stop it," I shouted. "Leave him alone."

"Get off me!"

He tried to shove me away, but it was too late: Gabe bounded back to his feet and rushed us. Though I levered myself between them, Jimmy cuffed me aside just in time for Gabe to tackle him. Jimmy was knocked backwards onto the muddy verge of the driveway, where Gabe scrambled on top of him, straddling his thighs and hurling rapid-fire blows to his face, ribs, kidneys. It was brutal, Mom. Jimmy was either too drunk or too stunned to defend himself. Spit and blood jettisoned from his mouth as he flailed helplessly beneath Gabe's onslaught, his body spasming with each cracking blow.

I heard Rozella scream from somewhere behind me, "Stop it! You'll kill him," and I leaped onto Gabe's back, grabbing at his arms and neck until he shouldered me off.

He staggered to his feet, his chest heaving, the blood and rain pouring down his chin as he backed away, glowering but triumphant. "You've had that coming for eighteen years!" he howled at Jimmy, who was rolling around on the ground and moaning, struggling with everything he had left to push himself to his feet. "How does it feel to get your ass handed to you for once?"

I crawled over to help Jimmy, but he shoved me aside.

Gabe circled us, itching for round two. "Get up!" he shouted at Jimmy. "Be a man for once and stand up to somebody who can fight back."

"Stop this," I said and scrambled to my feet. "He's down. Let it go."

"Come on, big man," Gabe sneered, glaring through me. "You gonna let a faggot like me wipe the floor with you? Or you gonna wait till I leave and take it out on him?"

"I'm calling the cops," Rozella warned.

I glanced over Gabe's shoulder to see that she was at the head of a small crowd of neighbors who'd gathered outside to watch.

"Just go," I pleaded with Gabe. "I'll be okay, I promise. He's just drunk. I can handle him."

"I can handle him better."

He tried to lunge around me, but I held my ground.

"No!" I slammed my fists into his chest. "You'll have to go through me to get to him."

For whatever reason, this pitiful display of machismo was enough to break Gabe's fever. He blinked a couple of times at me and backed away.

"Alright, beautiful," he said, wiping the rain from his eyes. "But if he lays a finger on you, you come get me, you hear?"

"You sick bastard," Jimmy sputtered from the ground behind me. "He's just a kid. I swear, if you come near him again, I'll—I'll kill you!" He somehow managed to push himself to his feet and staggered to my side.

"You can try." Gabe smeared the blood oozing down his chin with the back of his hand. His knuckles were already swollen. He spit more blood at Jimmy's feet and then stomped around the truck and threw himself behind the wheel. He revved the engine a couple of times and then peeled off in a tsunami of gravel.

I stood there watching him shrink into the distance, too shocked to move until I sensed Jimmy about to collapse beside me. I grabbed him by the forearm to keep him standing. He was a disaster: Soaked in mud and rain. Blood everywhere. His left eye already swelling shut. He winced when I tried to pivot him toward the house, and I feared Gabe may have broken his ribs.

"We should get you to the hospital."

"Just help me inside," he said and jerked his head at the crowd watching us.

Half the mobile manor stood beneath umbrellas, whispering to one another. I'd never seen so many of them gathered at one time.

Rozella came rushing back from her trailer with her cordless phone.

"Let me call you an ambulance, Jim," she said, her face drained of color.

"It's alright," he said. "I've got this under control."

"That's what I was saying," a voice piped up from the crowd. "You sure took care of him."

A ripple of laughter followed until Rozella roared, "Shut the hell up, all of you, unless you want a rent increase."

That quickly stifled the titters.

"Come on, Toby," she said, trying to grab Jimmy's other arm, but he shoved her away so forcefully she stumbled backward.

"Leave me alone," he growled. "All of you."

"It's alright, Rozella." I flashed her an apologetic look. "I've got this."

Of course, nobody else offered to do anything. They all just stood there and gawped. The fight would be the talk of J.J.'s tonight.

"Let's go," Jimmy hissed into my ear. "Now."

I grabbed his arm and looped it over my shoulder. Together, we hobbled across the driveway and up the steps to the door

When we reached the landing, Rozella called out again, "You sure I can't call someone, puppy? Or I could fetch ice or medicine or something?"

"No thanks," I called to her, and then added more loudly, "Show's over. Everyone go home."

I kneed open the front door, heaved Jimmy across the threshold, and hauled him to the couch, where it was all I could do to lay him down without collapsing on top of him.

He tried to sit up, but the pain in his side was too much, and he fell back moaning.

I slammed the door and turned to take stock of the carnage in the living room. A half-empty bottle of bourbon sat on the coffee table beside Jimmy's phone and a pool of what looked like spilled beer. The TV was on: a wrestling match splattered with drying beer foam from a bottle that lay drained on the carpet below it. Jimmy had knocked over your rocker, Mom, and kicked the pile of magazines I'd been reading across the floor. He'd hurled the college view books into the sink in the kitchen.

"It's funny how spooked you get about things," he said in a voice so low I could barely hear him. He glared at me with his good eye, his whole body practically vibrating with fury. "Donna called on my lunch break to tell me about your little visit. Said you snuck out on her as soon as she left the room. Said you were upset about seeing

Dylan like that. "Shaken" was the word she used. Shaken enough to do something stupid."

"So that's why you decided to redecorate the living room? You thought I was going to do what, exactly? Kill myself? Are you serious?"

"Shut up. Just shut the hell up."

He tried to sit up again and groaned.

"Let me call the doctor, at least."

He ignored me and grabbed the bourbon off the coffee table. He sucked down a two-fingered gulp, grimacing through the burn against the shredded flesh of his mouth. Then he closed his eyes, held his breath, and swung his legs out to heave himself upright, yelping like a kicked dog.

He took another swig from the bottle and then sat there glowering at me.

"You think I'm an idiot, don't you?" he sneered, his teeth showing red with fresh blood. "You think it's easy for me to watch you throw your life down the toilet? You think I like being like this?"

"Your mouth is still bleeding."

"This'll take care of it," he said and lifted the bottle to his lips.

"Don't you think you've had enough?"

He gave me a bitter laugh. "Listen to you, lecturing me about drinking after spending the day getting high and Lord knows what else with your new boyfriend. Does he know you just got treated for the clap?" He winced, though not from the pain. "Jesus Christ, I'm gonna have to drag you back to that clinic for more tests." He took another swig. "Didn't take you long to find a new one, did it? They haven't even unplugged the last one yet."

I didn't react. I didn't dare give him the satisfaction of showing how hard that hit me.

He wedged the bottle between his thighs and leaned back against the cushions. "You know he's human garbage, right? A fucking drug dealer. He used to get Mom stoned all the time when you were little. Now he's moving in on you."

"You're awfully high and mighty for someone hammered out of his mind."

"That may be," he said. "But he's no better than the lowlifes who sold her the shit that killed her. Besides, he's just using you to get under my skin."

"Yeah, right," I said bitterly. "It's all about you, isn't it? It's always about you, what you want, what you think is right and wrong."

"Damn straight it is." He took another swig and jerked his head like a horse shooing a fly. "Mark my words, you're never going to see him again. You can take that to the bank."

"I'm going to bed. I won't talk to you when you're like this."

"Get out of my sight. I can't stand to look at you right now."

"That makes two of us," I said before storming into my bedroom.

CHAPTER TWENTY-TWO
HAD iT COMING

I SPENT THE NEXT HOUR furiously ignoring the sounds of Jimmy's misery. He could barely move without hurting somewhere, and his gasps and groans echoed through the thin trailer walls like a chorus of scolds.

At first, I played music to drown him out, but then I began to worry he might cry for help, and I'd miss it. After that I just laid in bed, listening to him suffer. I consoled myself with the thought that at least Gabe had learned how to fight since the last time he tangled with his bully. It could be done. Maybe he should be the one to teach me how to throw a punch. That would serve my goddamned brother right.

Of all the things Jimmy had said to me, throwing your death up in my face was the lowest, Mom, especially since we both knew smoking pot was nothing like shooting heroin. Or getting shit-faced on bourbon.

But for once, none of this was really about you. Jimmy had shattered my remaining illusions all on his own. The way he'd lashed out at Gabe and me felt like confirmation of every awful thing Gabe had told me about him. All that ugliness and violence had burst into the open, and it was shocking to behold. What else might be lurking inside him? What more might he be capable of? I hated doubting him like that. I hated the desperate, awful emptiness of it. I hated knowing it was my fault. Jimmy would never be the same for me again. A part of me would always see him as he was tonight and ache with the memory of what I'd driven him to become.

I'd broken your good son, Mom. I'd broken him.

IT WAS WELL PAST TEN when he heaved himself off the couch and lumbered into the bathroom to clean up. I followed after him to help.

He had the good sense to keep his mouth shut when he saw me, deflating against the counter and leaving me to work. I'd never seen him so wrecked in my life. He'd somehow managed to pull off his tee-shirt and his entire torso was viciously inflamed. I dug out the truss he used the last time he'd broken ribs at work and gingerly secured it around his midriff.

This eased the pain enough that he was able to stand without gasping.

Next, I had him sit on the toilet while I worked on his face with a washcloth. Once I cleared away the dried blood, I realized the damage wasn't as bad as I feared. Though discolored and puffy, his nose didn't seem broken. He had a gash on his upper lip that'd already scabbed over and a few cuts on his cheek that still wept blood. A few daubs of alcohol and a couple of Band-Aids did the trick.

His left eye was another matter, with its socket encircled in an ugly swollen mound the size of a pork chop. I got some ice cubes from the freezer, wrapped them in a dishtowel, and handed it over. Then he popped the last two Percocet with a palmful of water, and we parted company, though not before he ignored my final offer to drive him to the doctor.

When I got back to my room, a flurry of new texts awaited me from Gabe:

I'm sorry, beautiful!

You alright? Is it over? Did he hurt you?

I didn't mean to do that. I just lost it.

Wanna come over and spend the night? I'll come get you.

I was serious about New York.

I'm serious about you.

Come over… please.

At least let me know you're ok.

I texted back *I'm fine. Talk in the morning.* I shut off the phone and slammed it on the bedside table.

I couldn't deal with Gabe right now. What Jimmy said about it not taking me long to find "another one" had knocked the wind out of me. He was right about that. I'd gone straight from Dylan's deathbed into Gabe's arms without so much as a twinge of hesitation.

What did that say about me?

I mean, it wasn't like I was completely shallow. I really did like Gabe. I liked his self-confidence. I liked his openness. I liked that he listened to me, understood me, and seemed to appreciate me. I wasn't just his home improvement project, like with Jimmy, or a dirty little secret he'd rather drink himself to death in the woods than admit he cared about. I was simply me. He called me beautiful.

But that didn't make it right, did it?

I grabbed Vergil from his perch on my nightstand and squeezed him to my chest. I didn't want this. I didn't want to feel like this anymore. I didn't want to go back to being a zombie either, but at least that hurt less than this did. This felt like rats gnawing holes in my heart. This felt like hanging off the edge of the Empire State Building by your fingernails. It was all I could do not to text Gabe to come get me and take me away to New York tonight.

Fuck my life. I slipped out of bed and crept back into the hall. Jimmy was parked in front of the TV in a stupor. He ignored me as I ducked into the bathroom and locked the door. I opened the medicine cabinet only to realize for the first time just what a number I'd done on it over the past week: There was nothing left but a half-dozen Benadryl rattling around in the bottle.

I swallowed two and then took a long, hot shower.

Back in bed, I tried to focus on the drumroll of the rain as I waited for the pills to erase me in sleep. But sleep refused to come. Instead, I lay there tossing and turning as the day's events reran themselves on a demented loop in my brain. The rats kept gnawing. I kept picturing Dylan wasting away in that hospital bed. I kept seeing Jimmy's face all twisted by hate and rage when he pulled me from Gabe's truck. Soon, I wanted to scream, to pound my fists into the wall. I wanted to hurl myself to the bottom of the swimming hole and never surface again. I wanted numbness. I wanted peace. I wanted to run away to the city and never look back; to never have to think, dream, feel about Dylan or Jimmy ever again. I was overflowing with poison, Mom, and I wanted to puke it all out of me before I choked to death on it.

But I couldn't… I just couldn't.

Maybe because I knew I had this coming for what I'd done.

Sometime after midnight, I couldn't stand it anymore. The storm had blown itself out. A trickle of moonlight streamed through the window, casting my bedroom in an icy silver glow. I scrambled out of bed and wandered into the kitchen. The TV was still on. Jimmy had passed out on the couch. He was snoring with agonized little gasps, and I realized that even in his sleep he must hurt. I splashed cold water on my face over the sink and then fixed myself a baloney sandwich and scarfed it down while watching a baseball round-up on ESPN.

But when I returned to my room, I was even more agitated than before. Guilt circled me like an exhausted seabird desperate for a place to land. Even Vergil glared up at me scornfully from my pillow, as if he were Dylan's proxy sent to judge me.

Except, I wasn't the one who'd checked out with a bottle of cheap booze, was I?

Who the hell did Vergil think he was?

Outrage suddenly bloomed inside me like toxic algae. So what if my asshole brother was right to be disgusted with me? So what if I was selfish messing around with Gabe while Dylan was still plugged into a ventilator? And so what if I had no business dreaming of New York or hoping for anything good out of my life ever again?

I was still alive, goddamnit. I wasn't the fucking zombie here. I wasn't the one who'd taken the easy way out. I was alive.

I grabbed Vergil by his feet and flung him under the bed. Then I flicked on my phone, fully intending to text Gabe to come pick me up at J.J.'s. But instead, I found a single new message waiting from Donna, just ten simple words that brought me crashing down to earth:

Will you come back and see us tomorrow, Toby? Please.

Goddamnit. Goddamnit. I dropped the phone on the bed, threw on a hoodie and jeans, and climbed out of my window into the stark chill of the night.

CHAPTER TWENTY-THREE
CONFIDANT

I FOUND ROZELLA OUTSIDE, GENTLY rocking on the side patio beneath the eerie glow of her bug zapper. She'd wrapped herself in an afghan with a cigarette in one hand and an expectant look on her face as if she'd been waiting all night for me to show.

"Hey," I said as I approached. "I'm glad you're still awake."

"I shouldn't be. I got a foot doctor's appointment first thing in the morning." She gestured to the stoop for me to sit down. "How's Jim?"

"Asleep," I said and settled on the steps, which were cold and still damp from the rain. "I think he broke a rib, but he won't let me take him to the doctor. He won't even talk to me."

She clucked her tongue. "Stubborn jackass. Let him suffer, then. He'll come around when it hurts bad enough." She flicked her ash onto the concrete and added, "How about you? How are you doing?"

"I'm okay."

"You sure about that?"

"Why wouldn't I be? It's not like I've ruined the lives of everyone I care about or anything."

She snorted. "You haven't ruined my life."

"Thanks for that." I smirked. "Why are you sitting out here in the dark? The air conditioner busted or something?"

She took a long drag off the cigarette and said, "I been cooped up all day. Besides, I like the smell after it rains. It's fresher, you know?"

"Sure," I agreed, though all I could smell was her cigarette smoke.

"So, you gonna tell me what that was all about tonight?"

"Do I have to?" I moaned and rubbed my face in my hands. "It's been such a shitty day. I'd really love to not think about things for a while, you know?"

I took her silence for assent and leaned away from her to suck down some clear air, hugging my hoodie close to suppress a shiver. I felt woozy, unsettled. Stray television voices murmured through the screens of neighboring windows. Traces of mist floated on the heaviness as the sickly glow of the bug zapper turned Rozella's skin mortuary-gray. I kept glancing at the trailer door hoping she'd take the hint and invite me inside, but she just sat there sucking on that damn cigarette.

"Got any beer?" I finally asked.

"Nope. All out of beer."

"Any good movies on TV?"

"Satellite's out."

"That's weird. Jimmy's been watching sports all night and—"

"Satellite's out," she repeated. "There's no TV, no beer, no ice cream. I got nothing."

I glared at her and said, "Alright, what's going on?"

She grunted. "We gonna talk about how you broke your promise about the Marsh Trail?"

"You're still pissed about that?"

She sucked so hard on the cigarette I thought the tip would burst into flames.

"You are pissed." I pushed to my feet. "I should go. I'm not in the mood for another fight."

"No," she snapped and jabbed the cigarette in the air. "Sit your scrawny ass down and talk to me. I don't give a shit about your moods. This ain't a free movie house, you know? You show me some respect for once and treat me like a person who cares about you. I'm not just the goddamned nightly entertainment."

"Okay, okay," I said and plopped back onto the steps. "I'm sorry I broke my promise."

"Thank you," she said, her expression softening. "Forget it for now. All I really want to know is that you're alright, puppy. That's it. I just want to know you won't end up like Donna's boy."

I groaned, more embarrassed than anything. "Shit, Rozella," I said, meeting her eyes. "I'd never do that to you or Jimmy."

She peered at me, like she wanted to believe me. "You sure you're alright?"

"Other than being strung out on pot and Benadryl, I'm fine. Really."

She sighed with audible relief. "That's good to hear, puppy," she said, flicking the butt of her cigarette onto the driveway. She heaved back in the rocker, wrapped the afghan around her shoulders, and shut her eyes. "Good to hear."

Maybe it was just the cadaver-like pallor of her skin in that awful light, but I caught a sudden glimpse of Rozella's mortality. It scared me to death, Mom. There it was, glaring me in the face in the shriveled skin of her neck, the tremor of her hands, the subtle wheeze with every breath she took. She'd always seemed like such a force of nature before, I'd somehow failed to notice how much the decades of smoking and drinking and loneliness had worn her down.

I knew I wasn't helping.

What must this be like for her, sitting on the sidelines, watching me careen from disaster to disaster while barely even knowing what was going on? I was the closest thing to family she had left without Nicki, yet our relationship was a strange one, defined more by boundaries than connections. In some ways, I felt closer to her than Jimmy, and yet we rarely spoke about anything deeper than the plunge of Jayne Mansfield's neckline in *The Girl Can't Help It*.

That suddenly struck me as the saddest thing in the world.

"What else do you need to know?" I said quietly. "I'll tell you anything."

She opened her eyes and peered at me, almost surprised. "I've been listening to the mouths around here flapping about you all week long. It'd be nice to hear your side of the story."

"I can do that." I smiled. "No problem at all."

And so, I took a deep breath, wrapped my arms around my knees, and spilled my guts. For the first time, I held nothing back—although I did PG-13 the X-rated bits with Dylan and Gabe. It felt so good to get it all out of me, Mom, better than I would've expected. I'd never opened up like that to anyone before, and knowing I could even do it was a revelation.

Rozella remained attentive but silent throughout, periodically lighting up a fresh cigarette, nodding occasionally, or clucking her tongue in interest or disapproval. And when I finally came to the end a half a pack later, she took a long, contemplative drag and said, "So, you gonna run away to New York or do the right thing and go back to that hospital tomorrow?"

This was the question, wasn't it? Only I didn't have a good answer. Seeing Dylan the first time had made everything so much worse. It'd taken something sterile and abstract, and given it the face of real, visceral pain. Now, I'd have to see him like that the rest of my life. Worse, I was afraid that if I went back again, the image of his pale, emaciated shell would crowd out every other memory I had of him, until there was nothing left but that hospital, the sound of those machines, the arid, fecal stench of death inching closer and closer.

And for what? It wouldn't change a damn thing.

New York was looking better and better.

"I don't know, Rozella," I said finally. "I just don't know."

"Well, maybe it'd be easier if Jim went with you for moral support." She said this as if it were a perfectly reasonable suggestion. "You should ask him again. I'll talk to him, too, try to smooth things over."

"Are you serious?" I gave a bitter laugh. "He's so pissed right now, I'll be lucky if he doesn't chain me to my bed. Besides, he doesn't give a shit about Dylan. He's already made that clear."

"Hmm," she said, bending down to massage the circulation back into her swollen ankles. "You probably don't want to hear this, but how about giving 'ole Jim a break? Seems to me like he's only been trying to protect you the best he knows how."

"Protect me or control me?"

"What's the difference?"

"He lied to me, Rozella." I realized as soon I said it that this was the thing I was still most angry about. "If it were up to him, Dylan would have died without me ever getting to say goodbye. As bad as it was today, I don't think I could've lived with myself if that'd happened." I sighed and squeezed the tension from my eyes. "Though I'm not sure how I'm supposed to live with myself anyway."

"That's why you need to go back, puppy," she said gently. "Face this thing. See it through. So long as there's any chance Donna might be right, you've got to try. Go and sit with that boy day and night if that's what it takes because running away won't make this disappear. This ain't the kind of problem you can turn your back on, and trust me, regret's a heavy load to drag behind you the rest of your life. Jim'll understand that."

"Are you kidding me? Jimmy *wants* me to turn my back. He wants me to forget, move on, pretend like nothing happened. That's his solution to everything. Ignore it, and it'll go away. That's how he treats Mom, too. He won't even mention her name unless it's to throw her up in my face. I hardly know anything about her except the awful shit people say around here. If he wanted to protect me so badly, he'd give me more than that, so when I look in the mirror and see her face, it isn't just what was so messed up about her that stares back at me."

She hesitated as if to consider what I'd said. "Maybe he's got nothing more to give, puppy. Maybe he's just trying to keep his head above water."

"Maybe I am, too," I said bitterly. "Maybe I'm drowning, but whenever I call for help, Jimmy doesn't listen to me. Instead, he buries himself under Baby's hood or drinks himself stupid in front of a ball game. I can't talk to him, Rozella. He doesn't hear me. It's like he doesn't even see me. Not the real me. All he sees is his cleaned-up, Disney gay version that's the stand-in for everything he ever wanted in life and could never have for himself. I'm just here to fulfill some role he never got to play. It makes me feel so invisible sometimes. Invisible and alone."

She bent down to stub out the cigarette on the concrete and said, "Sometimes you boys can't see yourselves—"

I snorted with derision. "I saw plenty tonight, believe me."

She frowned and fished out the last cigarette from the pack, rolling it contemplatively between her fingers. "I thought I saw things pretty clearly when I married Duke. I knew what he was like from the beginning. Hell, half the damn county knew. He chased anything in a skirt. Always had. Always would. But I figured it'd be okay, that I could suck it up and live with it. I was nineteen and pregnant. Getting married was just what you did back then. I figured I had it coming for being that stupid, so I played the obedient little wife. I let him use me as his doormat until he got bored and took off for good. Nicki was just four years old."

She lit the cigarette and gazed up at the crescent moon, which shined like the corner of a door cracked open onto a brightly lit room. "She was a lot like you growing up, you know? Smart as a whip. Beautiful girl. Kind heart. Had the whole world on a string. But she couldn't see it any better than you can." She paused to exhale, and the rocker began to creak back and forth, back and forth. "That was my fault. I shut her out. I was too ashamed to talk to her about Duke. Too ashamed to explain how I'd gotten myself in trouble with a man like that. Too ashamed to admit I maybe resented her a little bit for trapping me in a life I didn't want." She shook her head sadly and took another drag. "So instead, I worked. Busted my ass, twelve hours a day, seven days a week. I built myself a little business, put aside some money, and I neglected my daughter."

She peered down at the backs of her gnarled fingers and curled them into a fist. "By high school, she was drinking and partying, sleeping around. Usually, with scumbags old enough to be her father. Got herself pregnant the first time when she was seventeen by some loser down in Fonda, only a couple years younger than me. They got married, but it didn't last. By then, I was so angry at her for making the same mistakes I did I wasn't any help to her. It's been downhill between us ever since."

"Jesus, Rozella," I said weakly. "I'm sorry."

"Aww, don't be sorry, puppy. Just listen. You can waste your whole life thinking you see things clearly until you wake up one morning and realize you haven't seen a goddamn thing. I don't want you boys making that same mistake."

I leaned back against the steps and sighed. "Maybe you should tell that to Jimmy."

"Oh, believe me, I have. And I will again. But tonight, I'm telling it to you, so maybe you'll understand why you need to cut Jimmy some slack here. Maybe he's got troubles of his own he needs to figure out. Maybe he ought to have that talk with you about Bonnie I never had with Nicki about Duke. And maybe he needs to start listening to what you want instead of telling you how it's gonna be. But he's right to be scared for you because I'll tell you what, right now I'm pretty scared, too."

"What the hell's that supposed to mean?"

"It means end it with Gabe Fournier. Running away with him ain't gonna get you what you want. I don't know what his game is messing around with you like this, but it ain't right, and no good will come of it." She took one last fearsome drag off the cigarette and added, "Don't throw your life away over nothing, puppy. There's been enough of that already."

The edges of darkness were beginning to purple as I walked home. Rozella had made her point, however bluntly. I didn't argue. I figured the price of having a confidant was that they'd sometimes tell you things you didn't want to hear. Besides, I'd already come to the same conclusion about Gabe. Running away to New York was a nonstarter. Not because I'd be throwing my life away, or even because of Dylan.

No, I couldn't do that to Jimmy, no matter how angry I was with him.

Rozella had convinced me to talk to him about returning to the hospital with me in the morning. She said I should give him another chance to make this right, just like I should give myself one. She said she'd talk to him for me, too, persuade him that since I was jumping ship with the first sailor passing through town, now might be the last chance he ever got to start listening to me. Then she said if he still insisted on being a stone-headed jackass about it, she'd drive me to the hospital herself and let me crash at her place for as long as I wanted. I felt better about everything after that.

Now, all I needed to do was say goodbye to Gabe. As I slipped into the backyard, I noticed the living room remained aglow with the light from the TV. Jimmy must still be passed out on the couch. I'd have to wake him for work soon, even if he was in no shape to go in today. At least the Percocet and bourbon had helped him sleep through the night.

I flew up the deck steps, hoisted myself onto my windowsill, and gently lowered my body into the darkened bedroom.

But no sooner had my feet touched the carpet than my desk lamp flicked on.

Jimmy stood in his truss and boxer shorts, glaring straight at me. Behind him on the bed rested the cardboard box of your things, Mom, stuffed to overflowing with all of my Ravisha swag, my cosmetics, and the crumpled remains of my constellation he'd somehow torn down from the ceiling.

He held my phone in one quaking hand, and I knew he'd been reading Gabe's texts. "You change your mind and sneak over there to patch up his bruises?" He lunged at me, slapping my face so hard my head snapped back against the windowsill.

I crumpled to the floor.

"Don't say another word, you dirty little cocksucker," he hissed.

He heaved the box into his arms with a groan and hobbled out of my room, slamming the door behind him.

CHAPTER TWENTY-FOUR
SHATTER

THERE ARE A MILLION WAYS to break that don't show on the outside. A million kinds of hits to take that leave no perceptible marks. Silence keeps the cracks invisible. Distraction and routine are the glue that holds them together. TV. The Internet. Music. Drugs. Work. Sex. Love. They're all just diversions to prevent us from shaking apart, though we each shatter to pieces in the end.

I told myself I wasn't ready to shatter just yet as I stared at my face in yet another bathroom mirror. Even hours later, the swollen ghost of Jimmy's handprint—four fingers and a reddish glob of palm—still marred my left cheek.

If I had some concealer.... But he'd taken all of my makeup. Not that it mattered. Even if I could hide the physical evidence, slather myself in cosmetics, or don a paper bag over my head, nothing would erase what Jimmy's words had burned onto my heart. That was indelible.

My brother had called me a "dirty little cocksucker." Straight to my face. The sheer ugliness of it had stunned me mute, though even worse was remembering just how good I could tell it made him feel to say it. It was like he'd waited his whole life to speak those words. I don't know how I'd missed it for so long, Mom. I'd convinced myself he was different than the others, a better man, but I was wrong. I couldn't deny it anymore.

I showered and got dressed. He'd stolen all of my beautiful things, leaving me with little more than jeans and tee-shirts to wear. I tried not to dwell on the carnage in my bedroom, though it was impossible to ignore. My ceiling was bare, except for some pathetic paper corners still speared in place by stubborn tacks. He'd taken my phone. My money was gone, too, all $820 of it. My closet was completely ransacked, all of your things missing. He'd scooped up every last piece of you, even the stuff not inside the box. He must have known all these years what I'd saved of yours, mentally cataloged each relic, because he'd sniffed out every last trace of you like a bloodhound and carted it all away in the cardboard box when he hobbled out the front door for work. He'd even taken the truck instead of Baby because he knew I couldn't drive stick and wouldn't be able to follow him. I had no idea what he planned to do with it all. Burn it? Dump it in the garbage bins at the mill? Ditch it by the side of the road? Anything was possible. All that was certain was that I had nothing left of you now, not your picture or your clothes, not even a cheap plastic bangle to wear to give me courage.

He'd left me utterly helpless, Mom. Bereft and stone broke. The only thing I could think to do was to turn to Rozella.

I crammed a few of my remaining clothes into my backpack and stormed out the front door.

Even before I reached Rozella's trailer, I saw that her car was gone and remembered her foot doctor's appointment this morning. I went to the door and knocked anyway, but it was a futile gesture, and after a minute, I plopped into her creaky aluminum rocker to regroup.

My pulse wouldn't stop racing. I supposed I could wait here for her to get home, but then what? Sure, she'd take me in, but Jimmy would just come over tonight and drag me back home again, no doubt kicking and screaming. Rozella was old and frail. I couldn't expect her to stand up to him when I couldn't even do it for myself.

I'd put her through enough already.

I scanned the mobile manor, my heart aching with loss. The sun had risen above the trees in a misty halo. A moist chill clung to the piney air. The trailers lining the drive glistened in the sunshine, decrepit hulks, each saved from a trip to the junkyard by pride, stubbornness, or basic necessity, though dolled up with cheap curtains and plastic garden gnomes to hide the despair. It might be ramshackle and back-broke, but in the golden morning light, it was almost beautiful, too. At least I'd always felt safe here, sheltered from the brutality of the wider world by the home Jimmy had made for us. But that illusion of safety now seemed like a cruel joke. This wasn't my home anymore. I was homeless.

Fuck it all: I might as well run away to New York with Gabe.

I pushed myself to my feet, resigned to my decision. Rozella was wrong: I wasn't running away for nothing; I was running *from* nothing. In my heart, I knew it was too late for Dylan. Too late for my brother and me.

I decided to dash home to write Rozella a note. I'd slip it under her door and then go find Gabe at Harold's place. I'd call her from the city to explain things once I was settled. I wouldn't be gone forever. I'd come back here at some point, even if just to see her.

But right now I needed to get away from Jimmy.

I jogged back down the drive with a fresh sense of urgency, but as I approached our trailer, Baby caught my eye. Parked in the grass out front where Jimmy had left her the night before, she was perfect: her pristine black paint and sparkling chrome marred only by a few dusty splotches of dried rain.

God, I hated that fucking car....

A red mist settled over my eyes more intense than anything I'd ever experienced in my life. I wanted to take something from Jimmy that would hurt as much as what he'd taken from me. I bolted up the front stoop and disappeared into the trailer, returning moments later with a kitchen knife, a hammer, and a bottle of bleach.

Baby's headlights were the first to go. I howled at the top of my lungs as I busted out the taillights next, then clobbered the side mirrors until each dangled from threads of red wire. I smashed out the driver's side window, threw open the door, and dumped the bottle of bleach across the seats and carpet. I pulverized the gauge cluster and reduced the radio to jagged hunks of transistor and plastic. I battered holes in the windshield that radiated out in an intricate web of spidery cracks. I bashed craters into the sheet metal. I knifed slits into the sidewalls of all four tires.

When I was satisfied with my work, I jabbed the knife straight into the driver's seat and tossed the other implements of destruction onto the floor. Then I stepped back to survey the damage, my chest heaving and my arms screaming.

Baby looked like she'd endured a nuclear hailstorm; I hoped it broke Jimmy's heart.

A small crowd of neighbors had gathered outside to watch. As I grabbed my bag from the stoop, one of them called out, "Jim's gonna kill you when he sees what you did."

"I hope he tries," I screamed. "Call him if you want. Tell him. I dare you!"

But they all scuttled back to their trailers, the fucking cowards, and so I shouldered into my backpack and marched away, triumphant.

CiTY
OF
FALLEN
STARS

CHAPTER TWENTY-FIVE
SAY YES

As I HUNG OFF THE uppermost tread of the fire escape ladder above Gabe's fifth-floor apartment, I wondered what it would feel like if I let go. Five fingers, a tumble, and then a constellation of me splattered in brains and gore for the rain to wash away from the sidewalk below. A chalk outline, maybe some yellow tape, Rozella and Jimmy blubbering when the cops showed up in Shelter Valley with the news, while everybody else in town whispered that the dirty little cocksucker had it coming for what he'd done to Donna's boy.

Dirty little cocksucker.

I shook off the thought, squeezed my fist tighter around the iron bar, and peered down the street at the George Washington Bridge. If I squinted just so, I could almost trick my brain into believing that the bridge lights stretching all the way across the river to the wilds of

New Jersey were fallen stars, as if the Milky Way itself had plunged into the Hudson.

I clambered down the ladder to the narrow platform outside Gabe's bedroom and peered through the window to watch him sleep. He was snoring fitfully on his futon mattress beneath the gentle drone of an oscillating fan, his nude body tangled in the sheets, slicked with sweat and shimmering in the sodium glare of the streetlights.

I was too unsettled to go back inside. This was my first night in the city, and I was struggling to absorb the shock and awe of it. I'd just discovered from the roof that you could make out the tips of the hazily glowing spires of midtown in the distance, but from my vantage here on the fire escape, the gritty thrum of the street prevailed. Latin rhythms swelled from a pub down the block. Syncopated voices spoke in languages I didn't understand. The funk of ozone mingled with river rot and the aroma of smoked meats that wafted up from the rib joint around the corner. The atmosphere seemed to vibrate with a kind of menace, the murky sky all aglow like the churning belly of some deep-sea creature. Below me, a steady torrent of people spilled onto the sidewalks. How easy it would be to get carried away among them, just another in the ceaseless gush of bodies that coursed along these streets like blood cells through arteries of concrete and asphalt. It seemed as if more people were clogging this single block tonight than all the souls in Shelter Valley, though these were strangers, laughing, smoking, arguing with one another, each with secrets, longings, and dangers all their own.

In my wildest dreams I'd never anticipated the vastness of this city. The chaos of it. The noise. It made me dizzy just thinking about how small and fragile I was in comparison. I'd never felt so insignificant in my life, so easily swept aside, and yet, in some twisted way, this made the prospect of living with myself here seem almost possible, as if the wreckage I'd left behind back home couldn't possibly matter in a place so rife with disinterest in me and my fate.

At least there was comfort in that.

Despite the lateness of the hour, the heat remained oppressive. I felt unclean. I'd already taken two showers in Gabe's moldy bathtub, to little avail. That was something else I hadn't anticipated about the city: the grime of it. It was as if a thousand hands before mine had touched every square inch of surface here. Even the air felt greasy on my skin. What I wouldn't have given for a few cleansing laps in the swimming hole.

A police siren wailed down the street, the patrol car's reds and blues briefly illuminating the buildings like the walls of a canyon. Shouts broke out at the pub. A boisterous crowd gathered out front, laughing and speaking in Spanish. Gabe had said that mostly Dominicans and Puerto Ricans lived in this neighborhood. I'd never been more aware of my pasty-assed whiteness than in the hours since we'd arrived in Washington Heights. Everything was so different here. Everyone was so different. It made me feel isolated and even more uncomfortable with how utterly dependent I now was on Gabe.

The bedroom light flicked on behind me. I heard him stir and glanced over my shoulder to see him slip into a pair of boxers. Fuck. I turned back to the street as he climbed outside and came up behind me, wrapping me in his sweaty arms.

"Hey, beautiful," he said groggily. "Can't sleep?"

"It's so loud here." I tensed in his embrace. "I'm not used to it."

"It beats crickets." He chuckled lightly. "Come back to bed." His hand slid down my bare chest, his dick swelling against the small of my back.

"It's awfully hot for that," I said, redirecting his hand to my lips before it could slip beneath the waistband of my briefs. I kissed his fingertips. They reeked of sweat and pot, and I wondered if he was still high.

"How about a raincheck?" he said and swatted my ass playfully with his free hand before pulling away. "I need to piss anyway. What time is it? Shit." He yawned and then ducked back inside, where he disappeared into the bowels of the apartment.

My muscles slowly uncoiled.

Needless to say, Mom, it'd been a rough day. By the time I got to the Fournier homestead, Gabe had already left for the hospital. Luckily, I found the front door unlocked and let myself in. I was wrecked: hot and sticky from the walk, sore and miserable from my tussle with Baby. I drained the last beer in Harold's fridge and climbed into the shower, and that's when the magnitude of what I'd done hit me square in the chest.

I was all alone in the world now.

This sudden realization pierced me straight through the heart. Jimmy would never forgive me for what I'd done to Baby. All those years of blood, sweat, and tears he'd poured into restoring her—the money and passion and pride he'd invested in that stupid car, the only thing in his life I'd ever seen bring him joy, pure and sweet and unguarded.

And I destroyed it. Just like I destroyed everything else. I stood beneath that warm stream and cried for my brother.

When the hot water ran out, I dried off and wandered upstairs to Gabe's bedroom, where I cocooned myself in his sheets and drifted off into a deadened sleep. I didn't notice him return a few hours later until he slipped beneath the covers beside me and kissed the back of my neck.

With a yelp, I flew out of bed. That's when he saw the ghost of the slap still on my face.

"Did Jim do that to you?"

I nodded.

"I'll break his fucking neck!"

He was already out of bed and moving towards the door when I said, "No. I handled it. It's over. You need to forget it."

I managed to persuade him to sit back down and explained what had happened since the last time I saw him. I held nothing back, not one ugly detail. Yet, by the time I was finished, he seemed so delighted at the prospect of me coming to the city that his fury at Jimmy was all but forgotten. I laid back in the bed and let him crawl on top of me. He told me how much fun he was going to have showing me off to New York, how much fun we would have together.

I let him kiss me, Mom. Again and again and again. Eventually, I let him fuck me, too. To seal the deal. Sex was the last thing I wanted, but I was too afraid to tell him no. I'd never turned down anyone before except Dylan, and that'd immediately morphed into disaster. What if I hurt Gabe's feelings or made him angry? What if he changed his mind about taking me to New York? What if he threw me out, sent me home to Jimmy? What if I destroyed this last good thing in my life?

So, I just laid there inertly as he hammered away at me, though he barely seemed to notice, maybe because my heart was pounding so hard, or because I'd clamped my arms around his neck to fend off a rising panic attack: I'd just realized that from now on Gabe could ask me to do anything he wanted, and I would have to say yes. Yes, to getting fucked. Yes, to getting high. Yes, to running away to the city helpless, broke, and utterly dependent on him. Yes, to anything in the world, to a one-way ticket straight to hell, so long as he wouldn't let go of me.

As soon as he came, he tried to roll off me, but I clung to him like a baby. When he prized apart my arms so he could catch his breath, something inside me burst, and I began to bawl right there beneath him. It just came pouring out of me like it had in the shower.

I told him I was crying because of Dylan and Jimmy, what I'd done, the mess I was leaving behind. But the truth was far more pathetic: I'd lost everything else. I couldn't bear the thought of losing this, too, whatever it was.

Gabe was all I had left.

A light breeze swept up from the river, chilling the sweat on my back. I shivered and hugged my shoulders as Gabe stuck his head out of the bedroom window.

"I can't sleep on an empty stomach," he said. "You want some eggs?"

"Sure." I tried to smile. "Whatever you want."

"Alright, beautiful." He blew me a kiss. "Give me a couple of minutes."

A small woman in a floral print sundress and flip-flops leaned against the front window of the pawn shop across the street. She was smoking a cigarette, watching me. I felt suddenly naked standing there in nothing but underpants, and so I climbed back through the window, following the sound and light.

The narrow living area of Gabe's apartment featured ten-foot ceilings and wide-plank floors, with a cluster of sink and small appliances tucked into the corner against a brick wall. A sagging leather couch faced a cheap TV resting on cinder blocks. A pair of tall windows overlooked the fire escape on the far wall. A sorry bronze fixture with three bare bulbs dangled from the ceiling, casting the space in an unforgiving glare. Plastic bins where Gabe stored his clothes and personal belongings lurked in every corner. Dust coated surfaces like frost, and despite the wide-open windows, the odor of mildew pervaded the air.

The microwave's clock read 2:16. Gabe was on his knees peering into the mini-fridge. When he saw me, he asked, "Does a Western omelet sound good?"

"Sure, whatever you want," I said as I slipped into the bathroom.

After I finished peeing, I decided I had a headache, and rifled quickly through the medicines on the shelf below the sink. For a drug dealer, Gabe had precious little of value: Pepto-Bismol, four different kinds of over-the-counter pain meds, lineament, and a bottle of Viagra.

I settled for the Tylenol PM, swallowing two with a handful of water, and then examined my face in the mirror. At least Jimmy's handprint had faded, though my eyes were bloodshot from lack of sleep.

When I returned from the bathroom, Gabe was dicing an onion on the tiny countertop.

"You like green pepper?" he asked, not looking at me as I slumped onto the couch.

"Sure, whatever you want."

He stopped chopping and turned to face me. "Something on your mind?"

"No, why?"

"Well, if you tell me 'whatever you want' once more, I'm liable to take it personal. You don't have to choke down my cooking if you're not hungry."

"Sorry. I'm just out of it."

He humphed and said, "Is that why you were so stiff with Lon tonight?"

I gaped at him, unable to respond.

Between the interminable bus ride and the rush hour subway, it'd taken us nearly six hours to get here from Shelter Valley. Yet no sooner had we arrived at his apartment, dumped our shit, and taken quick showers, than he dragged me out again to "show me off" to his buddy Lon and his boyfriend Tiago at their tiny apartment in Inwood.

Tiago turned out to be sweet, twenty-three, and drop-dead gorgeous, with doe eyes and a faint, melodious accent Gabe later told me was Puerto Rican. Tiago said he was a dancer and had the body to prove it, although he fussed over me like a grandmother and kept trying to feed me leftovers because I was "too skinny."

Lon, on the other hand, was a certified creeper. Pushing fifty and already Botoxed, he smelled like he bathed in Drakkar Noir and wore more gold around his neck and wrists than a jewelry salesman at a pimp convention. He had a russet goatee trimmed to a demonic point, roving fingers, and ravenous green eyes that seemed able to see through my clothes to appraise every square inch of skin below. While Gabe and Tiago spent the evening laughing and smoking bowls together in front of Tiago's PlayStation, Lon cornered me on the couch, pawing at me and whispering nasty shit into my ear. I didn't know how to escape him, and so I just sat there and politely endured it. Now and then, I threw a stoned Gabe a helpless look, but it was pointless; he just grinned back at me.

"Well?" he said, still peering at me. "Lon's one of my oldest buddies. I wasn't going to say nothing, but you were kind of uptight with him. I was hoping you two'd hit it off, especially since he's getting us into the club tomorrow night."

He said this almost as if he were hurt by it.

"I'm sorry," I said carefully. "But he was kind of—" I hesitated. "He couldn't keep his hands off me. I was a little uncomfortable."

"That's just Lon." He smirked. "Don't pay him no mind. He likes 'em young. Used to be all over me, too, until I aged out." He chuckled at this as if it were funny instead of gross. "At least he hasn't let himself go like the losers on the Marsh Trail you're used to. Loosen up and enjoy the attention. I'll be right there. Nothing bad's gonna happen."

"That's not the point," I said. Then I lost my nerve. Maybe he was right. Maybe I was being uptight. What did I expect here anyway? Hearts and flowers and *Breakfast at Tiffany's?* I was hardly Holly Golightly. I needed to work on adjusting to my new reality. "Sorry," I mumbled. "I didn't mean to be rude. I'll be nicer next time. It's just not what I was expecting my first night."

"I know what you were expecting, beautiful," he said and came over and planted a sloppy kiss on my mouth with the kitchen knife still in his hand. He hadn't brushed his teeth, and his breath tasted of pot and sour milk.

"Tiago seems cool," I said, wiping my mouth as soon as he returned to the counter.

"Don't get too attached. Lon goes through boyfriends like underwear. They've been together eight months, which must be some kind of record. He won't be around much longer."

"Oh," I said, genuinely disappointed. I'd hoped to get to know him better. "How long have you known Lon?"

"Since I moved here. After the culinary school thing didn't pan out, I was out on my ass, so he took me in for a while." He flashed me an embarrassed grin over his shoulder. "Actually, I was one of his boyfriends. But don't get jealous. It only lasted a couple months, and by then I'd found myself a job and another place to live. We stayed buddies, though; now he's one of my biggest customers. We'll be seeing him a lot."

Great, I thought, though I managed to hold my tongue. That was the real reason we'd gone over there tonight: not to introduce me to his friends but to deliver Lon some pot and a dozen little green pills.

But since he'd brought the subject up, I decided to ask him the question that'd been gnawing at me since Jimmy first threw it up in my face.

"Why didn't you tell me before that you're a dealer?"

His neck snapped straight. "Didn't think I had to," he said sharply. "Besides, you didn't seem to mind when you were smoking up."

"I don't mind now. I just don't understand why you didn't level with me."

He sighed and rolled his shoulders. "It ain't the kind of thing you brag about, is it?" he said, sounding almost hurt again. "Not the kind of thing that makes your dying old man proud of his only son, even if it's what's keeping his lights on and his fridge stocked."

"No, I suppose not." My face burned with regret; I hadn't meant to humiliate him. "Forget it. It doesn't matter. I don't know why I asked."

I squirmed deeper into the cushions and gazed down at my hands.

"You know we're both full of shit, right?" he said and returned to attacking the pepper with the chef's knife. "You know damn well why you asked me, just like I know why I never mentioned it."

"Why?"

"Bonnie," he said matter-of-factly, leaving your name to hang in the air between us. He lifted the edge of the cutting board and scraped the vegetables and some diced ham into a frying pan sizzling with melted butter on the cooktop. "What Jim said about me got to you, didn't it?"

"Maybe a little, but not because of Mom," I said sincerely. "She made her own choices, just like I do. I only wondered why you didn't tell me yourself, that's all." I didn't mention that since I'd put myself at his mercy here, it would be nice to know that I could trust him to be upfront with me about stuff like this. "Anyway, it's no big deal."

"Good to know." He cracked three eggs into a glass bowl, added a dash of salt, and began to whisk them so violently I thought he would shatter the glass. "A little pot never hurt nobody," he mumbled as he dumped the eggs into the frying pan, releasing a cloud of steam. "Jim's one to talk. Donna's kid sure did a number on himself with just a bottle of B.V." A buttery aroma filled the room as he grasped the pan by the handle and began to swirl the contents. "A man's got a right to make a fucking living."

"I thought you were a cook?" I said hoping to change the subject.

He snorted. "I do cook. Fifty hours a week at a pancake house in midtown. In fact, I'm heading down there first thing in the morning to make sure they held my spot on the line. It ain't like I had all kinds of vacation days saved up, you know? I took off on borrowed time and favors." He grabbed a jar of dried oregano from the shelf above the cooktop and added a dash to the pan. "My secret ingredient," he said and gave the pan a couple of short jerks, using a spatula to fold over the edges of the omelet. "Anyway, you try living on a line cook's wages in this city. This shithole costs me $1600 a month, and that don't include lights or cable. I do the best I can." With a single flick of the wrist, he flipped the entire omelet on itself.

"What do you deal besides pot?"

His neck stiffened again. "Nothing but a good time." He unwrapped a waiting slice of American cheese and slapped it over the top of the omelet, which he slid out of the pan onto a plate yanked from the drying rack by the sink. He plucked a fork from a mason jar on the counter and strode over to present me the feast he'd prepared.

The omelet was beautiful to behold: fluffy, pale yellow, oozing cheese and dotted with jewel-like flecks of meat and vegetables.

"Bon appetit," he said and watched without expression as I tucked in.

"This is delicious," I said, nodding my head so vigorously I could barely swallow the first bite. "Thanks." I gave him a big thumbs-up and took another forkful.

"Hey, that's for the both of us." He smirked at me and took back the plate, and then slumped onto the couch and carved off half the omelet with the fork, shoving it into his mouth in three enormous gulps. He burped, handed me back what remained, and said, "Have you figured out what you're going to wear tomorrow night?"

I felt my face blanch as I forked more eggs into my mouth. I'd been dreading the subject of Manntasia since he asked Lon to get us in.

"Jimmy took all my best clothes. I mostly just have shorts, jeans, and tee-shirts with me."

"That won't cut it."

"I know," I said, and set the plate on the arm of the couch before launching into the spiel I'd mentally rehearsed on the subway ride back from Lon's apartment. "Maybe we don't have to go? It's not like I have my heart set on it or anything. I really don't want to put you and Lon out. Besides, I was thinking it would be kind of fun to just stay in." I laid my hand on his thigh and leaned in to nuzzle against his shoulder. "You know. The two of us... alone."

He smirked at me and patted my hand. "No way, beautiful. I can't let you miss that show. This is a once-in-a-lifetime deal. You'll have a blast, trust me." He leaned across me and grabbed the plate, scarfing down the rest of the omelet in one fell swoop. "Besides, it'll be a good night for me, too." He set the empty plate on the floor. "Lon says it's going to be a rich crowd."

"I know, but—"

"Look, I get it. You've got nothing to wear. But we can fix that." He squeezed my thigh and pushed himself to his feet. "Sit tight." He disappeared into the bedroom, shutting and locking the door behind him.

As soon as he was gone, I shot up from the couch and bolted to the window for fresh air. I felt like I was going to throw up. My heart raced. My throat squeezed tight. How the hell could I go to Manntasia like this? I wanted to be back home, in my own bed, staring up at my stupid constellation and dreaming of a better version of this someday. A version where Dylan wasn't on life-support and Jimmy didn't hate me. A version where the thought of being rewarded with my heart's desire didn't make me want to vomit up blood.

Nobody told me getting everything I'd ever dreamed of would cost me everyone I loved.

When Gabe returned from the bedroom, he carried with him a small metal lock box. "You wanted to know what I deal," he said, a little too aggressively as he threw open the box lid and thrust it at me. "Here. Take a look."

Inside was the large baggy of pot from before, now well depleted, plus a half-dozen smaller bags of Lon's green pills. There were bags of little gray ones, too, stamped with the face of Daffy Duck. Beside them was a thick roll of rubber-banded cash.

"See," he said, almost defensively as he reached inside to shift things around. "Nothing but high-grade pot and party enhancers. That's it. A good time. Once in a while, some acid or 'shrooms if I get my hands on them, but never anything serious. No coke or crystal, and sure as hell no smack. I don't deal in that shit, you understand? Never have, never will. It's my golden rule. I gotta sleep at night, too."

"I believe you," I said, my face flushing. I'd clearly touched a nerve. "I was out of line."

He looked at me a moment as if still hurt, but then flashed a mischievous grin. "No worries. I wanted you to see this anyway." He reached inside the box and peeled off a few bills from the wad of cash, and then shut and locked the lid and set it on the windowsill beside me. "I'll be busy all day tomorrow, so here, take this and go shopping. Buy yourself something sexy to wear to that club. Leather, maybe. Or lace. You decide. The more skin, the better."

He tried to hand me the money, but I refused.

"No, Gabe. I don't want your money. I can just—"

"Shut up and take it." He silenced me with a finger to my lips. Then he folded the bills into the waistband of my underpants like I was his personal stripper and peered into my eyes. "You buy yourself the sexiest outfit you can find, you hear me? I want every tongue in that club hanging out over you."

Maybe it was the Tylenol PM kicking in, but I felt my will to protest wither and die under the intensity of his gaze. "Yes, Gabe," I said, submitting utterly. Yes, to anything he wanted from me, yes to a one-way ticket straight to Manntasia.

"Good," he said and pulled me in closer. "Now, I'll have my raincheck."

I could feel his hardness press against my belly as he began to kiss my neck. I didn't recoil. What else could I do but say yes? After all, Mom, I was just a dirty little cocksucker.

CHAPTER TWENTY-SIX
THIS SHELTERING SEA

I AWOKE DROWNING IN A bathtub—*the* bathtub.

Powerful hands held me below the surface. I kicked and flailed to get free. I couldn't escape their iron grip, but just as my lungs were about to burst, they released me.

I lunged for air.

Gasping over the side of the tub, I saw Jimmy and Gabe watching me from the bathroom door, smirking, their arms wrapped around each other's shoulders like brothers. "Santa Baby" played in the harshly lit bedroom behind them. Fists pounded on an unseen door. The smell of death hung in the air. Gabe began to laugh as the tub overflowed, the dark water splashing onto the floor like blood. Jimmy said, "Drown the little cocksucker" to the unseen figure looming behind me, but just as those same strong hands reappeared, I jerked my head around in time to catch a glimpse of Dylan's corpse-white face before he pushed me under.

I bolted upright, sputtering.

Fucking Tylenol PM.

I sat up on the edge of Gabe's futon, grinding the heels of my hands in my eyes to smear away Dylan's ghost. Warm sunlight streamed through the window, washing away the chill of his touch. The miserable night stretched behind me in a stream of similarly vivid dreams: Gabe leading me through New York's sewers to find a secret dance club, only to ditch me in the dark without a flashlight. Sitting in the backseat as Jimmy and Rozella drove me to my first day of college, whispering secrets about me that I couldn't hear over the roar of Baby's engine. Donna bawling in my arms at Dylan's gravesite, whimpering, "Why did you leave us behind?"

I dragged myself to my feet and shuffled into the other room.

The time on the microwave read 10:47. Gabe had already left. I was glad of it, too. It'd occurred to me in bed last night—after we'd had sex again and he'd fallen asleep beside me—that I kept losing myself when we were together. I became this different person with him—submissive, compliant, eager to please—even when doing so made me unhappy. I was beginning not to like myself this way, but I didn't know what to do about it. The more time I spent with him, the more susceptible I felt, almost like he was a drug I'd developed a fast dependency on.

Still, I hadn't escaped his influence entirely this morning: He'd left behind a note on the counter with the names of a few bargain clothing stores he liked on 14th Street, plus directions on how to get there on the subway. He also left me a key to the apartment and the wad of cash he'd stuffed into my underpants last night. Jesus Christ. Why did he care so much how I dressed for Manntasia? Did he think I was going to embarrass him by showing up looking like a hick? I didn't even want to go anymore, let alone spend the whole day worrying about what I wore.

Yet, no sooner had this thought occurred to me than it brought me up short. When had I stopped worrying about my look? This was Manntasia we were talking about here, not Disco Night at the Kayoga VFW. A little over a week ago, I would've spent hours fussing over my ensemble just for some random outing to the Marsh Trail. Yet, here I was now, on the cusp of the most auspicious event of my life, and I somehow couldn't muster enough anxiety to break a sweat about having absolutely nothing to wear.

Maybe Gabe wasn't being controlling. Maybe he just wanted me to be *me* again.

Hell, for that matter, so did I.

I stumbled into the bathroom, and after another unsatisfying shower, I downed two Advil and lurched into the kitchenette. The larder was bare, but I managed to rustle up some toast and a cup of instant coffee and plunked onto the couch to eat. One thing was certain: I couldn't stay cooped up in this stuffy apartment all day alone. My skin was already crawling. After my nightmares, worries about Jimmy infested my mind.

Was he alright? Was he even sober? Would he show up here looking for me?

Probably not. After all, it wouldn't take a genius to figure out where I was. If he'd had any desire to come fetch me, he would've done so by now. No, he was finished with me; I'd lost him for good.

Rather than sit with how awful that made me feel, I choked down my toast, got dressed, and headed outside with the money and Gabe's directions. The day was warm, but not yet hot. A murky haze overhung the city, diffusing the sunlight into a chalky glare. The sidewalks bustled with pedestrians. Racks of fresh fruit had been set out in front of the bodega on the corner, attracting passersby like flies. I paused in front of the entrance and briefly considered whether to duck inside and buy a prepaid phone to call Rozella, but I had no idea what I would say to her.

Besides, I was terrified of what she might have to tell me about Jimmy.

Or worse, Dylan.

Was he even still alive?

This was the question I'd been carefully avoiding since I awoke, but by the time I settled onto a toxic orange bench on the A-Train twenty minutes later, it had all but consumed me.

Maybe my nightmare was an omen that he'd died.

What was I going to do with myself if that were true?

Would there be a funeral? Should I go back for it?

How would I even find out?

The train doors whooshed shut as I choked down my despair. I was sweating, my heart palpitating. I couldn't do this to myself. I couldn't drive myself crazy like this. I was sitting in a New York City subway car, and I could do nothing for him anymore.

I'd made my choice. Dylan was dead to me. Jimmy was lost. I was here.

The chilling clarity of these realizations calmed me. I closed my eyes and counted my breaths, feeling nothing but the grinding inevitability of my fate. Maybe resigning yourself to life's miseries and losses was the lesson every adult had to learn.

The car filled with more and more people the closer we got to midtown. Since I'd snagged a seat next to the window, I curled up against the hull and observed my fellow passengers in its reflection. They were pasty faces and beautiful brown skin, smudged mascara and fat Adam's apples, phones bleeping, bangles clinking, laughter. They were silver studs and earbuds, clicking tongues and glittery fingernails, gold teeth, onion breath, cherry gloss, and cold sores. They were hollow gazes peering through horned-rimmed glasses, pursed lips and pressed white Oxfords, man-spreading, knuckles cracking, sneers and menthol and silences.

They were so many things, all different, each unique in their combinations of ordinary and oddball, save for the single remarkable trait they all shared in common: not one of them paid the slightest attention to me. They looked past me, over me, through me, not seeing me at all, seeing nothing perhaps or merely registering a me-shaped object that took up space in the environment we all temporarily shared. It couldn't have been more different than Shelter Valley, where there was no place to hide from the constant stares and whispers. Back home, even a bad hair day was worth an evening's dragging around the bar at J.J.'s, but here it seemed that I could be a serial killer, or a dancing bear, or a sack of potatoes for all anyone noticed or cared.

I closed my eyes again and drifted on the sense of security this peculiar kind of shared aloneness provided. It was wonderful not feeling obliged to deal with anyone's bullshit or judgements, least of all my own, and so it was with surprising indifference that I marked the passage of each new station—Central Park West. Columbus Circle. The Port Authority—as the heart of the city of my dreams fell away above me, still unseen and unknown, little more than disembodied announcements over the subway PA system.

I didn't bother to get off at the 14th Street Station.

When I finally opened my eyes again a long time later, it was to change trains at the Broad Channel Station all the way out in the middle of Jamaica Bay. Though I hadn't planned to ride to the opposite end of the city, I'd studied the subway map thoroughly enough over the years to know where it was taking me. I'd been traveling for what seemed like forever, my body stiff from huddling in the same position, and so I paced the platform until the next train arrived, grateful for the flow of blood to my extremities.

I was almost beginning to feel like myself again.

On an elevated stretch of track, the Rockaway Park shuttle barreled high above the spine of the Rockaway Peninsula, a loose thread of land that dangled off the southwestern tip of Long Island. I soaked in the sights that flashed past the windows: a few nondescript blocks on either side of the tracks, bordered to the north by Jamaica Bay and the south by the endless expanse of the Atlantic. There was something precarious about that, as if at any moment a giant wave might flush all the cars and buildings straight into the bay.

When the train reached the end of the line, I emerged from the small brick station onto a wide boulevard lined with shops. The smell of the sea was ripe here. The light was hard and glassy, the way it sometimes gets near a large body of water like Lake Champlain. People in board shorts and sandals thronged the sidewalks. A few apartment blocks faced the beach. Some of the storefronts hadn't been renovated since the 1980s, and the neighborhood had a past-its-prime quality that reminded me of downtown Kayoga.

I followed the sidewalk, which quickly dead-ended at a kind of concrete boardwalk dividing the street from Rockaway Beach. Beyond it lay a world's worth of wide-open ocean.

I parked myself on a wooden bench on the boardwalk and just gawped for a while in silent awe. The water was a distance away across an expanse of marsh grass and creamy sand that stretched in an unbroken line for miles in either direction. A muggy breeze rich with the stench of fish and diesel fumes blew in from the water, stirring rows of whitecaps like sweeps of white and green frosting. The beach was surprisingly empty, populated by just a few sunbathers and two bare-chested boys tossing a Frisbee. One of them, maybe ten or eleven and a jumble of nut-brown knees and elbows, hurled the Frisbee in a rising arc straight into a headwind. It soared high above the arms of his friend, cutting through the air like a sail, and for a moment, just a moment, I thought it would keep on going, spinning out somewhere far over the ocean. But then the wind faltered, and it stalled, careening into the sand a few dozen yards away. The boys ran after it together, laughing, jostling each other, and as I watched them recede, I found myself climbing to my feet.

Fuck being an adult.

I descended a small set of steps that led onto the beach, where the sand was hot and pliant beneath the soles of my sneakers. Seagulls squealed overhead, gliding across the glossy sky. The wind whipped the water into a tumult of whitecaps and spray, the waves belching up plastic debris, empty beer cans, and seaweed onto the thin ribbon of muddy-wet shoreline. The silhouette of a freighter glistened on the horizon for a moment before seeming to dip below the surface and vanish altogether into the distance.

I kicked off my sneakers, shucked out of my shirt and jeans, and waded into the surf in nothing but my underpants. The sensation was shocking: briny, fierce, and bone gnawingly cold. This was nothing like diving into the swimming hole. These waves sucked mercilessly at my arms and legs, the saltwater stinging my lips and eyes. I could barely stand against the force of the onrushing tide, yet the smell of it, the roar of it, the raw power of it was too exhilarating to fear.

I wanted to let go, Mom. I waded out farther until the water lapped my shoulders, and then I kicked free of the sea floor, squirming into the embrace of the Atlantic as if I were a newborn wriggling into my mother's arms. A yearning inside me deeper than fear or self-preservation took hold. I longed to be set free into this abyss more than I wanted to keep breathing. I ached to feel my essence flowing out into this vast, unfathomable body, pure of water and life, of teeming oblivion, until there was nothing left of me, not even my knowing. Nothing left but this sheltering sea....

But I eventually crawled breathless and shivering back onto the beach, where I collapsed beneath the crackling sunlight and deflated. This is what I'd come here for: perspective. Short of drowning myself in the Atlantic, I could do nothing to resolve the emptiness gaping inside me. Everyone I loved was gone. Just like you, Mom, I would never get them back again.

I hadn't been ready to let them go. I hadn't been ready to do this, to leave everything behind me, to be here on my own with no safety net or backup plan, no goal for the future beyond surviving the scary, glittering night ahead. I wasn't ready for the city, Mom, but here I was, *ta-dah*, and there was nothing else to be done about that except mourn the losses and move on.

I climbed to my feet, whisked the sand from my body, slipped into my clothes, and marched across Rockaway Beach toward the subway back to Washington Heights and the only thing I had left to hold onto.

CHAPTER TWENTY-SEVEN
THE THINGS CHEMICALS DO

I DRAGGED MYSELF UP THE steps to Gabe's apartment around dinnertime, completely exhausted and drenched in sweat and irritation. I hadn't exactly rushed back from Rockaway. The day was too beautiful, the lure of the ocean too strong, so I walked along the beach for what seemed like miles, soaking up the sun and the invigorating sea air.

But the hellish train ride back broke the magical spell. Between MTA delays, a hair-raising breakdown in the tunnel, and the crush of rush hour bodies, it took me twice as long to get back to Washington Heights as the trip out had required.

I unlocked the front door to find Gabe on the couch in his boxers watching a baseball game and packing the bowl of a red glass pipe from a small baggy of weed.

His face lit up like a holiday billboard as soon as he saw me..

"Hey, beautiful," he said, flicking mute on the TV remote and setting the pipe on the cushion beside him. "How'd your big adventure go?"

"Fine." I kicked off my sneakers. "How about you?"

"Pretty good. Got my job back. I start Saturday."

"Congratulations."

He glanced at my empty hands, saw that I wasn't carrying anything that resembled a clothing purchase, and cleared his throat meaningfully.

"I couldn't find anything," I lied and fished his money out of my pocket and set it on the kitchenette counter. "Thanks, but I'll have to make do with what I've got."

He hesitated, his expression darkening, and smoothed the fabric of his boxers against his thighs, his toes scrunching against the dirty floor.

He seemed disappointed, maybe even angry.

"Any word from Shelter Valley?" I blurted before he could say anything else.

He flashed me an annoyed look. "Connie called to tell me how the old man practically jumped out of his death bed to hug and kiss her as soon as she waltzed through the door." He snorted, his voice tightening to a hiss. "I say good for him. Maybe she can do for him better than me. Not my problem anymore, is it? She found the envelope of cash I left for him. That's good enough. I told her I'd show up for the funeral when the time comes, but otherwise, I'm out." Though he tried to sound nonchalant about this, there was no disguising his hurt. He grabbed the pipe from beside him and lit the bowl with a cheap plastic lighter, taking a long hit and easing back into the cushions.

"Was that all she had to say?" I asked quietly.

"Pretty much." He exhaled a thick billow of smoke, glancing at me from the corner of his eyes. "What? You expect her to ask about you?"

"It's just, I thought she might have heard something about Dylan."

He shifted restlessly on the couch. "She didn't mention it."

My throat clenched. "How about Jimmy?"

"I told you what she said."

"Do you think he knows the address here?" I hated myself for how needy I sounded.

"This ain't exactly a safe house, is it? If he wants to find you, he will." He cocked his head at me curiously and asked in a softer tone. "Is that what's bugging you? You afraid he's gonna show up here and start trouble?"

"Who says anything's bugging me?"

His eyes widened. "Never mind," he grumbled, and took another hit off the pipe. "Forget I said anything."

My face burst into flames. "Um, I should shower," I said, making a beeline for the bathroom.

"You didn't go shopping at all, did you?"

I shut the door before I could answer him.

I took my time in the bathroom. After showering, I cleared out the entire medicine shelf until I found an old bottle of Tramadol tucked inside a rusty tin box with a single pill left inside. I swallowed it to ease the pounding in my skull and then squatted on the toilet with my face buried in my hands. Why was I lying to Gabe about this? Why couldn't I just level with him and tell him that no, I didn't go clothes shopping today because no, I didn't want to go to Manntasia tonight? The thought of attending felt obscene, like dancing on Dylan's grave.

But even as I pondered the possibility of leveling with him, I knew I wouldn't. I was the passenger here, not the captain. I would go with the flow tonight. What other choice did I have?

When I finally emerged from the bathroom, I found Gabe waiting in the bedroom. He'd dumped the contents of my backpack across the futon and held the only piece of my beautiful swag that had avoided Jimmy's purge: a frilly pair of pink designer panties I'd lifted from the clearance rack at the Albany Macy's. They'd been stuffed inside a pair of boxers at the rear of my underwear drawer. I hadn't even realized I'd packed them until last night.

"Here." Gabe tossed the panties at me. "I found your outfit for tonight."

"Where's the rest of it?"

"There is no rest of it."

I gawped at him as if he'd completely lost his mind. "There's no way." I laughed. "Come on. I'll get arrested."

"This is New York. Nobody's going to bat an eyelash."

I fingered the panties, savoring their coolness against my skin. They had see-through lace in the rear that transformed my normally feeble ass into something thirsty and a slightly more demure triangle of silk up front that managed to enhance my junk to eye-watering effect. They were just the sort of thing you wore when you were counting on them never being seen in public, which apparently made them ideal for what Gabe had in mind for me tonight. I guess he really did intend to show me off to New York—every square inch of me.

"I don't get it," I said. "Why do you care so much what I wear?"

"One of us has to care," he said, raising an eyebrow at me. "Look, I've been watching you since you got here. You've been walking around on eggshells, waiting for the other shoe to drop. I get it. You feel guilty about Donna's kid. You feel like shit about how things shook out with Jim. Maybe, in the back of your mind, you're even hoping he might show up here and beg you to come home with him. Am I right?"

Though I didn't reply, I felt myself flush, and a wry little smile crossed his lips.

"Listen, if Jim was coming for you, he'd have been here by now. My address ain't a secret, and we're what…? A four-hour drive from Shelter Valley? He could've shown up last night or anytime today, but he didn't. Just like my old man never showed up to fetch me at Bonnie's. I waited just like you, but he never came. That's how I knew where I stood with him. Now you know, too."

He took hold of my wrist. It felt more possessive than comforting.

"It's rough, I get that," he continued. "But it's also your ticket out of there, out of the past, out of feeling bad about yourself. You don't have to live by Shelter Valley rules no more—*his* rules. It's time to be yourself, beautiful. You're free. Start living like it."

He reached across the heap of my clothes and grabbed a plastic pint of Smirnoff's that was tucked beneath his nightstand. He unscrewed the cap, took a swig, and handed the bottle to me.

"Just relax, okay?" he said, waiting for me to gag down a sip before continuing. "You're here now. You're with me. Let's have fun tonight. That's why you came here, isn't it?"

"I'm just not sure I can do this."

"Aww, come on. You told me you were a raging exhibitionist." He pulled me close, nuzzling his lips against my belly as he yanked the towel from my waist. "Bonnie would've done it."

TWO HOURS LATER, I STOOD sizing up my radical look for Manntasia in front of Gabe's bedroom mirror. With the exception of the barely-there panties, I was basically naked. I'd slipped my feet bare into my pink high top Converse. I'd teased and gelled my hair into something resembling a spiky blonde hedgehog. Gabe had dug out a stash of old cosmetics from a past Halloween, and I'd set off my eyes with coal eyeliner and a wand of sparkly mascara. He'd even rustled up an old tube of silver body glitter, and I let him smear it into every nook and cranny of exposed skin from my face down to my ankles. The result: I glistened like the Tin Man ready to ease on down the road for a night of debauchery at Terminal City.

Still, it'd taken him a lot to get me here. More begging and cajoling, further chemical inducements, Chinese takeout for dinner, and numerous kisses. But though I'd let him think he needed to convince me, the truth was, Mom, he had me at, "Bonnie would've done it."

Besides, I couldn't say no to Gabe.

"Are you positive I won't get arrested?" I said, glancing at his reflection. He sat on the futon in skin-tight pleather pants and muscle shirt, flicking through screens on his phone.

"I told you, it's New York." He leaned back on the futon and yawned, bored with my insecurity. "You look hot. Just chill out, okay?"

But I was chill, or at least as chill as that Tramadol I'd swallowed, plus a bowl of Gabe's premium smoke, and several swigs of Smirnoff's could make me. The tip of my nose had gone numb, my jaw felt like overstretched elastic, and even the butterflies barely twitched on their little rubber-bands in my belly. This was a major improvement over an hour's worth of near-puking, shuddering panic.

Oh, the things the right chemicals will do! Ravisha purred the bridge from "Chemsexx" in my mind, and it occurred to me that one thing the right chemicals could do was persuade me that it was a brilliant idea to attend the hottest nightclub in New York City all but butt-ass naked.

Then again, as Gabe said, you would've done it, right Mom?

"Gabe, can I ask you something?"

He glanced up from his phone. "Shoot, beautiful."

"Why do you think Mom was the way she was?"

He hesitated a moment and then turned back to the screen. "What do you mean?"

"I mean, it's no secret she made bad choices. She hurt people. People she should have loved and protected, and not just me. I've always wondered if she knew what she was doing, or if, I don't know—shit just happened."

"Why are you asking me this all of a sudden?"

"Because I'm stoned," I said and laughed. This was partially true. My inhibitions were clearly compromised, and I doubted I would've had the courage to bring the subject up sober. I tugged at the front of my panties to try to stretch a millimeter or two more flesh coverage out of them, and added, "It's been on my mind a lot lately. You were her friend, and I've got nobody else to ask. Besides, you were the one who brought her up tonight."

Though his eyes remained fixed on his phone, I could tell he wasn't seeing what was on the screen. He shifted awkwardly and didn't say anything for several beats. But when he finally spoke, his voice had a distinct edge. "Bonnie wasn't real big on reflecting, you know? If she thought she was hurting people—and I figure you mean Jim—she didn't talk to me about it." He shoved the phone into his pocket and rubbed his hands together as if they'd gone cold. "I wish I could help, but if you're asking me to explain her to you, I can't. She had a tough life. She made a tough life. Just like everybody else."

"But she wasn't like everybody else, was she?"

"Nope, she wasn't. But then neither are you, beautiful, and that's what I like about you." He flashed me a smirk. "Anyway, enough of this buzzkill talk. I've been thinking you'd better not throw a boner in those tonight. There's nothing there to hide it."

He nodded to my panties, devouring the rest of me with hungry eyes.

"I'm not worried about that," I said and sighed, turning back to my reflection. I could tell I wasn't getting through to him, but that shouldn't have surprised me: I was too high to be lucid, and besides, I was losing myself to him all over again. Giving in too easily. Giving up without a fight. Gabe was only interested in hearing "yes" from me tonight.

I wondered if this was what had happened to you, Mom. Had you drowned in a flood of yeses? Yes after yes after yes? To the men, the booze, the drugs? Each yes a new wave crashing into you, until the night they all joined forces into one overwhelming tsunami of yes that drove that needle straight into your arm?

I stared harder at myself in the mirror, but all I saw was you staring back at me....

"I can't do this," I blurted and began to hyperventilate. "I look sleazy. Like a dirty little cocksucker. I'm staying here, okay? Can I please just stay here?"

Gabe leapt off the futon and pulled me roughly into his arms. "It's okay, beautiful," he said soothingly. He kept on saying it as he stroked the back of my head. "It's okay. It's okay."

"No, it's not. No, it's not."

He fished into his back pocket to retrieve the larger of the two baggies of Daffy Ducks he'd counted out while I was still fussing in the mirror. He plucked two of the little gray pills out, popped one into his own mouth, and then prized apart my lips and slipped the other onto my tongue. "Swallow this, and you'll feel so much better," he promised in his sweetest, most reassuring voice, though his eyes simply commanded me to swallow and say yes.

What was one more pill, Mom? I opened my mouth to show him Daffy was gone.

I said yes.

CHAPTER TWENTY-EIGHT
TERMINAL CITY

BOOM... BOOM... BOOM...

My heart pounded with something like joy as we cleared the Columbus Circle Station and entered the wild promise of the city at night. This was midtown Manhattan, the center of the universe. I was high on it. High on Gabe. High on tonight.

Thank God for good drugs, Mom. The Daffy Duck had kicked into high gear on the subway, with an ecstatic unraveling of nerves and inhibitions so swift it hit me like an orgasm. It left my body tingling all over with yeses.

The rumble and jive of the street swept us along. Horns squealed. Voices tinkled on the wind like tossed coins. Gabe squeezed my hand as he led us west toward the river between towers of glass and light. A pack of laughing girls elbowed by, bangles jangling, perfume sweetening the air. The occasional tourist stole a sidelong glance at me, careful to avoid eye contact as if whatever I was might be contagious.

My bare nipples prickled in the sultry breeze as we jogged across 11th Avenue, skirting down the side street past a car dealership toward Terminal City's nondescript rear entrance. A few hundred yards down the block, beyond the honking bustle of 12th Avenue, the river lay, its funk mingled with the exhaust oozing from Ravisha's hot-pink tour bus parked along the curbside.

A jolt of fresh adrenaline shot through me at the sight of the bus. This was happening. I was really here.

Boom… Boom… Boom…

The music inside rumbled through the walls like thunder. The show had already begun: an opening act, probably DJ Uri. Ravisha wouldn't take the stage before midnight. A small group of Manniacs milled around smoking a joint in front of the loading dock beside the stage entrance. They were beautiful. In their late teens or early twenties, they'd transformed their bodies into works of surrealist art. Glittering gels and electric wigs. Lace and metal and crepe de Chine. Makeup paved like neon boulevards across their faces. Heels as high as nose bleeds and a Mount Everest of attitude perfectly capped by snow-white teeth.

They sneered at us, necks craned, eyes dragging me from top to bottom as we drew near. I heard whispers and a few sniggers, but instead of crumpling under their scrutiny, my back stiffened. My head shot up like royalty. The attention was electrifying.

Gabe's hand slid to my ass. He maneuvered me in front of him as if displaying me to eager bidders at an auction. I liked it. I liked the rush of knowing I didn't give a shit what these bitches thought of me. I didn't require their approval because I had Gabe's.

He was proud of me. He was showing me off to New York.

He guided us past the leering mob to a black metal door with no knob. A couple of hurried texts later a crack of light appeared around the edges as the door inched open.

"Hey, Lon," Gabe whispered into the crack.

The door swung free, and Lon emerged into the night. He wore baggy jeans and a black tee-shirt with PROFESSIONAL GROUPIE splayed across the chest in white letters. He had on a Bluetooth headset atop his thick wave of coppery hair that he'd gelled into a Johnny Cash pompadour salted with glitter. He still stank of cheap cologne, his rings and bracelets glinting in the streetlights. His eyes were even more vulpine than the night before.

He chewed his bottom lip, quickly scanning the two of us with lordly indifference. "Hey," he said, then eyed the pack of glam boys edging closer like starving coyotes. "Come in, before these queens get ideas about muscling backstage. I need to tell security to clear them out. The talent doesn't like to be hassled."

He ushered us inside, slamming the door behind Gabe. Then he herded us across a grimy loading dock and into a narrow corridor that smelled of piss and bleach and was lit only by emergency lights. Gabe led the way. I stumbled closely behind, with Lon's hand pressed firmly to my ass as he shouted, "Keep going!" above the thud of electronic drums.

Boom... Boom... Boom...

Gabe came to a halt when the corridor ended in a pair of double doors. He turned to me as I slipped away from Lon, who was now staring straight at my crotch.

"You two look hot tonight," he said and literally licked his lips.

"Good to see you, too, man," Gabe said, patting him roughly on the back. "Thanks so much for this."

"Anything for you…. So, let's see what you brought me."

Gabe nodded and fished into his back pocket, retrieving the smaller baggy of a dozen little gray ducks he'd counted out.

Lon lifted the bag to his eyes and scowled. "What's with the duck?"

"It's Daffy," Gabe said proudly. "New shit out of China. Very pure."

"It better be. That junk I got off Marco last time gave some kid seizures. I don't need that kind of grief again."

"Aww, you know me, Lon. Only the best. I'd never fuck you over."

Lon wiped his lips as he considered him. "Alright then," he said and pocketed the bag. Then he squeezed Gabe on the shoulder and turned to me. "Gabe here's my man. You want to be my boy?" He looked me over from head to toe like I was a new car he planned to buy and then reached out to caress the upholstery with the backs of his fingers.

I shivered and pulled away.

Gabe laughed nervously. "Kid's all bark and no bite," he said to Lon, then slipped his arm around my shoulder. "Besides, he's mine." He swept me in for a kiss.

Although it made me feel a little like a tree getting pissed on by a dog, at least he'd claimed me this time. Maybe now Lon would take the hint.

"You two ought to get a room and invite me," he said, as a staticky voice chirped into his headset. "On my way," he barked into the microphone, and then to us, "I need to jet." He hurriedly produced a stamper from his pocket and branded the backs of our hands. Then he led us to the double doors, which vibrated within their frames from the force of the music on the other side. As he fiddled with the keys on his belt, I could barely keep my shit together long enough for him to unlock the alarm.

This was it… this was…it….

Lon shouted something to Gabe I couldn't make out, and then he pushed open the doors, and all at once my brain exploded in a barrage of light and color and sound as we emerged onto the dance floor.

The club was swimming in exotic bodies in motion, Mom, a full spectrum of genders, styles, and skin tones. Clothed and unclothed. Rolling, messy, joyous. The atmosphere hung saturated in a cloud of funk and jasmine, pot and clove cigarettes, laughter and breath and sex. Manniacs were nothing if not visionary in their attire, and no two looked alike. A bristling blonde queen glided across the floor in a gown made entirely of strawberry Twizzlers and fishing lures. A dazed stoner with facial tattoos and red neon horns swayed to his own beat in a kilt of blinking red Christmas lights. There were hoop skirts with blood-spattered bullet holes, furries wearing rhinestone tiaras, and lunchmeat codpieces decorated with glued purple sequins. I marveled at Day-Glo hairdos as wide as baby carriages, corsets fashioned from rawhide and chain mail, and man-sized wings handcrafted from bird bones and silver feathers.

Though my drugstore glitter and off-the-rack panties would hardly make the cut here, I was too swept up in the spectacle to care.

Boom... Boom... Boom...

The scene was transcendent, almost holy, like stepping into the middle of a deviant mass. The club's cathedral-like interior was enormous, awash in the beams of gyrating spotlights at least three stories above us. Glowing rods of yellow and pink pulsed along the walls in time to the beat. Gigantic swaths of billowing fabric, suspended from the rafters like upturned sails, glowed with projected images from gay and transgender porn. Chandeliers made of clear acrylic dildos and mirrored handcuffs hung above the stage, where a bare-chested DJ Uri spun furiously behind a thumping deck, a vortex of red and pink and violet light swirling hypnotically behind him. The air glistened with droplets of perspiration. Inflatable Hello Kitty heads bobbled atop a crowd made up of a thousand glorious bodies grinding in unison. The sampled voice of the legendary Loleatta Holloway wailed above the fray, as the—

Lon grabbed my ass again.

"I'll be over there if you need me," he shouted into my ear and nodded to the far side of the dance floor. Then he let go of my butt cheek and elbowed his way into the throngs of Manniacs, quickly disappearing from view.

Gabe leaned in and asked, "Where's he going?"

"Someplace far away, I hope... Come on, let's dance."

I grabbed him by the wrist and tried to lead him onto the floor, but he yanked me back and said, "Dancing later. Business first."

Reluctantly, I nodded. Gabe had already explained what was on the agenda for tonight. We were here for more than just fun. Though I wasn't sure why he needed me around to conduct his business, I was happy enough to oblige. I could dance later, save my energy for when Ravisha finally took the stage. Besides, I needed some water. What with all the excitement and chemical enhancements, I was burning up.

Gabe took my hand and guided me to a wide staircase along the far wall opposite the stage. It led to a kind of balcony partitioned as a VIP area with a commanding view of the club below. Two bored-looking women in latex dominatrix garb stood at the top of the stairs guarding a velvet rope. One of them kissed Gabe full on the lips and ushered him through with a pat on his ass. The other one insisted on examining my hand stamp like it was counterfeit money before she finally let me in. Beyond the rope lay a dozen leather and stainless steel booths lit by blue LED candles. A small bar at the rear was bathed in black light. A few cocktail tables built into the balcony railing overlooked the dance floor. A large circular platform cantilevered out into space at the far end, surrounded by thin brass bars like an empty birdcage. The whole balcony was murky and grim. Nobody was dancing, and if there were other Manniacs among the subdued crowd, they'd dimmed their high-beams to hang out with the VIPs.

Gabe led us to an empty cocktail table near the birdcage that Lon had reserved for us. It had an unobstructed view of the stage and dance floor below. I was glad to sit down for a few minutes. My head was spinning from our whirl through the crowd, and I'd begun to sweat like a beer can in the sun. I wrapped my legs around my stool and tried to steady myself.

Gabe pecked me on the cheek and wandered off to the bar, shaking hands and schmoozing at various booths along the way. I scanned the other VIPs. The Terminal City clientele was very different up here—almost exclusively white, male, and older—although I noticed a smattering of young men closer to my age who wore nothing but identical pairs of gold lamé hot pants. They flitted from lap to lap and table to table, flirting and laughing and occasionally making out with each other for the amusement of what I quickly understood were their patrons.

After a couple of them threw me looks of undisguised loathing, I turned my attention back to the dance floor.

A few minutes later, Gabe returned, sipping a draft beer. He handed me a highball glass filled with a murky green fluid he called a "Terminal City Corpse Reviver." He proudly explained it'd cost him twenty bucks and contained "two whole shots of Absinthe," among various other high-octane spirits. Though I'd only asked for water, I was too thirsty to turn it down, and I practically chugged the entire thing, nearly gagging on its syrupy sweet flavor of licorice and ass.

Then, I settled back to observe the spectacle below us.

Gabe seemed preoccupied, even anxious. I grew restless as the minutes ticked by and we weren't dancing. My stomach began to rumble from the assault of the Corpse Reviver. Sweat rolled down my back like a pig at a barbecue. I'd just begun to feel a little faint when a spotlight suddenly flared to life, bathing the birdcage beside us in a lava-red glow. A trio of the hot pants boys peeled away from their various tables, climbed inside the cage, and began to dance—if you can call all their humping and grinding, necking and groping "dancing."

It took me a moment to realize that one of them was Lon's boyfriend, Tiago. So this was what he meant about being a dancer. He looked even hotter with his clothes off.

All eyes in the VIP area were quickly glued to the boys in the birdcage. I couldn't pull my gaze away from them either. They were transfixing, dizzying, and a boner soon leaped to attention against the silk of my panties. My heart raced. My head swam. Gabe leaned in to whisper in my ear something I didn't understand, and then he was all over me, his hands crawling up my thighs, squeezing my crotch, caressing my back and neck. His mouth smothered my mouth until I couldn't breathe and had to gasp for air. Then I was somehow in his lap, straddling him, swathed in his heat and kisses. Though I vaguely understood that we, too, were now being watched, I didn't care. Between the drink and the Daffy Duck, the last of my inhibitions melted away. I felt free and alive, safe in Gabe's arms with the lights and music and leers of total strangers surrounding us, but not between us.

Nothing could come between us.

My erection thrust into his belly, and I began to moan, my tongue plunging deep into his mouth, my hands slipping beneath his muscle shirt, creeping up to his nipples and then lower and lower and—he stopped me.

"Whoa, tiger," he whispered and grabbed my wrist before I could unzip his fly. "Save some for later."

I blinked open my eyes and realized he wasn't even looking at me anymore. His gaze had migrated to a booth across the balcony where a couple of well-dressed men were now ogling us. One of them winked at me, his tongue practically hanging out of his mouth, while the other beckoned Gabe over with his fingers like he was summoning the waiter.

"Duty calls," Gabe said, and instructed me to hop down.

But I didn't move. I just gawped at him in shock until he literally lifted me off of him and set me down on my stool like a doll he'd finished playing with. Then he straightened himself out, mumbled "Back in ten," and sauntered off to attend to business.

I slumped against the table and tried not to topple over. Though the room had begun to spin wildly, the boys in the birdcage had stopped dancing. There'd been a lull in the music. DJ Uri invited Dandy-O and Nana Hughes onto the stage to perform their club hit "Love Fail." The crowd erupted in screams and howls as the pair strode out from opposite corners.

I felt an icy hand materialize on the small of my back.

Lon.

"Can I get you another one of those?" he hissed into my ear, so close I could smell the Binaca on his breath.

"I'm good," I said and tried to shrug him off. But I was too unsteady, and he had to catch me to keep me from toppling off the stool.

"I see you've had enough already," he said and laughed. "That's okay though. You did your job well. You can relax for a while."

"Job?"

"Your little performance. These horny queens ate it up. You're good for business. Better than that last stiff he brought in here with him. I was worried last night, but you really got into it after all. It was hot to watch. You'll see. He'll move shit quick tonight, then maybe the three of us can get together later and have some fun of our own, eh? I'd sure like to get to know you better."

"What are you... talking about?"

"This" he said, and slid his fingers beneath the waistband of my panties, diving deep into the sweaty crack of my ass.

I lurched forward, but there was nowhere to go.

"Oh, come on. Don't be a cocktease now. We both know why you're here. Gabe's the man. Got an image to project, and you're a walking billboard for a good time. I mean, look at you." He smacked his lips. "I bet he even picked out that getup to wear, no?"

I nodded. It was all I could do.

"Thought so," he said, as another staticky voice squawked over his headset. His hand jerked out of my panties, and he backed away from the table. "On my way," he spat into the microphone and then said to me, "Catch you boys later."

He gave me a little bow and melted into the darkness.

Boom... Boom... Boom...

DJ Uri had launched into the opening beats of "Love Fail," and as Dandy-O began to rap, its brutal concussion nearly rattled my skull to pieces. A fistful of vomit punched its way up my throat. I looked to Gabe for help, but he was now seated at the booth on the far side of the balcony with the two strange men.

They were all smirking at me.

CHAPTER TWENTY-NINE
COCKSUCKER

SWATHED FROM FLOOR TO CEILING in stainless steel and blood-red subway tiles, the club's VIP men's room gleamed like the lobby of Hell. I stumbled through the door and into the middle of a small, debauched party beneath the seedy flush of ruby lights. A pair of gaunt Wall Street types in white Oxfords snorted lines off a credit card at the sink. In front of the urinals, two ancient vampires kissed and fondled another hot pants boy, his gritted-teethed grin a sad parody of arousal. A third geezer leered at them from against the red wall, the words TERMINAL CITY emblazoned in ivory tiles above his head, his hand wheeling feverishly inside the fly of his crisply pressed slacks.

Grunts and moans reverberated from behind the closed door of one of the only two stalls, and so I darted into the other one, slamming and locking the stainless steel door behind me.

Then I was on my knees, heaving up licorice green bile into icy porcelain. It was like pulling the trigger on an automatic rifle: once I started, I couldn't stop, even after there was nothing left to bring up. My whole body shuddered like a fish on a hook, eyes bulging, vision glazed. Someone banged on the stall door and shouted, "Go die someplace else," followed by laughter. The bathroom door squealed open and closed, open and closed. The air stank of dried piss, urinal cakes, the vinegary musk of rutting bodies. I shut my eyes and listened to the moans and grunts next door until the first wave of nausea finally passed, and I managed to catch my breath.

The stall spun madly as I climbed off the floor and onto the toilet seat. Lon's words whirred like a meat grinder in my head, pulverizing my image of Gabe into a fleshy pulp.

"Better than that last stiff.... A walking billboard for a good time."

Surprise, fucking surprise.

The bathroom door squealed open again, followed by muffled whispers. Somebody grumbled, "He's in there." Fingertips scratched on the stall door, but instead of Gabe coming to beg for my forgiveness, a strange, drunken voice slurred, "Want some company?"

"No," I managed to say as the stranger tried the latch. Though the lock held, half of a crisp fifty-dollar bill snaked through the crack between the door and frame.

"There's more if you play nice," the stranger said, waggling the money at me like a dog treat. The tips of his loafers poked beneath the stall door, supple black leather with a soft, pliant sheen. English or maybe Italian, handcrafted, no doubt, and probably worth more than Jimmy brought home in a month of Sunday overtime.

I leaned forward and hocked a wad of phlegm onto the toe of the left shoe. Then I told its entitled owner to "Fuck off" as forcefully as I could, though my voice cracked from all the puking.

"Come on, open up," he said, not noticing my spit. "My money's as good as anyone's."

He tried the latch again, but the lock held.

"Leave me alone. I'm sick."

"I'll make you feel better."

A loud slam shook the entire stall. My heart leapt, but it was just the dudes going at it next door. Still, it felt like I was under siege. I pulled my legs up onto the seat and hugged my knees to my chest. DJ Uri's beats *boom... boom... boomed* like a barrage of gunfire through the bathroom walls. My eyes burned in the sour air, my stomach roiling again. There was a yowl from the couple next door, followed by whispers and a toilet flush. Water ran in a sink. The bathroom door squealed open and closed, open and closed. More whispers, laughter, then silence.

My head throbbed as my eyes struggled to focus in the devilish light. Thoughts became sludgy as my breathing shallowed, and it vaguely occurred to me I might pass out in here. I needed to get out of this bathroom, but Loafer Man still lingered on the other side of the stall, a stray dog stalking a trash can.

"I've got gonorrhea," I finally blurted. "Herpes, too."

Mercifully, this did the trick. He called me a "nasty cocktease" and slammed a fist against the stall door before shuffling out of the bathroom and leaving me in peace.

I waited a moment longer to be sure he was gone, and then I slipped out of the stall and stumbled up to the mirror. In the sickly red glare, my skin shone gray, my features sunken, my jaw gurning like a fiend. But at least the bathroom was empty. The booms outside had quieted. DJ Uri's set must be winding down. Ravisha would take the stage soon, but I was too fucked up to care.

I ran cold water in the sink and tried to rinse my face, but even just bending down to the bowl spun the room off on a rubbery axis. I was a bug trapped inside a poison jar—I needed clear air.

I braced myself against the sink and was about to push off toward the door when it swung open again, and Loafer Man sauntered back into the bathroom. At least he wasn't one of the dudes from the booth with Gabe. Just another fifty-something, silver-fox wannabe in black Versace jeans, a pale silk sport shirt stretched tight over an ample paunch, and a fat gold wristwatch that probably cost more than our entire trailer.

As soon as I saw the look on his face, I knew I was doomed.

"Figured you'd come out eventually," he purred. "Your friend out there's bragging about what a good time you are. Come on and show me."

I blurted something about getting back to Gabe and moved for the door, but he swooped in and pinned me against the sink, smelling of what I imagined to be crisp linen and cognac.

"He can wait. We haven't gotten to know each other yet."

He leaned in to kiss me, but I jerked my head away.

"I just puked."

"A little too much partying, eh? That's alright." He grabbed hold of my hand and forced it between his legs, where an erection throbbed against the fly of his jeans. "See how much I like you. Let me see if I can make you like me, too."

His hot tongue slithered up the side of my neck, and he began to chew on my earlobe. Though I tried to wriggle free, groaning something incoherent about Gabe as I reeled back, he held me fast as he slobbered into my ear, "You tricked me before. Lon says you're as clean as a whistle. A ripe little peach."

His hand slid into my panties, only this time, I didn't try to stop him because I was hard.

Why was I fucking hard?

"See, I knew you'd come around. How old are you anyway, beautiful?"

"Seventeen."

"Sweet," he whispered. "But let's call it eighteen between friends, shall we?" He licked my neck more fiercely as he ground his pelvis into my hip, fishing into his jeans pocket and yanking out two crumpled $50 bills that he slammed onto the counter beside me. "How about you suck me off?"

"I'm not a whore," I protested, although I'd already stopped trying to wriggle free.

"No, of course not. But who couldn't use a few extra dollars, right? Let's call it an exchange of gifts between friends."

He started kneading my boner again through my panties.

"What if somebody comes in?" I said.

"So what?"

He had a point.

"Why me?" I said.

"Why not you?"

Well, duh, Toby Ryerson. Why the hell not me? I'd certainly done more for less at the Marsh Trail. For free, as it happened. With other strangers not half as clean or rich or good smelling as this one. Who the hell did I think I was anyway? Gabe and Lon had me pegged all along: I was nothing more than somebody else's good time. Why bother getting uptight about it now? Besides, if I'd only done this for Dylan when he'd wanted it, I wouldn't even be here.

And he wouldn't be dead.

Jimmy was right: I was a dirty little cocksucker. I had this coming. I'd have them all cumming.

Loafer Man kept yanking at my erection—he must have thought I liked it, but my dick might as well have been petrified wood—I couldn't feel a thing. My mind had retreated to a cozy parlor at the back of the house while I left my body to deal with the pushy stranger at the front door. If all they wanted was to use my body for a while, then yes, fine, whatever. They could have it. Yes to anything they wanted. Yes and yes again, so long as I could just check out until it was over.

I wasn't getting out of there without a performance. I let Loafer Man push me to my knees.

"I won't—swallow," I managed to blurt as I hit the cold tile floor. My body swayed a little, too fucked up to hold itself upright, and so he grabbed a fistful of my hair and jammed his salty fingers between my lips to prepare the way. He pried my mouth open wide and slid himself inside. Then he crashed down my throat in waves, thrust after briny thrust, drowning my body in all that red, red light… the thrum of his moans… the sputtering bathroom fan… my hands seizing cold slabs of his flabby ass to pull him in deeper, to drown my body faster, please God, until my throat squeezed up so hard, I choked and had to spit him out.

"You're hungry for it," he cooed. I heard myself groan as if yes—but it wasn't really me, Mom. I was still kicking back in that parlor at the rear of the house, watching this sad porno movie where some dirty little cocksucker goes down on his knees for a bossy troll in the men's room.

When it was over, and he'd finished, he gave a sharp little gasp and then thumbed the tears from my eyes so tenderly it made me shudder. As I gagged up his bitter leavings onto the floor, he waddled away like a penguin, his pants around his knees as he grabbed a handful of toilet paper from the stall and wiped himself dry.

"My wife and kids are in London for the rest of the week," he said, tossing the wad of paper into the john. "Maybe I'll talk to your companion out there and see if you two would like to come back to my place later for more fun. I'm very generous with my friends." He hiked up his pants, rinsed his hands in the sink, and blew me a kiss before he slipped out of the bathroom door, disappearing into the music and chaos of Terminal City.

CHAPTER THIRTY
JUST ANOTHER USER

No sooner had Loafer Man gone than I dragged myself back into the stall to throw up again. My stomach burst like an overcooked sausage. Bile tinged with blood flooded the toilet bowl, turning my insides out. The door squealed open as traffic resumed to the men's room, but by then, things had deteriorated into little more than a blur of whispers and groans. Running water. Pounding feet. Zippers and cackles and coughs.

At some point, I rallied enough to heave myself onto the toilet seat, although I quickly collapsed against the stall, a wet smudge on the cool stainless steel. When I heard the percussion gun of Ravisha's cover of Sylvester's "Man[n] Enuff" fire the Diva onto the stage in a muffled roar of shouts and stomps, my heart sank inside my chest, and I finally blacked out.

Though I never fully lost consciousness, the universe reduced itself to a vague awareness of my breathing, punctuated now and then by a fresh thumping beat, a fist pounding on the stall door, a voice commanding me to, "Hurry the hell up in there."

In the end, Tiago came to fetch me, not Gabe. "Hey baby, you in there?"

I must have somehow fumbled open the latch because the next thing I knew, he was grumbling to himself as he held me over the sink, slapping me gently and splashing cold water onto my face. He smelled of almonds and lemon oil. No longer dressed in his gold lamé hot pants, he now wore navy blue sweats and a zippered hoodie over a LAST NIGHT A DJ SAVED MY LIFE tee-shirt. He checked my pupils and my pulse, asked me some random questions. He propped me against the counter and grabbed a fistful of paper towels from the dispenser. Wetting them in the sink, he scrubbed away the remains of my tear-streaked makeup and the vileness encrusted around my mouth. Then he shucked off his hoodie and zippered me up inside.

"We should get you some water," he said gently while wrapping a strong arm around my shoulder to help me out of the men's room.

The VIP area glared much brighter than before. The house lights were ablaze, the music dead. A greenish haze like poison gas overhung the space, which now looked more like a derelict warehouse than one of the hottest nightclubs in the city. The dance floor lay empty, save for a few staff sweeping up debris. I saw a gigantic scrim being dismantled on stage: Ravisha resplendent as a riding-crop-wielding dominatrix astride the back of a ball-gagged Donald Trump.

The remains of Manntasia melted before my eyes like a watercolor in the rain. I'd slept through the Diva's entire set.

Tiago maneuvered me toward a booth along the far side of the balcony where a small crowd of a half dozen men had gathered. The first face among them I recognized was Gabe's. He had his arm wrapped around the shoulder of a gorgeous young ginger whom I soon realized was one of the birdcage boys from before, only now dressed in sweats similar to Tiago's.

As soon as Gabe saw me, I could tell by his expression that he'd already talked to Loafer Man. He wasn't angry, just resigned, as if he should have known all along what to expect from me. It felt like a kick in the gut.

"There he is," he said to Tiago. "I told you he was off somewhere having fun."

All eyes turned to me.

"I found him in the bathroom," Tiago said, carefully depositing me into a chair one of the strangers had pulled up to the table. "What the hell did you give him?"

Gabe shrugged. "Nothing I didn't take myself." He was obviously drunk or still high. Possibly both. The ginger nuzzled in closer to him, sliding his hand possessively across Gabe's chest to whisper something into his ear. They both tittered like schoolgirls before a smirking Gabe added, "Oh yeah, he drank a Corpse Reviver, too."

"He sure looks like the walking dead," somebody said.

The whole table erupted in guffaws.

"Assholes," Tiago muttered and then leaned down to whisper into my ear. "You sit tight. I'll go find you some water."

As soon as he was gone, conversation resumed among the various strangers as if I'd never appeared. The ginger untangled himself from Gabe's embrace to fish into his backpack for cigarettes. Gabe took a sip from the beer in front of him. He was visibly agitated, bouncing in his seat to the rhythm of a song playing only in his head. He leaned across the table toward me, his pupils wide as pennies, and informed me that I'd missed "one hell of a show."

"I know," I replied hoarsely. "But that drink made me sick."

"I heard you made a friend, too."

My chest squeezed tight. I opened my mouth to protest, but Gabe held up a hand to shush me.

"Listen, no explanations," he said, as coldly as he'd ever spoken to me. "You're free to do what you like. It's cool. We both got what we wanted here."

Then he leaned back in his seat and rejoined the conversation, which had turned to the after-party we were all apparently going to as soon as Lon finished closing up the club.

I didn't say anything—I might have tried to explain or defend myself if Gabe had seemed wounded or jealous, but his indifference was withering. It wasn't even like he was all that disappointed in me. I just wasn't special anymore. I was just like all the others. I was just like him. Just another user.

I wondered how I hadn't seen it before, but you only really know someone once they show you who they are. Gabe was damaged goods. Damaged by a life lived all on his own. A life lived hustling to get by. A life of using and being used. He'd even admitted as much himself. *Everybody's got an angle.* I should have listened when he warned me most dudes only stuck around if they wanted something from you. I should have known he wasn't just confiding in me. He was confessing, too.

I slumped back in the chair and stared listlessly into space. It didn't matter if he cared about me or not. It was too late to fix this. Hell, it wasn't even worth the trouble of trying. I'd used Gabe to get to New York. He'd used me as his billboard for a good time. We were even now. There was no point in prolonging this any further. We weren't in love. Except through you, Mom, we barely even knew each other. Maybe he wouldn't kick me out, at least not right away, but whatever we had was done.

I was truly on my own now. Not that it even mattered. I felt so empty inside it was like a black hole had opened up within me and sucked away all the parts that made me human. Tonight was just a preview of what my future held in store. A future without Jimmy, where I had no one to look out for me but myself. I could see it all unfold in an endless stream of all-nighters like this one, parties and drugs and sex with a parade of Gabes and Lons and Loafer Men, whoever would slip me a few bucks or put me up for a few nights. Eventually, I'd get my feet under me, sure—maybe deal some drugs, flip some burgers, find a little place in Washington Heights I couldn't afford—and then I'd age out of circulation and become just like them.

Someday, I might even groom my own Toby into a walking billboard for a good time. The irony was so thick I could choke on it. I'd gotten everything I ever thought I wanted by running away to this city. The drugs the sex the men the scene.

Welcome to New York, Toby Ryerson! How does it feel to throw your life away on nothing?

Conversation simmered around me. Gabe and the ginger embarked on a flirtatious banter about how much money they'd each made tonight, though at least this made it easier to shut them out. I was beginning to emerge from my stupor, though an ungodly stabbing pain was rapidly replacing the fog in my head. Every inch of me ached or throbbed or burned. My tongue felt coated in wallpaper paste, and although my stomach had at least ceased its cartwheeling. Puke and blood still fouled my mouth. I could even still taste Loafer Man on my lips.

I scanned the balcony, briefly alarmed that he might suddenly materialize beside me, but he seemed to have vanished along with all the other VIPs.

The only creepers left up here were Gabe's friends.

I wondered what Loafer Man had said to Gabe. Not that it mattered now. Once he realized I wasn't following him home, he probably found some other dude to rent for the night. Hell, I hadn't even gotten paid for my services. Like an idiot, I forgot all about the cash he'd slapped on the counter when I locked myself in the stall. It was long gone by the time Tiago pulled me out again. Somebody had had a profitable night at my expense. More than one somebody, as a matter of fact.

I tried to catch Gabe's attention by asking him if we could go home now, but I realized he was avoiding eye contact with me. The ginger had taken root in his lap and was whispering in his ear like they were newlyweds. It seemed Gabe had already moved on. I wasn't jealous or hurt, just sick and exhausted. I stared even harder at him to see if I could force him to notice me, but the longer I looked, the more obviously he ignored me. What a coward.

When Tiago finally reappeared with two bottles of water, I gulped down the first like it was the antidote to a rattlesnake bite.

"Take it easy," he warned. "You'll make yourself sick."

"I'm alright, thanks," I gasped and began on the second bottle.

"See, he's fine," Gabe said, finally acknowledging my presence again. "The fresh air will sober him up. He'll shake it off." He took a long drag from the cigarette the ginger had lit for them to share, and then asked one of the other men at the table, "Where's Lon? Let's get this show on the road."

"Hey Gabe, pass me your keys," Tiago said. "I'll take him back to your place. He needs to sleep this off."

"Fuck that," Gabe said. "We're all heading over to Marco's to party. Aren't we, Toby?"

He looked at me, but I said nothing.

"Naw, he's not," Tiago said firmly. "I'm taking him back to your place, and then I'm going home. We're done for tonight. Now pass me your keys."

The others hushed as he held out his hand expectantly.

Gabe didn't say anything at first. He just peered at me, his expression unsure. I could tell he was struggling with whether to take me home himself. Maybe he wanted me to ask him to do it. Maybe he didn't trust me alone in his apartment anymore. Maybe he just felt guilty.

But whatever his hesitation was, it didn't last long.

"Let him go," the ginger said. He kissed Gabe on the neck and then caressed his cheek. "I promise we'll have more fun without him."

Gabe swallowed hard. He stared at me a moment longer, but when I still didn't say anything to stop him, he wrapped his arm around the ginger and said, "Fine, whatever," before producing his wallet from his back pocket and tossing Tiago his spare key.

Then he turned away in disgust.

Tiago helped me to my feet and led me across the balcony. I was still unsteady on my feet, but the farther we got from Gabe, the stronger I felt, the more myself again.

Yet, as we descended the staircase to the dance floor, I heard Gabe call after me one last time. "I'll catch you later, Little B?" in a voice as hollow as an open grave.

"Sure thing, Gabe," I muttered, without even looking back. "Sure thing."

CHAPTER THIRTY-ONE
PRETTY BOYS LIKE US

THE SUBWAY BACK TO WASHINGTON Heights lay empty. It was nearly four in the morning, and while the city wasn't exactly asleep, it'd kicked back for some quiet time before dawn. Gabe had been right about the fresh air sobering me up, though the result was hardly welcome: I felt like a picked scab flicked into the gutter, filthy and gross. Without the haze of drugs and booze to dull the edges, the wee hours had sharpened into slashes of steel and gray. My brain throbbed like a tender bruise. Cold gnawed my bones. My eyeballs ached. Even the grimness of the subway jarred me: the harsh yellow light; the stink of old sweat; the surfaces hard and unyielding, echoing with the shriek of the car along the rails.

Mercifully, Tiago said little once we left Terminal City. I couldn't tell if this meant he was pissed off at me, respecting my boundaries, or merely exhausted from dancing with the other hot-pants boys all night long. He sat beside me on the bench, flicking through screens on his phone. I huddled beneath his hoodie, grateful for his silence.

I didn't know what to say to him. Thanks for cleaning me up in the men's room? Cheers for rescuing me from the worst night of my life? What do I owe you for not asking awkward questions? It was bad enough to be this wrecked and pathetic, but having to acknowledge it'd taken the kindness of a total stranger to save me from myself was one humiliation too many in a night already hemorrhaging them.

Not that he'd actually saved me from anything. I'd been granted a temporary reprieve—I remained stone-broke and jobless, and utterly alone in this city without Gabe. I couldn't even afford a subway ticket—Tiago had to front me an extra swipe on his Metro card. I wished I hadn't lost those fifties Loafer Man had left for me on the counter. That was money I'd earned fair and square. Money I could've really used.

Besides, it hadn't made me any less of a whore by not taking it. *Fuck my life.*

"What'd you say?" Tiago asked and glanced at me.

"Huh? I didn't say anything."

"Yeah, you did. You been mumbling to yourself since we sat down."

"Oh—sorry." I bit my lip and tried to will myself invisible, but that was impossible with him staring at me.

"What you thinking about anyway?" he asked. "You been stuck in your head since we left."

"So have you."

"Eh," Tiago said and thumbed the side of his nose. "Just leaving you space to pull your shit together, you know?"

"Thanks."

"You want to talk about it now."

"Not really, no."

"Alright. That's cool."

Although he seemed perfectly willing to let the matter drop, the beat of silence that followed felt excruciatingly awkward, and I found myself blurting the first thing that came to mind. "Why did you come looking for me tonight?"

"Shit, baby. Somebody had to do it."

"Oh." I cringed inside. I wondered if Gabe would have left the club without me.

"You know he's a total player, right?" Tiago said, his eyes narrowing as he peered at me. "All that shit tonight, that's just a preview of coming attractions."

I hugged my elbows and stared at the floor.

"I know it's not my business," he continued, "but if you're hung up on him, you better get used to how he is. He's not a bad guy. He's just used to looking out for number one. You either take it or leave it with a man like that because he's not changing for nobody."

"How do you know so much about it?"

"I watch and I learn," he said and eased back in the seat. "Plus, Lon's no different."

"Why are you with him then?"

Tiago flashed me a wicked grin. "Look, ole Lon and me, we've got an understanding. Things are cool as long as we don't expect too much from each other. I don't put up with his shit. I respect myself, and I make sure he treats me with respect. I got rules and he follows 'em. He can have his trifling fun if he wants it, so long as he don't shove it in my face or bring any skanks home. I'm a fine piece of ass. I know what I'm worth. Lon's lucky to have me around, and I make damn sure he knows it, too. Know what I'm saying? You can't let a man like that try to use you cheaply because he will. He always will."

"But what if I don't want to be a fine piece of ass?"

He looked at me a moment, almost surprised, and then laughed. "Well shit, baby. You're in the wrong scene with the wrong man. Maybe it's time to reevaluate your life choices?"

"Yeah, maybe." I sighed and rubbed the cold from my face. "Anyway, I'm not hung up on Gabe. I wish it were that simple."

Tiago nodded like he understood and turned back to his phone.

I leaned my head against the hull of the subway and shut my eyes against the despair surging inside me. What was I worth to anyone around here if I didn't want to be a fine piece of ass?

I didn't have an answer. At least back home, I'd been worth something to Jimmy. He'd sacrificed everything for me, and I'd made him pay for that sacrifice every day of his life until he had nothing left to give. But without my brother to dream better things for me, all I had left was this, the best I'd ever dreamed for myself. And none of it had turned out to be worth a goddamn thing. A total stranger had shown me more respect tonight than I'd shown to myself. If Tiago hadn't been there, I probably would've gone with Gabe to Marco's place and done whatever he wanted me to do. That was how cheaply I thought of myself.

Maybe when Jimmy gave up on me, I'd given up on me, too. Or maybe I'd done that a long, long time ago....

When the subway pulled into the 181st Street Station, I told Tiago I could make it the rest of the way on my own, but he insisted on accompanying me back to Gabe's building. I was too exhausted to argue.

For the first few blocks, we walked in silence. The neighborhood slept. Windows were dark, and sidewalks were empty, bathed in sulfur and shadows from the simmering street lights. An occasional car whooshed past us, headlights burning holes in my retinas. Tiago had pocketed his phone, and his long, muscular arms dangled loosely at his sides. He held himself high, almost regally, his breathing easy and relaxed. He had a dancer's loping gait, with long, elegant strides that made it difficult to keep up.

I felt like Gollum beside him: hunched forward, lurching, my hands jammed so deep into the pockets of his hoodie it was like I was guarding my precious.

Since he seemed lost in thought, I focused on not tripping over the cracks in the pavement, though my mind wandered. I wondered what Gabe was doing right now. Would he bring that nasty ginger home with him when they were done at Marco's place? Would I have to listen to them going at it while I tried to sleep on the couch? Worse, what if Gabe expected me to join in?

Fuck that shit. *Fuck all of this shit.*

"You're talking to yourself again," Tiago said.

"Sorry. I need to work on that." My face reddened, and I quickly added, "I was just wondering what it's like being a go-go dancer."

"Why? You looking for a job?"

"No, no—I mean, I need one, but mostly I'm just curious."

Tiago snorted. "Well, the first thing to do is put some meat on you. You're too skinny. That jailbait look might work for Gabe, but most clubs want—" He eyed me with suspicion. "How old are you anyway? Nineteen? Twenty?"

"Seventeen."

"Shiiit." He sucked in his breath. "Why we even talking about this then? You need to be in school, not grinding for tips at Termite City. I thought you didn't want to be a piece of ass?"

"I'm not filling out a job application, okay? I just want to know what it's like."

Tiago shrugged.

"It's like a job. You show up, do your thing, earn your money, go home."

Though this made perfect sense, I needed to know something else. "What I mean is, how do you, um, handle all the strangers pawing at you night after night?"

Tiago took a deep breath. "It takes a while, but you get used to it. The money helps." He laughed. "To be honest, the first couple times, I was scared shitless. But I got over that. I'm kind of an exhibitionist anyway, so...." He flashed me a wink. "It can be a turn on. The attention. All those dudes looking at you, wanting you. I'd be lying if I said I never got off on it. So long as I say what's what, what I do and don't do, it's all good. Like I said, it's just a job. Some of the other dancers, they take it further, and that's cool, too. I don't judge. Their bodies, their business. But I don't play like that. I've got other priorities, know what I'm saying?"

"Like what?"

"Like college, for one."

"You're going to college?"

"Hell yeah," Tiago said proudly. "Getting my RN at CUNY in the Heights. A couple more semesters, and I start my residency.... Hey, don't look so surprised. You think all I know how to do is shake my ass for money?"

"No, no. I'm sorry. It's just ironic."

"How's that?"

"College is my brother's big dream for me," I said almost wistfully. "He's saved up practically my whole life to send me, but I never wanted any part of it. That's partly why I came here."

"And what the hell's so great about here?"

I gave a bitter laugh and said, "I thought I wanted all this."

He tilted his head at me curiously. "All this?"

"You know: big city life—clubs, parties, hot guys."

He flashed me a strange look, half-amused, half-irritated. "Man, if I had some brother waiting to hand me the keys to college, I sure as hell wouldn't be twerking at Termite City. You do know the clubs and parties and hot guys don't come free, right? If you're not paying for yourself, you're paying with your fine piece of ass. That's just the way it works, at least in this scene. Besides, this city's damn expensive. I've got another job waiting tables, and I still can't half afford college plus my own place. Lon's the only thing keeping me off my sister's couch."

"I get all that, I do." I nodded. "It's like one big trap, isn't it?"

He shook his head at me as if I didn't get it at all. "Being trapped is when you've got no other choices. Seems like you do. Why not go home and listen to that brother? He sounds alright to me."

"I can't go home," I said quietly. "I burned that bridge when I left."

"Oh, baby," Tiago said and gave me a gentle laugh. "You can't burn your bridges to home. Don't you know that's what makes it home?"

But I didn't reply. There wasn't any point. Though I knew Tiago meant well, he didn't understand Jimmy. Didn't understand how badly I'd messed things up with him. He hadn't seen the look in Jimmy's eyes when he'd said those horrible things to me. I'd seen it though. I knew where matters stood with my brother, and that was before I'd ever laid a finger on Baby. The fact that he hadn't come looking for me was confirmation enough of what was painfully obvious.

I'd failed him for the last time.

When we finally reached Gabe's block, the morning was just beginning to rise. The lights were on in the bodega at the corner. An elderly man in a white apron and Yankees cap was setting up the carts of produce on the sidewalk out front. The air smelled fresh with the promise of an early rain, and the sky purpled with the approach of dawn.

We paused at the stoop of Gabe's building. I invited Tiago upstairs to be polite, but he said he needed to go. He handed me Gabe's key, but when I tried to return his hoodie, he told me he'd snag it the next time he saw me. Then he said goodnight—no, *good morning*—and was about to leave when I stopped him.

"Why did you help me tonight?" I asked, genuinely curious. "I wasn't your problem."

A tired smile passed his lips. "You seemed lost is all. Like a puppy or something. I've been there before. Got myself into a couple of messed up situations when I was young and stupid too. I know how shitty it feels when nobody's got your back."

He looked at me sadly, and for a moment it felt like the sad porno I'd filmed with Loafer Man earlier was being projected onto my face. Maybe he knew what'd happened in that men's room. Maybe they all knew. Or maybe he was just replaying whatever humiliating porno of his own he'd had to live through once upon a time. Either way, Mom, I felt seen.

"Thanks, Tiago," I said quietly.

But he held up his hand. "Don't thank me, baby. Just don't let it happen again. You saw Gabe tonight. He ain't exactly boyfriend material, no? You seem like a smart kid. If you've got someplace to go back to, my advice is you think long and hard about it, and then get your ass on the next Greyhound. Go home. Go to college. Figure your shit out. Get your feet under you before you come back here. This city eats pretty boys like us alive if we let it."

I waved goodbye to him as he disappeared around the corner, and then I dragged myself up the several flights of stairs to Gabe's apartment, Tiago's words still echoing in my mind. I didn't know what to do. He was right about Gabe. Right about the scene I was in. Right about me needing to get my shit together before it was too late. If I stayed here much longer, I'd be lost. But I didn't know where else to turn. Sure, Rozella would take me in, but the thought of being so close to Jimmy terrified me. How could I face it, having him hate me like that? Having him shun me, day in and day out, just like he'd shunned you and your memory since the day you died, Mom?

It would be too much to bear. It would break whatever was left of my heart.

I would rather take my chances with Gabe and the Loafer Men of New York.

I would rather—but I had to cut myself off mid-thought, Mom, because at the top of the stairs, I found my brother, your son, curled up in a ball and snoring soundly against Gabe's front door.

CHAPTER THIRTY-TWO
MOTHER'S SON

WHEN I WOKE JIMMY, THERE were no apologies. He didn't yell or curse or lecture, and there were no tears or expressions of regret. He didn't ask about Gabe. He didn't demand to know where I'd been all night or why I was dressed the way I was dressed. He didn't say a word about Baby, question why I'd run away, or mention how low I'd obviously sunk.

He said, "Please, come home, Toby."

I told him, "Yes."

He waited on Gabe's couch as I jumped in the shower and packed, and then we left without further discussion, though not before I jotted Gabe a brief note telling him I'd gone back to Shelter Valley and asked him to please return Tiago's hoodie.

We climbed into the pickup and got the hell out of the city. As we crossed the George Washington Bridge into New Jersey, the rain began, washing the color from the morning and rendering our progress in grayish splotches of sky and asphalt. The traffic ran heavy close to the city, and Jimmy hunched over the wheel in his truss like an old woman frightened by aggressive drivers. We weren't even going the speed limit. The pickup bucked in the backwash from the semis barreling past us in gusty roars, blurs of white and red lights streaking through sheets of rain that glistened like cellophane.

I was no longer high, but I definitely felt strung out: too exhausted to sleep, too numb to speak, too wired to settle down. It was like I'd fallen into a waking dream, and Tiago had somehow conjured Jimmy into being simply by talking about him.

I kept pinching my thigh to remind myself I wasn't imagining this.

Jimmy seemed in even rougher shape than me. His left eye had shrunken down to a fat, swollen plum. Painfully hung over, with his face drawn and sallow, his hair dull and greasy, he reeked of flop sweat and beer breath in his dirty jeans and sad work shirt. Each mile aged him a little more, though I couldn't tell if this was down to stress or withdrawal. His body trembled noticeably. He fidgeted constantly in his seat, his ribs clearly aching. He drummed his fingers against the steering wheel in time to a song playing only in his head.

Fort Lee bled into Teaneck and then Paramus in a smear of gas stations, grimly cheerful chain restaurants, and garbage scattered like confetti along the roadside. When we finally crossed the border back into New York State, we slowed to a crawl, inching toward a busy toll plaza. Jimmy hadn't spoken or even looked at me since we left Gabe's building, but as soon as we'd collected our ticket and merged onto the

Thruway, he turned to me and said in a wary voice, "Dylan's about the same."

Mom, what could I say? Yippee? Thank God he's not dead yet? Maybe the news should've come as a relief, but instead, it felt more like learning that the Governor had refused to commute my sentence. Nothing had changed; there was nothing worth being relieved about.

Jimmy kept looking at me, though, expecting a response. Maybe he'd had that talk with Rozella about taking me to the hospital. He seemed almost desperate for me to fill the silence, but when I didn't say anything, he blurted, "I took three more days off work," and added hopefully, "We can still do our college visits."

"What?"

"We can squeeze in Delhi and Oneonta in one day. Cobleskill and Albany the next. Then maybe New Paltz? Though I was thinking you should probably reconsider Binghamton. With your grades, I bet you could get an early decision."

I gawped at him in sheer disbelief. Queasiness prickled through me like a pinched nerve. I caught my breath, faced the road ahead, and said in a small, tired voice, "Fine, whatever."

That's when Jimmy began to ramble, haranguing me about my application essay and the other colleges I might still consider. He forced a laugh and said Rozella threatened to evict him if he didn't bring me home. He rushed into an extended riff about my SAT scores before segueing into an update on work and a big new contract the mill had landed from China. He mentioned that Donna had called "to check in on me," as if I'd been suffering from a head cold. Then, without missing a beat, he pivoted back to our college visits and said we should splurge on motels rather than drive home each night.

I just sat there, numb, listening for the better part of fifteen minutes. His entire recitation was breathless. It seemed painstakingly rehearsed to avoid any troublesome references to Gabe, Baby, or anything that had transpired over the past 72 hours, and I came to realize these events would now be relegated to the dustbin of our history, best ignored and soon forgotten.

Much the same as you, Mom.

When he finally ran out of steam, I slammed my skull into the headrest and squeezed my eyes shut tight. The rain pelleted shrilly against the truck as weariness seeped into my bones. Nothing would ever change between us. I could see that now. Not even running away with Gabe had been sufficient kryptonite to overcome Jimmy's superpower of denial. We would go on the same as before, he and I, falling into our old grooves, trading the same familiar lies, until the future arrived like a meteor strike to smash all the sameness forever, spinning us off in opposite trajectories where our orbits would never cross again. Sure, there would be holidays and phone calls and visits home. But it suddenly felt as if we were saying goodbye, had been saying goodbye ever since the night you died. Two strangers who'd never really taken the chance to get to know each other. More roommates than brothers. More separate than together. The thought was unrelentingly bleak, so heartbreaking and hopeless that I found myself contemplating the merits of throwing open my door and leaping into the traffic to make it stop.

Instead, I committed a different kind of suicide: "I sucked off some old creeper for money last night." I heard myself utter the words with indifference, as if whoring myself out was a job any teen might do, like babysitting or dogwalking. "He paid me a hundred bucks for five minutes work, so maybe I can skip college?"

As soon as I said it, I knew I'd made a terrible mistake. I tried to laugh it off as a sick joke, but it came out sounding like a deranged cackle…. Or no, more like a choke or a sob. I'd revealed too much. I'd lived up to all of Jimmy's lowest expectations of me, though this could hardly come as much of a shock to him anymore.

He said nothing, just glared at the road ahead through the windshield. His knuckles flexed like cords of nylon cinching around the steering wheel, his lips churning, no words spilling out.

I covered my face. "You should've left me with Gabe. He doesn't care whose dick I suck."

"Fucking Fournier," Jimmy cursed and spun the wheel hard, veering the truck into the breakdown lane and flooring the brakes.

I slammed into my seatbelt as we screeched to a halt just beyond a hulking green overpass.

"What the hell, Jimmy?"

He killed the ignition. Then he hurled his arm behind my seat and glowered at me. "Why are you doing this? Just tell me that."

"Doing what?"

"This shit. Throwing your life away. I don't understand it."

"Why do you even care? I thought I was just a dirty little cocksucker to you."

His face blanched, and he leaned back in his seat. "You know I didn't mean that."

"No?" I almost laughed. "You could've fooled me." I sniffed at the wounded expression on his face and added spitefully, "Don't feel so bad. You were right about me anyway. When that creeper laid his money down, I dropped right to my knees. Nothing could've been easier."

"Please, stop this, Toby."

But it was too late to stop.

"He saw *me*, Jimmy," I continued, tears salting my lips. "He saw what you saw, what I am, what I'm worth. He saw what I had to give him, and he took it. Just like Gabe did. Just like all those losers at the Marsh Trail."

Jimmy grabbed me by the shoulder and shook me. "Look at me. That's not who you are, do you hear me? That's not what I raised you to be."

I sneered and wiped the wetness from my face. "Oh, I know what you raised me to be. I'm just another project to you, like Baby. You've made it your life's mission to fix me up, polish me into some shiny Disney gay you can show off to the world. But you don't care what I want. We never have a real conversation about anything. You lie, withhold, keep secrets. You shut me out every chance you get."

"You're not being fair, T-bird."

"Fuck being fair! It's true, and you know it. Shit, the realest you've ever been with me was when you slapped me in the face and told me what you really think of me."

"You're not being fair," he repeated, so meekly this time I almost didn't hear him above the hiss of the rain on the windshield. "I didn't mean that. I swear, I didn't mean it."

His face screwed up with anguish, and it dawned on me how deeply I'd wounded him. A hard knot twisted inside my chest. "I can't do this anymore," I muttered, unbuckling my seatbelt. "This is pointless. Go home. I'll hitch a ride back to the city."

I reached for the door handle, but he snagged my forearm and held fast.

"I'm not letting you go."

"Fuck off." I tried to wriggle free, but it was useless: he gripped me so tightly it began to hurt. "Jesus," I said, and slammed myself back in the seat. "Don't you see I'll never be what you want me to be? I'm nothing but a disappointment to you. I have been my whole life. You know I am. I see it in your eyes. When you look at me—I mean *really* look—all you see is her."

His grip withered, and he let go of me.

I didn't move.

He looked as if stunned and then muttered to himself, "I pushed you right out the door." He shook his head. "The things I did—said." His voice cracked as the fight seemed to drain from his body. "I nearly lost you…. I nearly let you go."

"Maybe you should have."

He laughed bitterly. "Do you really think that's what I want?"

"I'm our mother's son, so just save yourself the trouble. It's okay to give up on me. I'm giving you permission." I squeezed my eyes with my fingers to make the hurting stop. "Don't you see? You need to get away from me while you still can. I wreck everything I touch. Everyone I love. Dylan… Mom."

"Wait, what?" He grabbed me by the arm again, but his touch was more cautious, even tender this time. "What does that mean, T-bird? What do you think you did to Mom?"

"Seriously? You want me to say it?"

"Yes. I want you to say it."

I took a deep breath and spat, "Isn't it obvious? I fucked up her life so badly she had to end it." I punched the dashboard hard enough to leave a dent in the plastic. "Jesus, I can't believe you made me say that out loud."

Though I glared at him, he just stared at me dumbly. There was a beat of silence, followed by another. It was as if I'd announced I was pregnant.

"Never mind," I mumbled. "I'm gonna go." I tried to slip free of his grasp, but his fingers squeezed around my arm like a vice.

"Is that what you really think?" he demanded.

"Oh, come on!" I snapped and wrenched free of his grasp. "We both know the truth. All those lies I'm supposed to believe about how she died. She was sick. She wasn't thinking straight. It was an addiction, an accident. Bullshit. She knew exactly what she was doing. Why else was I even there? Tucked into that bathtub, asleep, just a useless little kid, all alone. She had to know I'd wake up and see her like that, all pale and bloated on the bed. That I'd keep seeing her that way for the rest of my life. She had to know what that would do to me, right? And if knowing that wasn't enough to stop her from… from… then… then…" I heaved to catch my breath. "It must have been the reason in the first place." My voice had shriveled into a dry, hard raisin, but I still managed to sputter, "I was the reason, Jimmy. I know it. I've always known it."

My brother looked dumbfounded like he was seeing me for the first time in his life. He released my arm with a heavy sigh and turned away, clasping his large hands in his lap like they held something precious and small he might lose or crush if he wasn't very careful with it. He was a bull holding a plucked daisy he didn't realize was already dead.

My Jimmy. So strong. So determined. So helpless.

He didn't say anything for a long while, just kept staring at his hands, his face as unreadable as new fallen snow. Still, I watched him, regretting what I'd said, wanting to take it all back. I wished it didn't have to be like this between us, that we could slip into some parallel universe where we could enjoy the peace and normalcy he wanted so badly to give me. But we couldn't, and knowing this made my heart swell for my poor, hapless brother, the only person in the whole world who would ever choose to give up his own life to save mine.

Yet, when Jimmy finally spoke again, something different had come over him.

Something fierce. Something dark.

"I could spend forever explaining to you what she was like and never make you understand," he said quietly, his posture stiffening. "All those nights of partying. Coming and going at all hours. Strange men. Losers she'd pick up from dives down in Kayoga or Gloversville or bring home from J.J.'s. Stumbling in at two or three in the morning, shit-faced and stinking of cigarettes, with some horny trucker or other low life in tow, and her dragging me out of bed, hollering my name as soon as she waltzed through the door. Jimmy, come on! Get out here now. Jimmy, sweetie, come meet your new uncle.

"I always played my part, her little man of the house. Making sure they had ashtrays and their drinks were kept fresh while they groped each other right in front of me on the couch and then slithered down the hall to her bedroom."

He peered at me with haunted eyes to see whether he was getting through to me, but I just said numbly, "Why are you telling me this now?"

"Because you accused me of throwing her away like garbage. But she threw herself away, T-bird. Day after day after day. She threw herself at the drugs and the liquor and at any scumbag who would take her. And believe me, they all did. It was like she couldn't say no. Wouldn't say no, not to any of it, no matter how much it hurt her—or me." He turned to gaze out the windshield, his face shadowed in the stormy gray light. "I don't know why she was like that. Earl's told me some rough stories about her home life growing up, why she ran away so young. But it doesn't matter anymore, and I just don't care. All I know is everything she touched, she dragged into the gutter with her, me included."

He slammed his fist into his chest so hard I jumped. "Look at me, T-bird. I know I'm a goddamned wreck. I *know* that. I drink too much. I can't hold down a decent relationship. I can't even get us out of Shelter Valley. But that didn't just happen, you know? I was a little kid once, too." His throat croaked, and he began to tremble. "I loved her so much. I really did. She was my mom, for Christ's sake. I spent my whole childhood trying to save her. To make sure there was food on the table and fresh clothes in the closet. To be there when she was lonely or needed a shoulder to cry on. To clean up the puke and cigarette butts and used rubbers when she passed out after whatever loser she'd spent the night with wandered home to his wife."

He paused long enough to wipe the image from his eyes, and in the weight of his silence, I sensed a tiny fraction of the crushing burden he'd borne alone for so long.

"As I got older, it got harder," he continued listlessly. "I turned bitter—angry. Started lashing out. Hurting people that maybe didn't deserve it. I was a terror in high school. I'm sure Fournier told you all about that. She and I fought all the time. I even moved out once, left my senior year to go live with Earl. Not that it even mattered. I moved right back in as soon as you came along. Just like she knew I would. But nothing had changed. There was always some new addiction. Another loser, another breakdown. Some fresh disaster or crisis only her little man could bail her out of until it was too much, and I worked up the nerve to say, 'No more, Mom. I'm walking away for good. I've got a plan, a fiancé, a future. And I'm taking Toby with me. I'll be damned if I leave him behind to take my place.' I even warned her I'd go to Social Services if she tried to stop me. I wanted a better life for both of us. I wanted to protect you. That's all I've ever wanted. I sure as hell wasn't going to leave you there to suffer what I'd gone through."

Though his voice remained resolute, he kept staring down at his hands as if, even now, he was ashamed of turning his back on her. As if he'd failed her somehow by saving me.

"I gave up on her, T-bird," he said. "I finally had enough, and I just walked away. She kept choosing her demons over us, and I couldn't forgive that. I still can't. Maybe I never will." He hesitated as if to let that sink in, though, when he continued, it was in a smaller, crushed voice. "And then she snatched you from daycare one morning while I was in class. You disappeared for three days. I was frantic. The cops were out looking for you. Rozella, too. My fiancé, Caroline. Even the guys from the mill. I couldn't sleep, I couldn't eat, and then, on that third night, she called me from the motel. She was so drunk, she could barely even talk. She wouldn't say where you were, but she told me about the smack and what she was planning to do with it. Said it was all my fault for abandoning her for Caroline. Said she'd never let me take you away from her. Said I'd only find your bodies when she was through. Then she hung up on me." He paused to gather himself and turned to face me. "It took another three hours before the cops finally spotted her car in the motel parking lot, but by then, it was too late."

I stopped breathing. My heart stopped beating. The world ended, and all became silent between us until I heard myself gasp, "Why— why didn't she kill me?"

He shrugged. "Because she loved you. She wasn't a monster. Just broken."

Coldness deeper than winter rushed in as the rain surged outside. A sharp pain in my arm sent stars shooting across my vision. I'd dug my fingernails into my flesh without even realizing it. They drew back wet with blood, though Jimmy didn't notice.

He was still staring into the past.

"Some people convince themselves they're too broken to be fixed," he whispered, then his eyes focused on mine. "I won't let you become one of them. I won't let you be like her. When I look at you, I see a bright, beautiful light that will set the world on fire. That's all I've ever wanted you to be. No matter what you decide to do with your life, no matter what stupid shit I might say in anger, I'll never give up on you. Do you hear me? *Never.* Just please, please don't give up on yourself."

Fierce tears blazed trails down his cheeks as something like pride rose inside him. "I know we've made mistakes. I've made mistakes. I know you're hurting because I'm hurting, too. But you need to let her go. She checked out on us a long time ago. But I'm still here. I may be damaged goods, but I'm here." He reached out and pulled me into a crushing bear hug that made him wince. "You're *my* son, goddammit. Do you hear me? You're mine, not hers and I'll be damned if I let you go another second believing anything else."

Though I couldn't bring myself to speak, I squeezed him back as hard as I could.

I never wanted to let go again.

EPiLOGUE: BEAUTiFUL BOYS

CHAPTER THIRTY-THREE
FORGIVENESS IS A RIVER

DECEMBER IN THE ADIRONDACKS HAS always bullied me. Come Halloween, and the winter tests its weight, tentative at first, taunting the earth with frost and dustings of white until it swings for the gut with full-on flurries and squalls. As the season builds in swagger, it strong-arms itself into every corner of my life, all that snow, cold, and darkness bearing down off the mountain like a boot on the back of my neck.

By the solstice, I'm down for the count.

That's not to say it can't be beautiful at times. Like now, as I write this, gazing out my bedroom window at the twilit snow blanketing our backyard, cross-stitched with the prints of deer and foxes vanishing into the shadowy woods beyond. There's something about a December dusk. The elements pause to catch their breath. The wind calms, almost mercifully, like it's making a gesture to you, offering you a chance to appreciate the stars winking to life above a snowscape that, in the dying rays of skylight, glows the palest, palest blue.

It's the closest winter ever comes to an apology.

When I awoke this morning, Mom, it was well before dawn. I scrambled out of bed in a cold sweat to retrieve the box of your things from my closet. Except for the shreds of my poor constellation, everything else remained intact: my cosmetics and beautiful-boy wardrobe; the envelope with my life savings; your clothes and relics and photographs. Jimmy never destroyed any of it; I found the box returned to my closet when we got back from New York. It's been there waiting for me ever since.

But as I rifled through the artifacts that once defined me, they made me feel… different, empty—like a battery made useless after its charge has faded. My new therapist, Simon Willow, says traumatic experiences can change us into brand new people overnight—people we no longer recognize in the mirror. He may be right about that.

When Jimmy's alarm went off, I followed him into the kitchen, my head still swimming and my cheeks raw with tears. He didn't need reminding about today's anniversary, though in the past he always pretended it was just another day. But ignoring you has never done us a damn bit of good, so I told him to call around and find somebody else to pick up his Sunday overtime because I was treating him to breakfast.

An hour later, we elbowed our way through the church crowd to a cramped two-topper by the kitchen at the Kayoga Denny's. Jimmy seemed anxious at first, glancing expectantly at me over the top of his menu as if waiting for a dam to burst. But when the waitress finally took our order, I asked for hash browns and two eggs "over-sleazy," and he cracked a grin. We both knew where I'd gotten that expression from, and so I smiled, too, because it felt like a minor miracle to be able to share one harmless memory of you without it having to mean anything more.

As it turned out, it was the last time you even came up.

Instead, we chatted about random stuff while we waited for our food. Jimmy told me a funny story about helping his new A.A. buddy, Roger, rebuild the transmission on the Firebird that Roger's been restoring. I updated Jimmy on the courses I plan to take at K.C.C.C. next month. When our food arrived—his toast burned, my eggs overcooked—we ate in a silence that, for once, didn't feel the least bit angry or awkward or sad.

When we finally left Denny's, the sun shined down a warm, buttery yellow on the powdery snow outside. I didn't want our day to end just yet, so I suggested taking a drive. We headed out to the Albany mall, where I bought Rozella a pair of cozy fleece slippers for Christmas and stocked up on nail polish for myself at Hot Topic. Then we went to Macy's, where I treated Jimmy to new gloves and a scarf, and he bought me a lovely pink cashmere sweater for my first day at K.C.C.C. He even made me try it on for him. I haven't felt much like wearing anything beautiful since New York, but when I came out of the dressing room to gauge his reaction, he said he was happy to see me looking so much like myself again.

Better still, when the saleslady asked him if it was a present for his girlfriend, he said, "No, it's for my brother."

We listened to Christmas carols on the drive back to Shelter Valley, something we'd never done before. When we got home, we ate grilled cheese sandwiches with cans of Pepsi in front of a football game on TV. Jimmy nodded off on the couch while I painted my fingernails Blackheart Beauty Bright Fuchsia and listened to Dolly Parton songs on my phone.

It felt good to add some color back into my life.

Jimmy's doing better, Mom, although it's taken a lot of work. For weeks after we got back from the city, he was downing a six-pack a night, sometimes more. He still had a really hard time talking to me. So much so, he didn't even put up a fight when I announced I was skipping senior year at Kayoga Unified and would start early admission at K.C.C.C. in January to finish my diploma and earn credits towards an Associate's Degree (though I still don't know in what). Instead, he nodded wearily and packed away the stack of view books left to gather dust on the kitchen counter.

It took an intervention from Rozella and me to get him to go to his first AA meeting. I had to threaten to move in with her just to make him see how worried I was. Simon Willow helped me get him started, but Jimmy's been doing the hard work himself, going to his meetings and tackling his twelve steps. He's made a couple of new friends there, too, including Roger, an auto-mechanic from Kayoga who's been sober for two years and is helping Jimmy plan Baby's restoration in the spring.

Speaking of Baby, when we got home from the city, I saw that he'd thrown a tarp over her battered body like a corpse in a morgue and left her in the driveway to rot. We've never talked about what I did to her, but it's turned out okay because at least fixing her up has given him something positive to focus on. He and Roger spend Saturdays looking through parts catalogs together, while drinking cases of Pepsi instead of beer. It's been good for Jimmy to have a life of his own again. He even got his two-month sobriety chip last week.

Still, I worry about him, Mom. He looks like shit. A small bald patch has surfaced on the crown of his head. He's lost a ton of weight, and he doesn't sleep well—I hear him tossing and turning until three or four most mornings. Yet, he still insists on pulling every hour of overtime he can get his hands on. He says it's to pay for my therapy. My Simon Willow visits aren't covered by our insurance, and I know it can't be cheap sending me to the only gay family therapist in a three-county area. But sometimes it just feels like he's avoiding me. I can't blame him for that. We still don't know quite how to relax around each other, although we're working on that, too, which is why today felt like such a beautiful achievement.

Baby steps.

I'm in it for the long haul with Jimmy. I'm not going anywhere until I see him well again and finally happy. I've started applying for part-time jobs in Kayoga, so I can help out with the bills. I want him to pull back on his hours and return to college to finish his own degree. He only needs a few more credits, and the admissions counselor I talked to at K.C.C.C. said there are night and online classes he can take. We can even do it together. I already have the view book to show him.

Long term, I want him to quit the mill and leave Shelter Valley. I want him to find a better career that brings him satisfaction. I want him to move to a house in the suburbs with a white picket fence, marry a kind and intelligent woman, and have a bunch of rotten kids who'll drive him crazy and bring him joy. I want him to have his dreams for himself. It's not too late, and there's nobody on earth who deserves a piece of his own happiness more than my brother.

That's my New Year's plan for Jimmy.

My plan for me is still a work in progress, though.

Simon Willow is the one that got me started on this little writing project back when Jimmy first dragged me to see him back in September. I've worked on it most days since then, and it's been satisfying to sort through my memories and feelings this way, outside the popcorn popper of my brain. With some time and distance, I've gained perspective on these messy chapters of my life.

Simon Willow says our stories are the most precious things we own. They're all we have and all we leave behind us. We are our stories. They are our superpower, our only power, and I've felt powerless for way too long.

Maybe that's why I haven't gone back to the Marsh Trail.

Maybe I don't feel like being used anymore.

Maybe I'm tired of believing I deserve it...

Okay, so my phone just buzzed with this text:

Please, T-bone. Answer me. I just want to talk.

Yes, Mom. Dylan is alive.

More than just alive—he's nearly recovered. One minute he was a human vegetable withering on life support, and the next he was sitting up and slurping a ginger ale. Even the doctors couldn't believe it. He's faced lots of complications since, but his long-term prognosis is good, although Donna tells Jimmy his rehab has been tough. He's basically had to relearn to walk. She says he still has terrible nightmares, memory lapses, and difficulty concentrating, but with hard work he should be able to resume a normal life.

Yet, even though I'm happy he's alive, my feelings remain—complicated.

The morning after we got back from New York, I made Jimmy drive me to the hospital to see Dylan again. He even offered to come up to the room with me, but I'd already decided this was something I needed to do on my own, and so I told him he could leave, that I'd take the bus home.

I spent that whole day at Dylan's bedside, talking to him in his lifeless state just like Donna had asked me to. I told him all about Gabe and New York and how badly I'd fucked everything up. I went back the next day, too, and the next, and then every single day after that. It became a kind of routine, with Jimmy dropping me off on his way to the mill, and me taking the bus home in the afternoon. I'd bring books and magazines to read to Dylan. Sometimes I'd play old movies on the TV in his room, telling him all the gossip I knew about the stars. Shad and I called a truce, and he stopped by on the weekends to fill us in on the latest news from Kayoga Unified or what new community service Scarface and Owen were performing in lieu of charges from the D.A. Donna and I would talk occasionally, too, although she often took the opportunity of my visits to go home and shower, consult the doctors, or try to figure out how she was going to cope with the mountain of bills that awaited her at home.

But as soon as Dylan's coma broke, I stopped going to see him. It felt like the right thing to do. The only thing to do. I didn't belong there anymore. My job was done, my debt repaid, and so, that last evening, as he lay there snoring in bed after a full battery of tests, I snuck into his room and nestled Vergil on his nightstand right next to Dante.

Then, I faded away.

I haven't seen or spoken to him or Donna since.

There's this stupid motivational poster on Simon Willow's wall: *Forgiveness is the river that will carry you home.* But, Mom, here's the thing: I still don't know who I'm supposed to forgive, Dylan or me.

Can I come over and see you? Just five minutes?

We're leaving in the morning.

Let me say goodbye, at least.

Donna and Dylan are moving to New Jersey to live with their cousins. They've had to sell their place to cover some hospital bills, but it won't be enough. Theresa is putting them up while Donna recovers from her bankruptcy, and though I hate to sound like a cold-hearted bastard, I'm glad they're leaving. Maybe then he'll stop texting me like this. Rozella says he probably wants to thank me for being there for him or maybe to apologize for everything he put me through. He's been texting like this for days, though I've taken a page out of his playbook and haven't answered a single one so far. It feels cruel to keep ghosting him like this, but what else can I do? Jimmy says Dylan may need to walk with a cane for the rest of his life. How on earth can I ever let him thank me or apologize to me knowing that?

I have until the morning to figure it out, but for tonight I'll just shut off my phone...

Not everything has been this confusing, though.

For example, I'm going over to spend the evening with Rozella. It's Betty Grable's birthday today, so we're planning to watch *How to Marry a Millionaire* on Turner Movies and eat ice cream and dish about who had the best wardrobe in the film: Grable, Monroe, or Bacall.

Thank God for Rozella. She's kept me sane. I'm not sure I could have coped these past few months without her. She's been a rock, an oasis of calm and common sense in a whirlwind of upheaval. Though we haven't talked much about what happened in New York, that's okay because it doesn't feel like we *can't* talk about it anymore.

We just haven't needed to.

Fun story: The other day Rozella received her first-ever Christmas card from Nicki! It included pictures of the grandkids, both with families of their own now. It said they were all looking forward to calling her on Christmas, and I was so happy for her. I didn't even mention how I'd Googled Nicki's address in Florida a while back and written her a letter. I told Nicki all about you. I told her about Jimmy and me, too, and how I thought she and Rozella had made some of our same mistakes. I told her it wasn't too late to fix things, though considering Rozella's age, it might become too late, too soon. Then I told her how I'd learned that you can't throw away the people you love, no matter how much they've hurt you, because they'll always be a part of you no matter what. So, if they're willing to change, why not let them try?

And my God, Mom, she listened to me.

It's easier to let go of your anger like that after so much time and misery have passed. I wouldn't know. I'm still trying to find my anger about what happened to me. Simon Willow says that anger is good and that it's an appropriate immune response in a healthy psyche. He says that finally feeling angry will mean that I've stopped blaming myself for what others have done to me—what Loafer Man did. Simon Willow once called him my rapist. He says coerced consent is not consent. He says intoxicated consent is not consent.

But while I understand what he means, when I try on that word for size—rape—my own shame and self-loathing swamp whatever anger I ought to feel towards Loafer Man. I want to hate him, I do, but I keep on hating myself. I want to burn with rage, but, inside, I have no heat to start that fire.

I'm still too exhausted, too empty, too embarrassed. Maybe someday I won't be, but I'm not there yet. Like I said, I'm a work in progress.

At least it's been less complicated with Gabe. Harold died last month, but Gabe didn't even attend the funeral. I worried that I'd kept him away, which broke my heart. But I can't blame myself for him. Tiago was right: Gabe isn't a bad man; he's just had to survive too long on his own with no one to trust or love. What a sad, lonely existence he must lead alone in the city. It's like what he said about you: He's had a tough life. But he's also made a tough life tougher than it needed to be. I don't think he understands this any better than you ever did.

Gabe's a broken man, and it's hard to stay angry with somebody so broken.

That's the way I feel about you, too.

Lately, I've been thinking a lot about those last three hours that played out thirteen years ago tonight. I think about what Jimmy went through after you hung up on him like that. His fear and guilt and rage and frustration until the cops found us. How that experience nearly destroyed him and shaped everything between us afterward.

I think about myself, too, about how clueless and helpless I was, sound asleep in that bathtub while you debated with yourself in some half-drunk, half-mad rage whether I should live or die along with you.

Don't get me wrong, Mom: I'm grateful you spared my life. But I'm also sorry you couldn't battle your demons for us. Sorry we weren't enough for you. Sorry I wasn't enough.

Maybe I still blame myself for that, although I'm done punishing myself for your mistakes. Maybe I'm angry, too, disappointed, abandoned. Maybe I feel so many things I can't even put into words yet. And maybe, just maybe, forgiveness is a river, but it's an endless one that never reaches any destination, and Jimmy and I will be navigating its bends and rapids for the rest of our lives.

But even if that's the case, it's still a worthwhile journey.

Speaking of journeys, I have a new destination in mind for the Fourth of July next year: Central Park. Ravisha announced that the new MANN of the People Tour will be kicking off there. Tickets are free, but you have to donate a minimum of $100 to one or more of a dozen charities working to support queer youth. She's also donating all the proceeds from her upcoming *Angry Young Mann* album to the Trevor Project.

When Trump won the election last month, she got very political. Many others have, too. Nobody knows what's coming next. There's a lot of confusion out there right now, a lot of fear—although you'd never know it in Shelter Valley, where most folks haven't stopped gloating. There were so many hoots and hollers and shotgun blasts on Election Night, I thought the world was coming to an end.

In a way, it did.

Jimmy was up all that night yelling at the TV, but I just stayed in bed with the lights out, wishing I could somehow wake up from the nightmare. Even Rozella called to check on how we were doing. (She doesn't like Trump, doesn't like the way he treats women, but I haven't had the heart yet to ask her how she voted.) We're all still in shock. It's hard to know what to do. A few folks have organized protests. Others spend hours rage-tweeting online. Most, however, just shrugged and went back to their lives. When you haven't lived with a target painted on your back it's easy to ignore the consequences of your indifference for people like me.

At least Ravisha is taking her anger and turning it into activism. Maybe I'll join her.

Come to think of it, maybe I won't have to do it alone…

I've heard New Jersey's not far from the city. If you want to see me so badly, this is where I'll be on July 4th. Come find me.

I added a link to the MANN of the People site and hit send. Then I shut off my phone.

We'll see what Dylan does with that.

But for now, it's getting late, Mom. Twilight's long since faded, and the blue snow outside my window has turned charcoal gray as the darkness settles in. Jimmy just knocked on my door, and when I told him to come in, he saw me at my desk and asked, "What are you doing?"

"Nothing," I replied automatically, but then I thought better of myself and admitted, "Actually, I'm writing my goodbyes to Mom."

He looked at me a moment, but I couldn't tell what he was thinking. I'm not sure why I've kept this writing project a secret from Jimmy for so long or what I expected him to say when he found out.

But all he said was, "Good. That's really good, T-bird."

Then he turned to leave me in peace.

"Wait," I said. "Did you need something?"

He paused in the doorway. "I was just wondering if you'd mind if I joined you and Rozella for that movie tonight."

I could feel the grin spread across my face. "I'd like that."

He beamed at me. "I'll be in the living room when you're ready."

My brother still finds new ways to surprise me, Mom. We're going to be alright.

Which means I've finally said all I need to say to you. This goodbye has been a long time coming—thirteen years, to be precise. But Rozella is waiting for me. Jimmy's waiting. The rest of my life is waiting.

Tonight feels like my story can finally become, well, mine.

It's time for me to let you go. So, as soon as I'm done writing this, I will pack up these notebooks inside your box and put them away in my closet where they belong. I've set your photograph on my bedside table where Vergil used to stand, and where I'll get to look at it each night before bed instead of staring up at my ceiling. You'll make a suitable replacement for my constellation.

Ravisha would approve.

And besides, I'll probably be writing more to you soon enough, or at least when I have something worthwhile to tell you. Maybe after my first day at K.C.C.C., maybe when I go to MANN of the People next summer, or when Jimmy earns his college degree. Or maybe when I finally move to New York City for good, because I won't abandon that dream. What's best about the city still beats in my blood—the music, the energy, the freedom. But this time, I'll make sure I only say yes to me, what I want, whom I choose.

Besides, this shithole town is too small to contain Jimmy and me for much longer. We're climbing out together. We'll reach the sunlight soon. We've been in this darkness too long, Mom, and we're never falling back again. Not ever.

We can see the light of the clear blue morning.

But you have yet to hear the last from me. I promise I won't make Jimmy's mistake: I'm not going to push you out of my life. You just can't be the center of it anymore, okay? I think you'd understand that. In fact, I'm sure you'd understand it, because Jimmy was right about one thing: however broken you were, you still loved me.

And that's all I ever needed to know.

AUTHOR'S NOTE

As a queer man, I once hoped that Martin Luther King Jr. was right when he said that "the arc of the moral universe is long, but it bends toward justice." Yet, in 2016, our country veered away from justice and decades of growing queer acceptance down a darker, more hateful path.

This story is set there, in the summer of 2016, in a dark corner of the MAGA heartland. Queer teenager Toby Ryerson wrestles with both his identity and a family legacy of shame. He misunderstands his past, misinterprets his present, and misjudges himself and others. He hurts the people he loves and makes huge mistakes about whom he can trust. His journey ultimately leads him through the predatory underbelly of the queer experience. To some readers, this unflattering portrait of one ugly part of the queer community may seem to run counter to the crucial message of hope and affirmation that queer youth so desperately need today. But it's an equally necessary part of telling them the truth.

Teenagers need and respect truth, even when it's upsetting. Even when it makes adults uncomfortable. At a time when there are growing calls for censoring even the most innocent of queer books, queer teens urgently need stories that address the specific traumas many of them still face. When we shy away from telling such stories, we reinforce the terrible message of the censors that certain queer experiences are shameful and should be kept hidden. That the queer teens who endure them are problematic and don't matter.

In this book, Toby deals with homophobia, bullying, outing, sexual predation, and assault. His world includes pervasive alcoholism and substance abuse, promiscuity, homophobic slurs and violence, and even suicide. Toby's story is not for everyone. Ultimately, however, he discovers his inner strength, leading him to a place of family and forgiveness, self-respect and love. He learns that it's never too late for hope. He finds his way.

This is a book for readers who need it, and who need it for that classic reason: to know that they are not alone. I want those readers to draw their own strength from Toby's story. I want to say to them, "I see you. I love you. I honor your struggle, and I know that you will find your way."

—Rob Costello, October 2024

Although we've made much progress since I was Toby's and Dylan's age many years ago, the sad truth is that it's still an ugly world out there for far too many beautiful young people.

I wrote this book for you. I wanted you to know that I see you. I wanted you to know that you are not alone.

Toby's journey is a story of survival and resilience. But sometimes it's hard to be resilient, especially if you don't have a Jimmy in your life to lean on. The good news is that many wonderful people and organizations are out there to help.

If you or someone you care about is struggling with sexuality and/or gender identity issues, you can find resources, help, and advice at The Trevor Project (www.thetrevorproject.org), the It Gets Better Project (www.itgetsbetter.org), InterAct (www.interactadvocates.org), and Trans Lifeline (www.translifeline.org).

Counselors at The National Runaway Safeline (1-800-RUNAWAY) are available 24/7 to offer support and assistance to runaway and homeless youth and young people in crisis who are thinking about running away.

You can text HOME to 741741 to reach trained professionals at the Crisis Text Line (www.crisistextline.org) who will help if you or someone you care about is facing anxiety, depression, emotional abuse, loneliness, self-harm, bullying, or thoughts of suicide.

Finally, the Substance Abuse and Mental Heath Service Administration's National Helpline at 1-800-662-HELP offers free, confidential treatment referral and other resources to both English and Spanish speakers wrestling with mental health issues and/or substance abuse and addiction.

ACKNOWLEDGMENTS

THANK YOU TO STEVE BERMAN, my editor, for taking on the challenge of publishing a difficult book that scared away so many others. I am so thankful for your editorial wisdom, your confidence in me, and your support for my work. Most importantly, I'm grateful that you've given Toby and his story a chance to reach the readers who need to find them.

Thank you to my fiercest champions in publishing, Jennifer De Chiara and especially my agent, Marie Lamba. Marie, this is the novel that brought us together. For a long time it seemed it might not happen, but you never gave up believing in Toby—or in me. The road of an author can be long, hard, and rocky. I am so lucky and grateful to have you as my guide.

Thank you to my dear friend Anne Mazer who did the kindest, bravest thing a writer friend can do: tell the truth. Without you, this book would literally not exist. Your honestly and wisdom helped me to see what I couldn't. Toby owes you so much, but not nearly as much as I do.

Thank you to the students, faculty, and staff of The Highlights Foundation, my writing home-away-from-home. You've provided me with a safe, loving, and supportive community for more than a decade now. I might well have given up on this writing dream a long time ago if it weren't for you. Specifically for this novel I need to thank Sarah Aronson, George Brown, Alison Green-Myers, Jennifer Richard Jacobson, Nicole Valentine, Nancy Werlin, and Melissa Wyatt. I couldn't ask for better friends or a more enriching creative environment. You inspire me!

Thank you to my fellow Secret Gardeners and the community of the Writing for Children and Young Adults MFA Program at the Vermont College of Fine Arts for being my writing fam. Special thanks to Franny Billingsley, Elizabeth Partridge, Coe Booth, and A.M. Jenkins for teaching me how to write a book. Your fingerprints are all over Toby's story.

Thank you to Millay Arts, The Constance Saltonstall Foundation for the Arts, and the Ulysses Philomathic Library where chunks of this novel were written.

Thank you to Shelby Hogan and Ritch Savin-Williams for your help in researching aspects of Toby's story.

Thank you to all my friends and family who have encouraged and supported me over the years. Though there are too many of you to name here, there's a little piece of each one of you in Toby's story. I am so fortunate to have you all in my life.

Thank you to Sonja, Seamus, Roxy, Willow, Barnabas, Billie, and Silas for being the most loyal writing companions any human could ask for.

Finally, my deepest, most inadequate thanks go to my husband (and best reader), Werner Sun. Everything I write exists because you believe in me. Without you none of this would matter. My heart and home are with you always.

ABOUT THE AUTHOR

ROB COSTELLO (HE/HIM) writes dark speculative and contemporary fiction with a queer bent for and about young people. He's the contributing editor of *We Mostly Come Out At Night: 15 Queer Tales of Monsters, Angels & Other Creatures*, nominated for a 2024 Bram Stoker Award® and named a 2024 CYBILS Award Finalist, as well as a Notable/Recommended/Best Book of 2024 by the New York Public Library, Ginger Nuts of Horror, PseudoPod, Reactor Magazine, and Locus Magazine. He's also author of the dark fiction story collection *The Dancing Bears: Queer Fables for the End Times*, named a finalist for The Whirling Prize. His stories have been nominated for the Pushcart Prize and have appeared in *The Dark*, *The NoSleep Podcast*, *The Magazine of Fantasy & Science Fiction*, *PseudoPod*, *Hunger Mountain*, *Cape Cod Review*, and *Narrative*, among other publications.

An Ugly World for Beautiful Boys is his debut novel.

An alumnus of Millay Arts, he holds an MFA in Writing from the Vermont College of Fine Arts and has served on the faculty of the Highlights Foundation since 2014. He is co-founder (with Lesa Cline-Ransome, Jo Knowles, and Jennifer Richard Jacobson) of the R(ev)ise and Shine! writing community, and he lives in upstate NY with his husband and their four-legged overlords.

www.ingramcontent.com/pod-product-compliance
Lightning Source LLC
Chambersburg PA
CBHW022245020726
47496CB00004B/1068